PRAISE FOR THE NOVELS OF

MAYA BANKS

"Heated investigative romantic suspense . . . Intense, transfixing."
—*Midwest Book Review*

"Definitely a recommended read . . . filled with friendship, passion, and most of all, a love that grows beyond just being friends."
—*Fallen Angel Reviews*

"Grabbed me from page one and refused to let go until I read the last word . . . When a book still affects me hours after reading it, I can't help but Joyfully Recommend it!"
—*Joyfully Reviewed*

"I guarantee I will reread this book many times over, and will derive as much pleasure as I did in the first reading each and every subsequent time."
—*Novelspot*

"An excellent read that I simply did not put down . . . A fantastic adventure . . . covers all the emotional range."
—*The Road to Romance*

"Searingly sexy and highly believable."
—*RT Book Reviews*

"A must-read author . . . her [stories] are always full of emotional situations, lovable characters and kick-butt story lines."
—*Romance Junkies*

sweet addiction

MAYA BANKS

Heat / New York

THE BERKLEY PUBLISHING GROUP
Published by the Penguin Group
Penguin Group (USA) Inc.
375 Hudson Street, New York, New York 10014, USA
Penguin Group (Canada), 90 Eglinton Avenue East, Suite 700, Toronto, Ontario M4P 2Y3, Canada
(a division of Pearson Penguin Canada Inc.) • Penguin Books Ltd., 80 Strand, London WC2R 0RL, England
• Penguin Group Ireland, 25 St. Stephen's Green, Dublin 2, Ireland (a division of Penguin
Books Ltd.) • Penguin Group (Australia), 250 Camberwell Road, Camberwell, Victoria 3124, Australia
(a division of Pearson Australia Group Pty. Ltd.) • Penguin Books India Pvt. Ltd., 11 Community
Centre, Panchsheel Park, New Delhi—110 017, India • Penguin Group (NZ), 67 Apollo Drive,
Rosedale, Auckland 0632, New Zealand (a division of Pearson New Zealand Ltd.) • Penguin Books
(South Africa) (Pty.) Ltd., 24 Sturdee Avenue, Rosebank, Johannesburg 2196, South Africa

Penguin Books Ltd., Registered Offices: 80 Strand, London WC2R 0RL, England

This book is an original publication of The Berkley Publishing Group.

This is a work of fiction. Names, characters, places, and incidents either are the product of the author's
imagination or are used fictitiously, and any resemblance to actual persons, living or dead, business
establishments, events, or locales is entirely coincidental. The publisher does not have any control over
and does not assume any responsibility for author or third-party websites or their content.

PUBLISHING HISTORY
Heat trade paperback edition / April 2012

Library of Congress Cataloging-in-Publication Data

Banks, Maya.
Sweet addiction / Maya Banks.
p.   cm.
ISBN 978-0-425-24565-1
1. First loves—Fiction.   2. Triangles (Interpersonal relations)—Fiction.   I. Title.
PS3602.A643S825   2012
813'.6—dc22   2011037774

PRINTED IN THE UNITED STATES OF AMERICA

10 9 8 7 6 5 4 3 2

To everyone who wanted to read Cole's story

PART 1

lucas

CHAPTER I

$\mathcal{H}$er laughter was the first thing that caught his attention. Vibrant and shining. So effervescent and full of unfettered joy that it arrested him and he couldn't remember what he'd been thinking just moments earlier.

He turned, seeking the source of the captivating music. And then he thought he'd heard it before. When he was much younger.

A lifetime ago.

Ren.

The memory of her still had the power to make him ache.

So much regret. Guilt. Wishful thinking. If only he had it to do all over again.

He hadn't thought about her in a while now. Not because she'd slipped from his mind, but because he'd willed himself to stop thinking of the beautiful, shy eighteen-year-old girl who'd meant the world to him when he was in his early twenties.

It still hurt him to bring her to mind years later. She reminded him of mistakes he'd made. How he'd hurt her when it was the very last thing he'd ever wanted or intended.

He scanned the interior of the restaurant, his eyes sharp as he took in each table. But he couldn't find the source of the burst of laughter, nor did he hear it again.

"Is something the matter?" Damon Roche asked.

Cole turned back to his friend and dinner companion and cast an apologetic glance in Serena Roche's direction.

"No, nothing. I just thought I heard . . . I was reminded of someone I once knew."

Damon slid his hand from Serena's arm and picked up his glass of wine. His touch never strayed far from his wife. His now pregnant wife. If Damon had been possessive before—and he was forbiddingly possessive of Serena—he was even more so now that she was round with his child.

The two shared a nontraditional relationship. Serena was submissive to Damon's dominance in and out of the bedroom. It was a relationship that made Cole envious, dangerously so. Spending time with the couple he called friends made him face his past mistakes. Made him realize that if he'd only been more careful and mindful in the past, he could even now be enjoying a relationship like Damon and Serena's with a woman he'd loved with everything he had.

But he'd hurt her in his impatience and ignorance.

He'd met many women in the years since. Women who were beautiful, submissive, willing to submit to him on a permanent basis, but none had captured his heart like Ren. The one woman he couldn't have.

Until recently he hadn't done more than touch or prepare women who frequented The House, the exclusive club devoted to sexual largesse, owned by Damon Roche. Cole was a frequent visitor. Damon trusted him. Only Cole had been trusted with Serena, Damon's beloved wife, and even then his role was just preparation.

Only with Angelina had he allowed himself to become more intimate, to actually have sex and open himself to the pleasure of having a woman go quiet at his touch and command. But a part of him realized that Angelina had reminded him of Ren. And Angelina belonged to Micah, another of Cole's friends, one he shared with Damon.

All of the women he'd allowed himself to soften around belonged to other men. Maybe that was why he was willing to indulge with them, because he knew they were no threat to his heart and soul.

"Is the food to your liking, Serena mine?" Damon asked.

Serena smiled. "It's divine. I only wish I could eat more. I swear this kid is wrapped around my stomach, squeezing for all it's worth. I can't eat more than a small amount at a time, but then I get hungry. The result is I eat all day!"

Damon chuckled and lifted a glass of water before pressing it gently to her lips. "You need to eat. You've not been sleeping well lately. Our child is wearing you out. The calories will give you more energy."

"Or just make me fat and lazy," Serena muttered.

"Are you still set on not knowing the sex?" Cole asked, trying to maintain polite conversation. But he was rattled and the laughter had opened the door to his past that he tried to keep shut at all times.

A wistful light entered Serena's eyes. She was a beautiful woman. Startling blue eyes and shiny black hair. He'd been drawn to her as well even though there had never been a question of her belonging to Damon. But again, there was something about her that had reminded him of his childhood sweetheart, and he often found himself unable to look away from Serena. And wish that he hadn't messed up so badly with Ren, that they could have been older. Cole could have been wiser. Could have guided her as Damon had guided Serena. Maybe Ren would still be with him now. His. Beautiful, submissive, his treasure.

"There are days when I really want to know," she said. She glanced over at Damon and smiled. "I made Damon promise not to let me cave even though he wants to know very badly whether we're having a son or a daughter. He really wants a girl. I don't care and maybe that's why I want to be surprised."

"Another girl in the fold would be entertaining," Cole said. "I imagine Damon will be just as bad as Micah when it comes to his little girl."

Serena rolled her eyes. "Oh God, don't you know it?"

"She's threatening to make me wear one of those damn baby carriers that Micah parades around in," Damon said dryly. "He's lost his goddamn mind ever since Nia was born."

Cole snickered. "I'm going to remind you of this conversation when your own child is born. You're overprotective of Serena as it is. I can't imagine you'll be any less so of the baby. Especially if you have a daughter."

"Maybe, but that doesn't mean I'm going to wear her twenty-four seven," Damon said darkly.

Serena just grinned and stroked her fingers over Damon's hand. Cole winked at her as if to say he agreed with her private assessment.

Distant laughter sounded again, sending a cascade of chill bumps up his neck. This time he reacted much quicker and jerked around, his gaze honing in on the source.

Finally, he saw her.

All his breath left him in a ragged rush. She was facing away, which was why he hadn't been able to find her the first time. He could just see the hint of her profile. Smooth, dusky skin, creamy, beckoning his touch. A cascade of black hair tumbled down her back, going so low that he lost track of it.

She was petite. He could tell from here that she was a small woman, probably not much more than five feet. Her features were delicate. As she turned, he caught a glimpse of the slim column of her neck, but then she reached up and pulled her hair over one shoulder, baring the expanse of her back.

Her dress was backless and he froze as his gaze lighted on the tattoo trailing down her spine.

He couldn't breathe. His fingers curled and uncurled as he stared, riveted to the sight. Almost in dread, he raised his gaze to her right shoulder, just over the blade. Would it still be there? Had the years been kind and diminished the reminder of his inexperience?

He couldn't tell from this distance. Or maybe he didn't want it to be there. A scar. Evidence of the care he hadn't taken with a woman who trusted him with her heart and body.

Ren.

What was she doing here? It was her. The tattoo was unmistakable. Delicate and feminine. Just like her. A thin, scripty flowering vine from the small of her back to her nape. He'd traced it many times with his fingers, his mouth and his tongue.

Before he could get to his feet, the man sitting with Ren stood and extended his hand to her. She took it and gracefully rose from her seat. The man's hold was possessive and intimate, a clear signal that he considered her his.

But when Ren turned where he could see her fully, Cole saw the wide silver band encircling her neck. It was a fist to his gut and he could only stare, so stunned that he couldn't draw a breath.

He knew the significance of that piece of jewelry. It wasn't decorative, although it was beautifully rendered and drew attention to her delicate features.

It was a sign of ownership.

A gift from a master to his submissive.

Serena wore such a symbol, but hers was a band that encircled her upper arm. Damon wasn't a fan of collars. He found them demeaning. Cole agreed.

The surge of jealousy—and anger—that bolted through his veins took him completely off guard.

The man put his arm protectively around Ren, and she smiled up at him as they made their way to the exit. Power emanated from the man—a worthy adversary.

"Do you know him?" Cole asked urgently, glancing quickly back at Damon.

Damon's gaze jerked up, his brow creased in confusion.

"The man there, with the Asian woman. They're walking out now."

"Why would you think I know . . ." Damon frowned and leaned forward. "Yes, I do, actually."

"Who·is he?" Cole demanded.

"He's visited The House before, but not often. He prefers to keep to himself."

"Who?" Cole asked again, his impatience an edgy burn under his skin.

"Lucas Holt."

"What's his story? Is he into the scene or is he just someone playing at the game?"

"He's serious," Damon said slowly. "His background checked out or he wouldn't have been admitted to The House. He's wealthy. Successful businessman. Owns several clubs both in Houston and Dallas. I think he recently opened one in Vegas. He spends a lot of time in Vegas but he has residences in Dallas and Houston as well."

"Have you ever seen *her* at The House?" Cole asked. How close had she been all this time? Had they barely missed each other? Had she been present in the very place he frequented?

His pulse ratcheted up and he stood, the urge to go after her so strong that he was almost in motion when Damon spoke again.

"Sit down, Cole. Don't make a scene. I'll tell you what I know."

Reluctantly, Cole retook his seat but watched the pair until they disappeared from view.

"Who is she?" Serena asked in a low tone.

She put a gentle hand on his arm, a gesture of comfort he appreciated, though it took everything he had not to snatch his hand back
and go chasing after Ren.

Ren.

God. He couldn't believe it. She was here. And she belonged, *really*
belonged, to another man. There was a clear stamp of ownership for
the world to see. He couldn't even wrap his mind around it. He'd never
imagined that Ren would have gone from their failed experimentation
into a submissive relationship.

Jealousy. Anger. Rage.

Excitement.

Longing ate at his gut until his stomach churned and the food he'd
eaten knotted into a giant fist.

"Tell me," he rasped in Damon's direction. He ignored Serena's
question for now. He had to know all he could about Ren.

Damon calmly sipped his wine, almost as if he were trying to infuse
some of that calm into Cole. "I haven't seen her at The House. But it's
been quite some time since I've seen Lucas. He isn't big into the scene
or into public displays for that matter."

"Who did you see him with?" Cole bit out.

"He doesn't bring his submissives to the club. When I saw him last,
he was simply there to observe. He's extremely private. He only has one
woman at any given time. He's loyal and he demands the same, but his
relationships aren't permanent."

Cole frowned. "He's a player?"

Damon shook his head. "I never got that impression. I've spoken to
him before. Had drinks with him. He finds comfort in the women in
his keeping. Most interestingly, he is completely faithful to his submissive. However, he has discreetly inquired in the past as to men for his
woman. I think he likes to watch. Perhaps he even participates. But he
himself only has sex with the woman in his care."

"How the hell do you know all of this?" Cole demanded.

Christ, like he wanted to imagine Ren with other men while the bastard watched? He was a flaming hypocrite. He wasn't so pissed he didn't recognize the blatant hypocrisy in his anger. He'd had sex with a woman who belonged to another man. He'd indulged in Angelina more than once at Micah's urging.

Damon shrugged. "We've talked on occasion. He's asked for recommendations."

Serena's brow furrowed. "Are you trying to delicately state that you've been with some of his women?"

Damon smiled and lazily ran his fingers over her shoulder. "No, Serena mine. You of all people should know I don't share. Even another man's woman. I don't look down on the practice. However, it isn't for me."

"I need to see her," Cole said tightly. "I . . . have . . . to see her."

"Is she important to you?" Serena asked, her blue gaze studying him intently.

"She used to be everything to me."

Damon lifted an eyebrow. "I wondered."

Cole sent him a questioning look.

"Let's face it. You've had your pick of beautiful, willing women all but throwing themselves at your feet," Damon said dryly. "And yet you've shunned them all. That speaks of a man whose focus is elsewhere."

"I hurt her," Cole said in a low voice. "I was young, arrogant, stupid. I abused her trust. She gave herself to me. She believed I wouldn't hurt her. I did."

Serena's face crinkled in sympathy. Damon simply stared back, silent.

"I need to know how to find her," Cole said. "I have to see her."

Damon sighed. "I can invite Lucas to The House. That's all I can do. I can't give you anything else. He's extremely private. Such a breach would be unforgiveable to him."

"Then invite him. Make damn sure he brings Ren," Cole growled. "I'll turn this whole damn city over if I have to."

Damon leveled his gaze at Cole. "What will you do if Lucas comes?"

"I don't know yet. But I'm damn sure not going to sit back and do nothing. I have to see her. Damn it, she was mine."

"And yet you didn't keep her," Damon returned.

Cole flinched at the reminder. No, he hadn't kept her. He'd walked away. And he'd never found anyone who could occupy the same place in his heart.

CHAPTER 2

"*O*n your knees."

Ren slid gracefully to her knees, thighs open, lips parted, hands resting palms up on her legs. She waited patiently for Lucas's next instruction, her gaze trained straight ahead.

"You were beautiful tonight, Ren. But then you're always beautiful and graceful. I've no complaint in that area."

"Thank you, Lucas."

"As a reward, I'll let you choose tonight's instrument."

"Your hand," she said without hesitation.

He smiled and she thought he liked her choice. "Tell me why."

"I like having the imprint of your hand on my skin. It's a reminder that I belong to you. That you possess me."

He nodded his agreement. "Open your mouth. Wider. No teeth. If your teeth touch me, you'll be punished."

The words were said more for effect than a true warning. Arousal rose, sharp and aching, within her. He knew how his words would fan the flames of her desire. Above all else, she enjoyed the sweet kiss of pain when he saw fit to give it to her.

If she weren't so disciplined, she'd graze her teeth across his rigid length, but they played no games. No silly pretense of disobedience so he would punish her. They both had needs and they fulfilled each other's need perfectly.

She supposed in a way that Lucas cared for her. Emotion had little to do with their relationship. He gave her something far more powerful than love. He provided security and comfort. He protected her, and in return, she gave him her submission, her complete obedience and her respect.

His cock slid over her lips and then over her tongue. She savored the first burst of musk and inhaled his masculine scent. He was rougher tonight, not as patient as he typically was.

He thrust deep, holding there until her chest burned. Then he pulled back and she sucked in a deep breath. He framed her face in his hands and slid his fingers around to the back of her head until they dug into her scalp. Then he thrust again, harder this time.

It was then she realized he was trying to draw her teeth. He wanted to punish her. He was in a mood tonight. He wanted to exert mastery over her, push her limits. For a moment she considered giving in and allowing him the bite of her teeth, but he wouldn't want that either.

He was her master, yes, but he didn't want a weak woman or one who gave in too easily to his silent demands. Yes, she was obedient, absolutely. But only to commands he voiced. If he wanted to punish her, he would, but she wouldn't be an easy conquest for him.

She relaxed further around his impressive girth and allowed him to slide deeper into her throat. He made a sound that was a mixture of approval and frustration. He didn't want her to give in.

And for that reason, he withheld his release for longer than usual. He was rough, relentless, and he showed no mercy. He was determined to push her past her limits, and she was determined to show him she had none.

She purposely blanked herself to everything but the task at hand. Outlasting him.

With a muttered curse, he tightened his hands on her head and poured himself into her throat, forcing her to swallow every single drop. When he finally released her, she rocked back on her heels, dazed by the power of the exchange.

Lucas breathed harshly as he slowly withdrew from her mouth. His grip gentled and he slid his fingers back along the line of her cheekbones before wiping his semen from her lips.

"So fiercely determined," he murmured. "I wonder what it would take to break that restraint."

Ren didn't flinch because she knew Lucas wouldn't do it. He had no interest in breaking her. Eventually he'd grow bored with her just as he'd grown bored with his previous possessions. And when he did, she would be cast adrift again.

He saw her as a challenge. She knew without false modesty that she intrigued him far more than the previous women he'd owned. It wasn't intentional. It was just who she was. She knew what she wanted and what she needed. She had nothing to prove. She wasn't interested in impressing her master. She did only what she needed to do in order to have her needs met. Pleasing the man she gave herself to *was* a need.

He held his hand down to her and she accepted the wordless command. He helped her to her feet and then guided her toward the plush leather chair where much of her pleasure and pain were doled out.

He settled onto the seat, still nude, his muscular legs splayed. His cock was semi-erect. Thick and long, it lay over the top of his thigh and she stared, suddenly overtaken by the urge to have it deep inside her body, taking, demanding.

More likely he would thrust it into her ass when he was through spanking it.

He pulled her between his legs, allowing his hands to smooth up her body, wandering over her curves, up to cup her full breasts.

Her breasts were a source of fascination for him. She was otherwise slender. Slim hips, flat belly, slender legs. She was slightly built and delicate, and he loved that sense of fragility about her that hid a core of steel.

But her breasts were full and plump, a contradiction to the rest of her otherwise boyish figure.

He toyed with her dark nipples, plucking gently at them until they were hard and pointed. But he didn't do as she wanted. He didn't take them into his mouth and suck.

"I'm glad you chose my hand."

He bent her over, positioning her so that she was draped across his lap, her head toward the floor. He tucked his leg over the backs of her knees and then rubbed his hand over her buttocks.

She shivered and he chuckled softly. He loved to draw out her pleasure. Tease her mercilessly. He was hard. No doubt about that. He was ruthless, even. But he was fair and a generous lover. He knew what pleased her and never hesitated to give her what she needed.

Were their needs not so closely aligned, perhaps it would be a different matter. Perhaps he wouldn't be as generous as he was. But they craved the same things. Him taking his pleasure spurred her own.

The smack of his hand against her behind startled her from her sensual thoughts. Fire licked up her spine when he followed the first blow with another in rapid succession.

He alternated splaying his fingers and keeping them tightly held together so the sensation was different each time he struck her flesh.

She moaned and stirred restlessly but his hold tightened on her until she was powerless to move and it only heightened her desire.

This was what she craved beyond all else. To be held completely in a man's power. To know that she had no choice but to accept whatever it was he wanted to do to her. The knowledge was dark and edgy. It made her skate along that forbidden line where it was easy to fall off into complete darkness.

How far would she go? How far would she allow Lucas to go? She'd never answered that question. Had never entertained allowing things to go that far.

She trusted Lucas. Implicitly. But maybe even he didn't trust himself to push beyond the tightly controlled boundaries they'd erected.

He continued to mete out the spanking, but it was a ludicrous word that in no way described the dance they performed. This was no spanking for an undisciplined sub. This was as sexual as fucking, more powerful than kissing.

This was where she got her high. Where she got so pumped on lust that she'd literally let him take her wherever she wanted to go.

She was barely aware when he pushed her to the floor, forced her cheek to the carpet and held her head down, his hand tangled in her hair.

He mounted over her—rough, crude, possessive—like she was a bitch in heat. He thrust first into her pussy and then dragged his cock out and up the seam of her ass. With his free hand, he applied a liberal amount of lubricant, but tonight she didn't even want that. She wanted it hard. She wanted it to hurt. She craved the rough bite of pain when he forced his way past her unwilling opening.

His hand tightened in her hair and he growled low in his throat. "Open to me. Let me take what's mine."

As he knew they would, the words sent her over the edge. She arched up, desperate for his possession. He fit his cock to the tight ring and pushed hard.

She cried out but he yanked upward on her hair until she quieted.

"That's it," he said in a harsh, low voice. "Be silent and take it. You're mine, Ren. Never forget that. I own you."

He powered inside her and held himself deep, cupped over her body, covering every inch of her flesh.

She trembled. Her entire body shook as she fought the orgasm that built like a hurricane.

He laughed and reached underneath to press the flat of his hand to her belly. He slid his fingers down to the juncture of her legs and lightly touched her clit.

She clenched her teeth, closed her eyes and willed herself to control the reaction.

He was a master at knowing her body. Knowing what she loved. He knew how to talk to her, what words aroused her. How hard to take her. When to be rough and when to be gentle.

His fingers slid even lower, toying with the entrance to her pussy. He fingered her roughly as his cock twitched deep inside her ass. Then he withdrew, dragging that huge erection over distended flesh.

She moaned again and let out a sigh.

"No, Ren, you don't get to come yet. I'm going to fuck you for a good long while and you're going to be a good girl and you're going to take it up the ass and keep taking it until I tell you to come. And then I'm going to fill your ass full of my cum and you're going to beg me for more."

And she would. She closed her eyes. She'd beg him never to stop. He'd come inside her and then he'd go back to fucking her until his hot liquid ran down her leg. And she'd love every damn minute of it.

CHAPTER 3

*R*en stretched and glanced up at the clock. She grimaced. It was time for a break. Lucas insisted she not work to the exclusion of all else. It annoyed her sometimes, but the simple fact was, that if he didn't interfere, she'd forget to eat, wouldn't sleep and would work tirelessly until she collapsed.

And well, she was in touch enough with her feminine wants and needs to know that she loved that he took such good care of her. She needed that.

She put down the pencil she'd made preliminary sketches with, carefully pushed her drawings into an orderly pile and closed her sketchbook so the weight would prevent them from falling out.

Deadlines had little meaning to her. Once she got inspiration for the story she wanted to tell and the images began dancing in her mind, she was driven to work until the book was completed. Often that meant finishing well ahead of her deadline. It was an illness, this compulsion to be early. But it was who she was and it served her well in her career as an author of children's books.

Rennie Michaels. A slight variation of her real name. It sounded light and fun and on the level with the children who she wrote for.

She got up from her desk and rubbed absently at a kink in her neck. When she looked up, to her surprise, Lucas was leaning against the doorframe, his lazy gaze stroking lightly over her body.

He didn't often come into her studio. It was the one place that was hers. It was provided by him and he insisted that she be able to maintain her privacy here. Anywhere else in his home, she was his. There was no privacy. She belonged to him and he could intrude at will. But here was her work place and her place to be alone with her thoughts. It was off limits to him, a condition he himself had put into place.

She stood still, unsure of what he wanted her to do.

He pushed off the doorframe and walked into her studio, hands shoved into his jeans pocket. He was barefooted, as he typically was in his home. For a man as wealthy and cultured as he was, in his private sanctuary he was a creature of comfort, usually in well-worn jeans, a T-shirt and sometimes flip-flops.

"We've received an invitation," he said when he stopped in front of her.

She arched one eyebrow. She didn't know anyone here. She and Lucas had met in his Las Vegas nightclub a year ago. She'd been out of sorts because her last relationship had been a complete disaster and he'd been an immediate source of security. He'd taken her home with him that night and they'd been together ever since.

She was honest enough with herself to know she'd used him in the beginning. He knew it also and was unbothered by it. She cared about him now. In a lot of ways, he was her best friend. Theirs was an odd friendship to be sure, but it worked for both parties.

"A friend of mine who owns a private club has invited us both to attend an intimate gathering in three nights' time."

She frowned. "What kind of private club and what kind of intimate gathering?"

He flashed that lazy grin. "You know very well what kind of club. You aren't stupid, Ren."

"Have I met this friend?"

He shook his head. "The last time I saw him was right before I left for Vegas the time you and I met."

"And what are we supposed to . . . do . . . at this intimate gathering?"

He touched her then. Smoothed his hand up her arm, a gesture meant to reassure her. And it did.

"You know very well I'm not into public displays of dominance. I sense you aren't either, though we've never really discussed it. I've been blunt about the fact I find it distasteful and we've adhered to my wishes on the subject. But tell me, Ren, does the idea of being played with in front of others turn you on?"

She wrinkled her nose. "What we do isn't playing, Lucas. It's not a game. And it's . . . private. At least to the extent of it not being a public spectacle. Is that what your friend wants?"

She knew that it was a particular kink of Lucas's to watch while another man fucked the woman he owned. He'd told her about his past submissives and how turned on he was by watching another man not only possess her but command her.

Interestingly enough, he'd never invited another man to fuck her, and Ren couldn't decide if she was happy or disappointed. She wouldn't lie. In some ways the idea titillated her and made all her girly parts tingle. There was something extremely naughty and forbidden about having the man who owned you give you to another man to do with as he wished.

A shiver went up her spine and she decided that yes, the idea did turn her on. It turned her on very much. But the public display of mastery? Not so much. It reeked of showmanship. Of some fake, hyped-up display of testosterone that did nothing for her. She loved the quiet relationship she shared with Lucas.

"No, I don't think that's what he wants at all. I think what he wants is our company for the evening. He's a lot like I am. We share a lot of the same tastes but perhaps he's a little more possessive than I am when it comes to his woman."

Both her brows rose at that and Lucas smiled. "He doesn't share his woman under any circumstance. I find I don't mind if the situation is right."

"So he wants our company, but he wants us to come to his club," she said slowly. "Why not invite us to dinner? Or out for drinks?"

Lucas shrugged. "For the same reason I entertain guests at my clubs. We're both private people and as such I'm sure he's as picky about who he allows into his sanctuary as I am. It's a neutral place and yet perhaps more intimate than a restaurant or a bar."

"If you wish me to accompany you, you know that I will."

He nodded. "I know this. But I'd like to know if you have a desire to go or if you will go only because you think it pleases me."

Her brow furrowed. This didn't sound like Lucas. He was a man who commanded. He was arrogant. Not obnoxiously so, but he was very comfortable wearing the mantle of authority. He expected obedience. He'd never been particularly concerned with whether she truly wished to accompany him someplace.

It made him sound like an unfeeling bastard. It wasn't so. If she wasn't feeling well or was busy with work, he didn't expect her to accommodate his wishes. He was very good at picking up on her moods and her health. He often knew before she did when she was getting sick.

He took excellent care of her. She had no complaint there. But if there was no solid reason for her to be unable to attend something he wished her to be present for, she went. He didn't offer her a choice.

"I don't know that I have a preference one way or the other," she said honestly. "You know I love to please you. I don't know this friend, so obviously I have no investment in seeing him. I suppose if there is kinky sex to view that might entice me to be more eager to go."

She finished with a small grin and he laughed, shaking his head.

"I love how uninhibited you are and how unapologetic you are about loving sex. I wonder if you even know how desirable it makes you in my eyes. There is something intensely sexy about a strong woman who's confident in her sexuality and furthermore celebrates it."

Her cheeks grew hot at the uncharacteristic praise. His eyes were warm and he seemed so mellow today. It made her want to please him even more.

"Then we should go. You never know. Maybe we'll learn something new and can practice it after we return home," she said cheekily.

He pulled her into his side and stroked his hand down her back and down to cup her ass. She loved that he frequently touched her. And not just touched her but was possessive about it. He often did so in public, like he was telling the world that she belonged to him. That he was proud she belonged to him.

With his other hand, he absently ran a finger over the platinum collar around her neck. Then he slid his finger between it and her skin and pulled her forcefully forward until their mouths were a mere breath apart.

He kissed her, savaging her mouth until her lips were swollen and tender. After a moment, he removed his hand and carefully eased her away.

"We'll go. I'll buy something new for you to wear. I have something killer in mind. I may not want to demonstrate my authority over you in public, but I want every male in the place to look at you with lust in their eyes and know that you belong to me."

She smiled because she loved it when he got all growly and possessive. He oftern took her to his clubs and for all practical purposes he kept her on a leash. There wasn't a person in the club who couldn't clearly see his stamp of possession all over her.

And for her part, she didn't give a damn who knew the nature of their relationship. She felt no shame whatsoever for anyone to know that she served Lucas in all aspects and that she looked to him for absolute protection and care.

"Now let's go eat. You need a break and I've encroached on your private quarters long enough. Afterward I feel a distinct need to fuck you for the entire afternoon."

CHAPTER 4

amon laced his fingers through Serena's and brought her hand to his lips. It seemed such a natural action and Cole wondered if Damon even knew how frequently he touched and kissed his wife. It was done absently as if the habit was so strong he did it without realizing.

Serena was dressed tonight. Cole had noticed that since Serena's belly had begun to swell and the evidence of her pregnancy was so clearly visible that Damon had clamped down, almost as if he wanted no one but himself to see his pregnant wife.

Before, it was a common sight for Cole to come into The House when Damon was present and see Serena spread, waiting for the kiss of the flogger. Often Cole prepared her for Damon, clamping her or tying her in various positions.

But these days, no one but Damon touched her, and he'd become intensely private about putting his lover on display. He damn sure hadn't so much as touched her with anything but the most gentle of hands since the start of her pregnancy. He showered her with affection both in public and in private. Cole wondered if having a child would alter Damon's practices on a permanent basis.

In fact, were it not for Damon having invited Lucas and Ren and wanting Serena to act as his social hostess, Cole doubted Serena would even be at The House. The further Serena got into her pregnancy, the more protective Damon became of her. He himself didn't spend very much time at The House these days. He left the running to his manager and gave Cole leeway to oversee as he pleased.

Cole shoved his hands into his expensive slacks and looked at the entrance to the social room for the hundredth time since he'd arrived. Damon had assured him that Lucas had accepted his invitation and that he would be present, but Cole's impatience was a living, breathing demon within him.

"Cool it, man," Damon murmured beside him. "Go get a drink. Relax. Have you even given a thought to what you'll say? You don't want to cause an awkward scene. I don't think that's the impression you want to make when you haven't seen her in so many years. And it wouldn't do to insult Lucas. A submissive is quite protective of their master. If she feels you're disrespecting Lucas, it could go badly."

"I know all of that," Cole said. "I may have been stupid once. But—"

Damon held up a hand in apology. "I have every faith in your knowledge, Cole. Or I would have never trusted you with what I treasure most in the world."

Cole turned, taking Damon's suggestion that he go collect a drink and calm the fuck down. He wasn't used to the wildness of his emotional state. He was calm. He lived his life in a calm, reflective manner. Nothing rattled him.

Except Ren.

Always Ren.

She alone had the power to unhinge him.

He picked up a glass of wine and brought it to his mouth. The flavor was excellent. Damon had very good tastes. Expensive tastes.

He sighed and turned around, his gaze taking in the room once more. And then he froze.

Lucas Holt stood in the doorway, Ren at his side.

Cole drank in the sight of her. He couldn't look away. While she'd always been beautiful, she'd grown into a gorgeous, mature woman who lacked the slight edge of youth to her features.

She was petite—she'd always been a small thing—barely reaching Lucas's shoulder. Her shiny black hair was flowing over her shoulders and down her back, wild and beautiful like her.

And her eyes. The slight lilt at the corners signified her half-Korean heritage, but they weren't dark. Instead they were a lush green with flecks of warm brown swirled until they became an unusual shade. They were vibrant, almost glowing, even across the distance.

She was so perfect she made him ache.

His gaze wandered over her as Lucas made his way toward Damon. She wore tight jeans that molded to her slim hips and ass. Low slung so that her belly button ring was bared and winked daringly at him.

Her top was barely much at all. She wore no bra and the silky material of her top clung to the generous swells of her breasts. It tied around her neck and completely bared her back and that tattoo Cole was so intimately familiar with. He'd taken her to have the ink done. To mark the occasion of her eighteenth birthday.

She smiled at Damon as Lucas introduced her. She sparkled. There was no other word for her. She wore a vivacious, confident smile. Not once did she look around to see if others were watching her or were curious about her. She was focused entirely on Lucas.

Jealousy knotted Cole's gut. He hated that feeling. It was irrational. Jealousy was a stupid, pointless emotion that never brought anything but more frustration and a sense of helplessness. It wasn't something he was familiar with. Until now.

He wanted her to look at *him* that way. She had once. She'd looked at him as though he were the only man in the world.

Why had she sought out a relationship like this? Cole hadn't imagined that she'd ever want any part of the lifestyle. He had botched things so badly with Ren. He'd been nothing more than a boy playing at being someone's keeper. He'd abused her trust and it was something that still ate at him to this day.

Damon glanced his way, but Cole was still rooted to the spot, unable to move as he stared at Ren. He suddenly felt unsure and he hated that feeling above all others.

He considered himself a confident man. He'd been successful early in life, driven by ambition that certainly couldn't be attributed to insecurity. His only missteps had been with Ren, and maybe that was why he was now faced with hesitancy.

Ren and Lucas moved away from Damon. Lucas put his hand to Ren's bare back and shot her a quick look of affection—and approval. Then he directed her toward the bar. Exactly where Cole was standing, staring at the only woman to ever fully capture his heart.

Ren glanced around the room, a little surprised by how posh and . . . sedate . . . it looked. It was like attending any other cocktail party. Who would even know that this place was devoted to sexual practices that didn't fall into the traditional realm.

Damon and his wife had been exceedingly gracious. Serena was elegant and most definitely submissive, but it was obvious that Damon adored her. And truly there was nothing more attractive to her than a man who clearly adored his woman.

"What would you like to drink, Ren?" Lucas asked.

She blinked and turned back from her perusal of the room. It was then she saw him, standing just a few feet away, his blue eyes burning into her. She stared back in shock, in awareness. Even after so many years, her heart leapt and her skin tingled in remembrance.

He hadn't changed. Well, maybe that wasn't entirely true. The youthful, handsome features of his early twenties had been replaced by the handsome ruggedness of age. He was tall but not as lanky as he'd been when she'd been with him. He'd filled out. Solid. Strong.

Power emanated from him. Controlled power. It was as though he boiled just below the surface but outwardly projected calm and confidence.

She shivered as his gaze skirted over her. He recognized her too, and she was instantly aware of the hunger in his eyes. She felt hunted, and it was a *delicious* sensation.

"Cole."

It came out as a whisper, barely discernible in the quiet din of mingled voices and random conversation. But he heard her. Acknowledged the address with a step forward.

"Ren."

She nearly moaned. Her name was a caress, sliding off his tongue with all the practice that had made her name an endearment. He'd always said her name like she was the most special thing in his world. With reverence. With . . . love.

Lucas's hold suddenly tightened on her. She knew that touch. It was possessive. A clear hands-off to an intruder. It was his way of saying *mine*. It was rare indeed for Lucas to assume such a posture. He didn't often see another man as a threat. The fact that he did so now told her all too clearly that the electric tension between her and Cole was plainly evident.

"It's good to see you again," Cole said quietly. "You look beautiful. But then, you always have."

Her heart squeezed and for a moment she worried that she'd be rendered unable to speak. She swallowed and tried to control the fact that her knees shook with nervousness.

"You're looking good too, Cole. How are you?"

It was an awkward, stilted conversation that only grew more uncomfortable with each passing second. Lucas sensed her disquiet and pulled her further into the protection of his body.

"Ren, introduce me to your friend," Lucas said in an easy, casual tone that completely belied the tension she felt in his coiled muscles.

Ren broke her gaze and looked up at Lucas. Then back at Cole. "Lucas, this is Cole Madison, an old friend of mine. Cole, this is Lucas Holt."

Lucas made no move to release her so he could shake Cole's hand, but then neither did Cole make an effort to do more than nod in Lucas's direction.

"A former lover," Lucas said, a slight lift at the corner of his mouth.

Ren nodded. She was always truthful with Lucas. Theirs was an open and honest relationship. She'd met Lucas's previous lovers in the past. He hadn't tried to hide them from her. Neither would she hide her previous relationship with Cole.

"We were a hell of a lot more than that," Cole said bluntly.

Lucas's eyebrow arched and he stared coolly at Cole. "Were you now?"

"*Were* is the operative word," Ren said quietly. "Cole chose a life that didn't include me. It's in the past."

It was strange to be having such a direct conversation. Weren't encounters with former lovers supposed to be filled with silly small talk and clear avoidance of the depth of the relationship? Weren't they supposed to pretend that neither mattered to the other?

"I made a mistake."

Nothing Cole said could have shocked her more than this. Her eyes widened and she went still against Lucas. An action that didn't go unnoticed by the man she belonged to.

"Then I must be very grateful for your mistake," Lucas said in a deceptively soft voice. "For she is now my greatest treasure."

Ren's eyes narrowed and she looked up at Lucas, baffled by his statement. They simply didn't have that kind of relationship. Did he value her? Absolutely. Ren had no doubt as to that. Friendship. Respect. He offered her protection. She gave him her absolute obedience and submission. But never had they been into flowery descriptors that came far too close at hinting at deeper feelings.

Or maybe it was a male posturing thing that had to do with entirely too much testosterone.

Suddenly the tension was too much for her to bear. She didn't want Cole to see how undone she was by his presence. By his admission that he'd made a mistake!

She turned her chin upward so she could look at Lucas. "Excuse me. I need to go to the ladies' room."

His hold loosened on her and he pressed a quick kiss to her forehead. "Of course. I'll be waiting here. What would you like to drink?"

"Something strong," she said, not realizing how much it said about her current state. "You choose."

She slipped away, not even knowing where the bathroom was, but more important, she just needed to get away to collect herself.

Once in the hallway, she glanced right and left and chose right since she and Lucas had entered from the left and she hadn't thought they'd passed a bathroom.

She finally found what she was looking for and slipped inside, locking the door behind her. She leaned against the vanity, her hands gripping the edge as she stared at her reflection in the mirror.

She looked . . . shocked. Unsteady. Her eyes had a bewildered look. Her pulse was too rapid and the pressure in her chest was ever increasing.

It wasn't as if she thought of Cole on a daily basis. Quite the opposite. She'd made peace with his defection a long time ago.

Really, Ren? Is that why you're standing here out of sorts? Because you made peace with the man you adored beyond reason who left you after awakening a fire inside you that has never been extinguished?

She ran water over her shaking hands but was careful not to mess up the light makeup she'd applied before arriving. She didn't want any sign of her disturbance to be evident.

When she finally managed to hold out her hand and see no noticeable tremble, she turned off the water and dried her hands.

A knock at the door startled her.

"Ren, open the door."

Lucas she might have expected. But it was Cole standing just two feet away and suddenly her hands shook so hard that she had no hope of regaining her composure.

CHAPTER 5

*R*en briefly contemplated refusing but then she realized she was huddling in a bathroom *hiding* for God's sake. She opened the door, flicked her hair over her shoulder and arched one eyebrow as she stared back at Cole.

He filled the doorway. Big. Broad shouldered. So damn good-looking that she couldn't help but stare.

Time had been extraordinarily good to him. It wasn't fair. If there was any justice, he'd be balding, sporting a potbelly and married with two point five bratty children and a wife who nagged him on a daily basis.

"What do you want?" she asked.

He stared at her a moment longer, his gaze stroking over her as surely as if he caressed her with his hand. "You, Ren. I want you."

Her eyes widened in surprise. If she weren't so flabbergasted, she'd laugh. Lucas. Cole. Herself. All apparently blunt people who didn't play coy games and pretend they were unaffected.

So many things were on the tip of her tongue, but in the end, none of them mattered and all were better left unsaid. They solved nothing. So instead, she spoke a simple truth.

"Even if I wanted such a thing, I belong to another man. I don't just belong in the symbolic sense of having a relationship. He owns me. I am his possession."

She watched to see if he so much as blinked. He didn't. But then perhaps he too had followed the path they'd struck out on together all those years ago. He was after all in a private club for just such practices.

"You said 'even if I wanted.' Do you want it, Ren?"

She frowned. Again, she hadn't expected that approach.

"No," she replied honestly. "We're two very different people now, Cole. We can't just pick up because we once shared something special. You can't just walk back into my life after ten years and expect me to open my arms."

Cole's eyes glittered and his jaw tightened at her response. "Tell me this: If there was no Lucas, if you didn't belong to another man, would you be holding me at arms' length right now or would you be willing to see if there was still a spark between us?"

She'd already been honest. There was no point in fudging the truth now. She closed her eyes, breathed out and then reopened them again, hoping she sounded steady and calm. "Maybe? I can't really answer that. My loyalty lies elsewhere. The point is there *is* a Lucas. I'm not free. This conversation is pointless."

"What about your heart?" he asked in a quiet voice. "Where does *that* lie, Ren?"

She held up her hands. "Enough, Cole. Nothing good can come of this. It was nice to see you. The years have been good to you. I would never be disloyal to Lucas. He *owns* me. I'm happy to be his. I'm his by choice. My choice. There is no other place I want to be more."

"I'm glad to hear that what belongs to me can't be swayed by the pretty words of others," Lucas drawled.

Ren jumped, took a step back and stared over Cole's shoulder to see Lucas leaning against the opposite wall. How long had he been there? And why did she feel so damn guilty?

She rubbed her hands down her jeans, dismayed at how this evening had turned out. She simply hadn't been prepared to see Cole again after so long and definitely not to be bombarded by memories of them together and his bluntness about wanting . . . What did he want? It all sounded so crazy. They see each other again, in some sex club, and he wants her back just like that?

She pushed forward and frowned as she automatically went to Lucas's side. He slid an arm around her but it was a gesture of support, not a movement meant to signal his possession to another man. She appreciated that. At the moment she didn't feel like being in the middle of some pissing match. She needed comfort and Lucas had sensed it.

As she stared back at Cole, he looked . . . tortured. Again, why? None of this made sense. Unless . . . ?

"You knew I'd be here tonight, didn't you? Did you plan this? How did you know? You weren't surprised to see me. This didn't come out of the blue at all."

Lucas's hand tightened on her upper arm and he pulled her in closer, as if to tell her not to worry. But he too waited for Cole's response, his dark eyes staring intently at the man who'd boldly encroached on his territory.

Maybe he was curious. Ren wasn't entirely certain why Lucas was allowing this to go further. At times he was absolutely unreadable. This was one of those times. She didn't sense that he was angry. She didn't want him angry.

Cole's lips drew into a firm line. His jaw grew tight, which only accentuated the strong lines of his face. Gone were the traces of youth.

He was a formidable man. One that she'd absolutely be drawn to. That promise of dominance. The quiet strength in those intense eyes.

She'd had a taste. Just a taste. Mixed with youthful innocence. It had been bittersweet. She'd loved him so much, but they'd been too young to know what they were getting into.

"I asked Damon to invite you," he said by way of admission. "I saw you the other night when I was eating with Damon and Serena. I knew I had to see you again. I couldn't walk away . . ."

Like he had before.

The words lay unspoken and heavy between them. The air was electric, the silence unnerving. She swallowed but couldn't rid herself of the sudden knot that was closing her throat.

"And yet you knew she belonged to me," Lucas said mildly.

"She was mine first."

Lucas nodded. "That may be so, but you're her past. I'm her future."

Ren glanced up in surprise but Lucas admonished her with a quick squeeze of her arm. It was the first time he issued any sort of order since they'd arrived. He wanted her silence.

She lowered her gaze and his grip slowly loosened.

Cole's eyes glittered in challenge. "So you say. But I've not heard Ren say the same."

Lucas studied him a moment, his expression odd. "Interesting that you'd make such a distinction. As the one who owns her, body and soul, the two are the same. What I say *is* what she says. Clearly you are a man of similar tastes and yet you'd expect her to refute my word. Would you tolerate the same if she were yours?"

"I would want her to be happy," Cole said from behind tightly clenched teeth. "Even if it wasn't with me."

"In that we are agreed," Lucas said. "Ren's happiness is of utmost importance to me."

"Then allow her to make the choice."

Lucas smiled. "She already has."

Cole stared at Lucas, the man who *owned* Ren. It wasn't an alien concept. It could be argued that Damon owned Serena, although she owned his heart, body and soul as well. He was hers every bit as much as she was his.

He'd never given the idea of ownership much thought. It was something that over the years he'd contemplated. He'd seen. He'd experienced. Though he'd never owned a woman. He'd never been close enough to one to feel proprietary over. He'd only ever wanted to possess one woman.

Now, faced with a man who was very clear in his ownership, and backed by Ren herself, who seemed very comfortable with the label and the sentiment, he was . . . appalled? Dismayed? Frustrated?

He was a flaming hypocrite because from the moment he'd laid eyes on Ren again, he'd been seized by a force so strong that it staggered him. A voice inside his head that told him to claim her. That she belonged to him. That *he* wanted to own her.

He wanted to be able to show her that he wasn't the same boy playing at dominance. He would never make such a brutal mistake now. He would never hurt her as he'd done when he was young and inexperienced and had no business testing the waters with a girl he adored.

He'd been arrogant and self-assured. He didn't need to be taught and certainly not by another man. Ren was his and he needed no instruction when it came to her, did he? He knew her body intimately. Had spent hours exploring it, tasting it, possessing it.

He'd been so stupid. So very *wrong*.

He couldn't accept that Ren was beyond his reach. But he also knew that there were different rules for the world he lived in. The world Ren lived in.

He nodded slowly, but his gaze locked with Lucas's in a clear message. This wasn't over. Not by a long shot. Lucas dipped his head in acknowledgment.

"I think perhaps it's best if we go now," Lucas said in that quiet, controlled voice. "I don't want to cause Ren any further upset. Give my regrets to Damon and Serena."

He turned to Ren as if giving her permission to speak. She was a disciplined submissive. So beautiful. Elegant in her obedience and her respect for the man who mastered her. It made Cole ache.

She touched Lucas's arm as if to thank him and then she turned to Cole.

"It was nice to see you again, Cole."

It took all of Cole's restraint not to reach out and touch her. Not to take her hand and feel the softness of her palm. Turn it over in his hand and kiss it. He wanted to rub her hand over his cheek and down his neck. He just wanted to touch her. To feel her against him.

And now she was turning to go. Panic flared in his chest. Spread to his throat, squeezing relentlessly until his pulse thudded rapidly, each beat like a hammer at his temples.

Lucas nudged Ren away and as she started down the hall, Lucas held out a business card to Cole.

With a frown, Cole took the card. He was still holding it, staring down at the name and contact information for Lucas Holt when Lucas turned and disappeared down the hall after Ren.

CHAPTER 6

*R*en wasn't herself. Lucas knew her intimately. Better than he'd ever known another woman, which he found interesting given the length of their association.

He'd had longer relationships. Their year together was actually one of his shorter agreements. But they meshed well.

And yet, as well as he knew her, he also recognized that there was still so much of her to learn. Maybe that was why she still fascinated him so much.

He watched her frown over her sketch, chew absently at her pencil and then with disgust, ball up the paper and toss it across the room.

Yes, his Ren was distracted, and he knew well the source of her preoccupation.

If he asked, he knew she'd be truthful. It was what he liked most about her. She was refreshingly honest even when she thought he'd be unhappy with her response. He never grew angry over the truth, though. It was a clear invitation for lies, and he hated untruths above all else.

But he wouldn't force her to voice the source of her distraction. He sensed how unsettled she was and he worried about her happiness.

With a sigh, he turned away, knowing what he needed to do, but at the same time, reluctant. His reluctance intrigued him as much as the idea that he didn't yet know all there was to know of his Ren.

It would seem that he did indeed possess the ability to feel jealousy. This was new for him, and while he recognized it for what it was, he was mystified by it.

Perhaps he'd allowed Ren to get closer than he'd intended. But then he hadn't done it consciously. Somehow she'd managed to slip past his defenses and he doubted she'd tried to do so. She seemed as content with the status of their relationship as he was. Or had been. Now he wasn't so sure what he wanted or expected. And that bothered him.

The question was, what did he want?

He walked quietly away from the doorway of Ren's office, went into his own, closed the door and then sank into the chair behind his desk.

He fingered the message left by his secretary, who came in half a day to take care of paperwork. Cole had called as Lucas had known he would.

He laid his hand over the phone receiver, staring at that message for a long moment. Then he picked it up and keyed in Cole's number.

CHAPTER 7

$\mathcal{L}$ucas entered Ren's office to find her asleep at her desk. Her
cheek rested against the polished mahogany and her silky hair splayed
out over the piles of paper that littered the surface.

He'd left her to contemplate for the last two days. She'd immersed
herself in her work and she seemed deep in thought even when she was
away from it and in his presence.

Normally he wouldn't tolerate such inattention. But he found himself unable to punish her for the confusion she was feeling. It was also
becoming increasingly clear that he had a soft spot for this particular
woman.

He reached down, slid his hands underneath her slight body and
lifted her into his arms. She came to rest against his chest with a small
sigh and she immediately snuggled into his hold.

He smiled and kissed her brow as he strode out of her office toward
the bedroom they shared. Once there, he placed her on the bed and
then began undressing her.

She roused and stared at him with sleepy eyes as he slid her jeans over her hips.

"I did it again," she mumbled.

He nodded. "You did. You worked too hard and too long without a break. When did you eat last?"

She frowned and her lips pursed in concentration. "This morning, I think."

He scowled and she smiled. She reached up to feather her fingers over his brow, brushing aside his hair.

He removed her jeans and stared down at her nearly naked body. She was down to only her panties. They wouldn't last long. She had a drawer full of expensive lacy confections because he did love to tear them.

He ran his hands up her legs until his thumbs brushed over the thin material covering her pussy. He dipped one finger underneath the band, ran it downward and then he ripped, rending the material in two, the ends fluttering outward to bare her to his gaze.

The diamond teardrop glittered from her navel. Above the hood shielding her clitoris was a triangle of dark hair, trimmed short and neat. Her pussy lips were bare. Silky soft to the touch. Waxed smooth every week.

He warred with himself over how he wanted tonight to go down. There was a part of him eager to reassert his dominance. To take her to the very edge of her boundaries until they were both satisfied that he owned every inch of her body.

The other part of him wanted to be gentle with her. Shower her with tenderness. And ask her to bare her secrets.

The last gave him pause. Ask. Not demand. Somehow it seemed important that she willingly give him what he wanted to know. He could demand, yes. And she'd willingly oblige him. She was perfect in that regard. He'd never met a woman quite so comfortable in her skin. So open. So . . . at peace.

But now he wondered about that peace and what it had cost her. Her meeting with Cole had rattled her. He'd seen it. Known it. Hadn't exactly known how to digest what he'd witnessed.

One thing he knew. He wanted to know more about the much younger Ren. The Ren who'd once belonged to Cole Madison, a man who clearly hadn't forgotten her in the many years since they went their separate ways.

"What are you thinking?"

She lay beneath him, quiet, soft. Her gaze on him. Her attention focused solely on him. He leaned down and pressed a single kiss to the soft lips of her pussy and enjoyed the quick shiver that rocked through her body.

So responsive. So in tune with his wants and needs. He wondered if he'd ever find a woman more perfect for him. And yet, he'd never given much thought to the permanence of their relationship. Her role in his life.

Now he was going to be made to do just that, and he wasn't sure he liked the circumstances that were going to force his hand.

He shifted his body up until he lay on his side next to her, his head propped in his palm as he stared down into her eyes. She was still staring oddly at him, obviously perplexed by his mood.

He touched his finger to the soft skin of her cheek and traced a line down to her jaw. "Tell me about Cole Madison."

He didn't miss the sudden flare in her eyes or the slight tension coiling through her body. She was tempted to look away but her discipline didn't desert her. She kept her gaze steady and fixed on him.

Then she sighed. "We were childhood sweethearts. I say childhood. I was young. Just sixteen when we first met. He was twenty. In college. I adored him. He was everything a sixteen-year-old girl dreams of. Athletic. Gorgeous. Sweet. Protective and very alpha. Even then I knew I wanted and needed a very strong man. I didn't have an explanation or even a name for it at the time, but I was instantly attracted to him."

Lucas continued to stroke her cheek, more to offer her comfort and to let her know he wasn't threatened by the retelling of her first love.

"Were you intimate at such a young age?" he asked. "That could have gotten him into serious legal trouble in most, if not all, states."

Ren shook her head. "He never pressured me for sex. In fact, he was adamant that we wait. It would probably make him sound weak or Beta to most people, but he was confident, self-assured. All he cared about was me and he thought I was too young for a sexual relationship."

Lucas nodded in grudging respect. Not many young men would have cared whether their pretty girlfriend was too immature for sex.

"I thought perhaps we would consummate our relationship when I turned eighteen. I was positively breathless as my birthday neared. We'd been together for two years. He was about to graduate college. I loved him. I was sure he was the one I wanted to be with sexually and emotionally.

"But he surprised me by taking me to get the tattoo on my back. My parents were very strict and perhaps this was another reason Cole held off and didn't pressure me. He didn't want to cause problems for me with my mom and dad. They were very conservative. They forbade me from even getting my ears pierced until I turned eighteen."

He tweaked one earlobe. "You never did get them pierced."

She shook her head. "I got the tattoo instead. It was exactly what I wanted. I designed it myself. Cole insisted that I not go to some fly-by-night, back-alley tattoo parlor, so he took me into the city to a very expensive artist who did the ink. It was the best birthday gift I ever received. In a lot of ways it wasn't just a tattoo. It was a mark of my independence. A new milestone in my life."

So far Lucas wasn't seeing the problem in her relationship with

Cole. He seemed like a pretty decent guy, which annoyed him, truth be told. He wanted—needed—a reason to back out of the decision he'd already made.

"Only after the tattoo was completely healed did we make love for the first time. It was so perfect. He was my first and he made it so very special for me."

She went silent a moment and though she still looked up at him, she was no longer seeing him. She was somewhere else. Lost in her memories. Sadness entered her eyes and he suddenly wanted nothing more than to hold her and shield her from hurt.

"After that first time, we became inseparable. Cole took over. Not in a negative way. I welcomed it. I loved that he took care of me. He anticipated my needs. He provided for me. It was like a fairy tale. It was precisely what I wanted in a relationship.

"We began to talk about it. We didn't just slip into it. We knew what we were was . . . different. And exciting. We were young and we weren't even sure exactly how to define this type of relationship. We began to experiment. Sexually. We quickly discovered what we did and didn't enjoy. We embraced what turned us on and satisfied us emotionally and quickly discarded what didn't meet a need."

Again she broke off and went silent.

"What happened?" Lucas asked.

"One night things went too far. It was an accident. He was using a whip and he didn't have much experience."

Lucas winced. A whip wasn't for an inexperienced hand. Not at all. It took long hours of practice to be able to wield it without injuring your partner. He didn't use whips. He didn't like them. He liked leather. Crops. Belts. Or the flat of his own hand. He also liked wood. Smooth, treated wood so there was no chance of Ren being injured by splinters or rough surfaces.

Then he frowned as a thought occurred to him. He turned her so the scar on her shoulder was visible. It was about four inches long, curving over her shoulder blade.

He traced the scar with his fingertip and then leaned down to kiss it. "Did he do this?"

She swallowed visibly and nodded.

Lucas gripped her shoulder, kissed her again and softly nuzzled the barely raised area of flesh. Had she been badly frightened? Had it broken her trust?

"It must have scared you."

Ren rose up on her elbow so they were eye level. "That's just the thing, Lucas. It didn't frighten me. It hurt, yes. No doubt about that. Cole was devastated. I mean, truly devastated. He was so horrified that he'd hurt me. But I loved him. I trusted him. I knew he hadn't meant to. I knew he'd cut off his right arm before ever willingly hurting me. I *knew* all of this. But he was the one who couldn't get past it."

Lucas's forehead wrinkled in confusion.

"He was the one who walked away," Ren said softly, pain evident in her voice. "I begged him. God, I begged him. He hated himself. I think it made it worse for me to tell him it didn't matter, that I loved him and knew he hadn't meant to. He made this comment about how often women forgave their abusers over and over and how they were willing to say it was an accident when they were hurt. In his mind, he crossed an unforgivable line and nothing I said could change his mind.

"He began to question every aspect of our relationship. How he had complete control and dominance. How I complied with his wishes. He worried I'd lost my individuality, that somehow he'd swallowed me up. He was horrified that he'd become this monster who held me on such a tight leash that I had no life outside of him."

"Did he?"

Her denial was immediate and he believed her. She was honest in all things. About herself. Her mistakes. Her shortcomings. If she truly believed that she'd been abused, she would tell him so now.

"He made a mistake," Ren said painfully. "One mistake. We were young. We were inexperienced. We were testing the waters of a relationship we knew defied societal norms. We decided together what did and didn't work for us. He and I were both drawn to the idea of pain as pleasure and how much pain was too much before it overrode all else and simply became . . . pain. He was always so careful and he simply made a *mistake*."

"Was that the only mark?" Lucas asked. Cole's reaction seemed extreme, but then he'd been a much younger man and it appeared as though he'd had a deep sense of responsibility toward Ren even at that young age. It was hard to know if Lucas would have felt the same if he'd made such a mistake in his youth with a woman he hadn't cared for as deeply as Cole had cared for Ren.

Ren frowned and her eyes glittered with unshed tears. "No. But it was the only mark that left a scar. My back was striped. The skin was broken in three places but the place on my shoulder was the worst. The whip sliced open the skin and I bled a lot. Cole took me in to be stitched."

Lucas pulled her in closer, offering his warmth and the strength of his body. He knew it was something that comforted her, and her sadness was unsettling to him. He didn't like the look in her eyes or the sound of her voice.

He felt . . . helpless and it was an odd sensation. Not at all one he was accustomed to.

She was getting to him. Worming her way deeper and he found it perplexing. Why her? What was it about her?

"So he left?" Lucas finally asked.

Ren sighed against him and again, her unhappiness struck a chord deep inside his chest. "Not at first. He took care of me. Dressed the wound every single day. Went with me to have the stitches removed. But he didn't touch me sexually. Not even once. He drifted further and further away. It was like he felt he wasn't worthy of me anymore. It was so frustrating. I tried to talk to him but I just couldn't get through. The harder I tried, the more convinced he was that he wielded too much power over me and that he wasn't responsible enough to shoulder it and wield it properly. He blamed himself for 'pushing' me into the lifestyle. He seemed to forget that it had held as much interest to me as it had to him from the very beginning. It was a need I had, one I recognized, even before we ever embarked on the sexual side of our relationship. But he didn't see it that way. He thought he'd forced me into something I didn't want. That I'd done it all just to please him. And I know I'm making him sound like a martyr and that now, years later, it may sound ridiculous, but you have to understand, this affected him profoundly."

"Yes, I see it did," Lucas murmured.

"He truly felt like the best thing he could do for me was to walk away when in fact it was the one thing that hurt me far worse than any whip to my back. Cole changed me. He awakened something within me that has never died. He is a large part of who I am today."

"I think you don't give yourself enough credit," Lucas said.

She shook her head. "I know what you're saying. I do. But the thing is, he was my introduction to dominance and submission. Would I have gotten there eventually without him? Oh yes, definitely I would have. It was a need inside me before he awakened it. But through him, I tasted what it was like to have a man utterly cherish me. Protect me. Love me with everything he had. Would my experience have been the same with another man? Absolutely not. What if I had chosen the wrong man? What if I had experimented with someone who didn't care for me as much as Cole did? Or someone who wasn't as patient as he was. Or even someone who wasn't willing to listen to what I liked and didn't like, and what I needed and didn't need? Because of him, I knew exactly what I wanted and needed from a relationship and I refused to settle for less. I'm honest in my needs and wants because of *him*. Because he showed me that there are men who will give me exactly what I want sexually and emotionally."

Her impassioned speech shook him. Her eyes had darkened and she leaned forward, her voice cracking with emotion. This wasn't a woman who'd moved on and forgotten the man she'd once given her very soul to.

A sensation that felt very much like dread settled heavily into his chest. The weight was uncomfortable, like a rock pushing down on him.

Cole had said he'd want Ren to be happy. Could Lucas say the same? He'd told Cole as much. But were they just words? A week ago he would have said without question that her happiness was everything to him. He spared no expense to ensure she had everything she could possibly need or want. He anticipated her moods, protected her, cared for her and yes, he cherished her.

But could he really take that step to ensure her happiness? To give her a choice?

His mouth was dry and he loathed the indecision that racked him. He'd already taken the first step. Ren was his. She wouldn't question what he chose to do with her body. But he couldn't control her heart and that realization unsettled his carefully ordered existence.

What he planned to do could very well mean losing her, and he wasn't at all sure he could ever live with that.

CHAPTER 8

$\mathcal{L}$ucas chose the meeting to happen at Cole's offices. Cole wouldn't have expected Lucas to come to him. The more expected move would have been for Lucas to have made a power play, invited Cole into his sanctum so that the confrontation occurred on Lucas's turf.

Lucas wasn't one to be threatened by the power of others. He could easily meet Cole on his own terms and where Cole felt most comfortable. The outcome wouldn't change regardless of where the meeting was held.

He parked on the street outside the tall downtown Houston office building and strode inside. He checked in with security, got a visitor's pass and then took the elevator to the thirtieth floor.

He'd done his homework on Cole Madison. He was a successful real estate developer but he had his hands in many other pots. He had a Midas touch when it came to business and what he touched turned to gold, making him a sought out investor for up-and-coming enterprises.

In recent years, he'd focused quite a bit on the timber industry in Southeast Texas and had partnered with Damon Roche in quite a few projects.

When he stepped off the elevator, Lucas was greeted by Cole himself. Apparently Cole wasn't into power games any more than Lucas was. Cole didn't make Lucas wait and showed him directly into his office.

Lucas declined Cole's offer of a drink but took the seat in the sitting area away from the desk when Cole issued the invitation.

Lucas leaned back and simply waited, his gaze tracking Cole as he took the seat across from Lucas.

"I want her," Cole said bluntly.

Appreciative that there would be no skirting the issue, Lucas nodded. "I know you do."

"What exactly is the nature of your agreement with her?"

Lucas lifted an eyebrow. "You don't expect me to tell you that, do you?"

"Is she your lover or is she simply your submissive?" Cole asked, his eyes narrowing.

Lucas understood the differentiation but he didn't appreciate Cole delving into what Lucas considered very private territory. Even though he well understood why Cole did so.

"She's both," he said simply.

"You care for her."

"I care for all the women in my keeping."

The vague response irritated Cole. Lucas wasn't sure why he led Cole to believe that Ren meant nothing more to him than any other woman he had. Maybe it was said more to himself than to the other man. But either way it was an untruth, and Lucas despised liars.

"Tell me, Madison, what makes you think Ren would want you back? Have you ever considered that she's happy where she is in her life right now?"

Pain darkened Cole's eyes and he looked away briefly. When his gaze returned to Lucas, it was cold and unyielding, giving nothing away.

"I can make her happy."

It was on the tip of Lucas's tongue to argue the point. To tell Cole that it didn't matter what he thought because Ren was Lucas's. But that wasn't why he'd come. It wasn't at all what he was going to say. There was little point in needling the other man.

"I'm agreeable to giving her to you for two weeks' time," Lucas said.

Cole went completely still, and his eyes suddenly blazed. It was clear that he was shocked by Lucas's offer. Lucas experienced a moment's satisfaction that he'd been able to catch this man off guard because he sensed it didn't happen often.

Cole finally found his tongue and his response was explosive. *"What?"*

Lucas remained silent, allowing Cole to process the sudden declaration.

Cole's eyes narrowed and he leaned forward. "What's your angle, Holt?"

"No angle," Lucas returned calmly. "Ren has been out of sorts since her meeting with you. It's clear that you and she have unresolved feelings. I'd prefer for those feelings to be resolved so the past can be put to rest."

"And if they aren't?" Cole challenged.

"One way or another, they will be."

Cole stood, then ran a hand through his hair and turned his back to Lucas to stare out the window. When he turned back around, Lucas could see how unsettled he was. Whatever the past, he obviously did still care deeply for Ren.

"I have conditions," Lucas said before Cole could say anything further.

"Of course," Cole said dryly.

"For the first meeting, I will be present. I won't simply turn over a woman I care a great deal about to a man I'm not sure of. You'll demonstrate your handling of her and I'll be satisfied that she'll be well cared for or we leave together."

"You want to watch me fuck her?" Cole asked in disbelief.

Lucas shrugged. "If that's what occurs, then yes, I'll watch you fuck her. You won't disrespect her. You will treat her with the utmost care. If I sense anything, and I mean, anything at all that would lead me to believe I'm making a mistake, I'll pull the plug and Ren leaves with me."

Cole shook his head. "What's your game? Why would you do this? It doesn't make any sense. You have to know that I'm going to do everything in my power to make damn sure she stays with me."

"Yes, I know."

Cole's look of absolute *what the fuck* amused Lucas.

"If you're able to take her from me then she never really belonged to me now did she?"

"You're crazy," Cole muttered.

"I want her to be happy even if it's not with me. I wonder if you can say the same."

"I don't know," Cole said honestly.

Lucas rose. "I realize I run the risk of having Ren not return to me. She could choose you. I would be lying if I said I had any confidence of knowing how she'll choose either way. But know this: If she does indeed return to me when her time with you is over, I'll never let her go again."

"Yeah, I understand. In your position, I wouldn't either."

"I'm giving you something very precious to me," Lucas said quietly. "If you do anything to hurt her, I'll come after you."

Cole nodded his understanding. "Just so you understand, though, I don't take orders from you. If you're truly giving Ren to me, that period of time will be on my terms."

"I think Ren would be very disappointed if the man charged with taking care for her ever allowed another man to dictate his actions. Ren needs a very strong man. Don't think to wrap her in cotton and pretend you aren't a dominant man. She won't thank you for it and it will immediately drive her away. Ren is a woman who is very comfortable with her needs and wants. She doesn't like games and she won't appreciate you pretending to be what you're not in an effort to woo her."

Cole's breath huffed out in a sound that came between confusion and exasperation. "You're a twisted son of a bitch, you know that? You're giving me a primer to seducing the woman you care about away from you. You're bitingly possessive one minute and lazily accepting the next."

A slow smile twitched the corners of Lucas's mouth. "But you need no such primer. You were Ren's first. You should know how to please her. And if you don't, she'll simply come back to me that much faster."

Cole settled onto the couch and after a moment, Lucas took his seat across from Cole. For the space of a few seconds, Lucas studied the man who'd meant so much to Ren.

"Tread carefully, Madison. It puzzles you that I'd provide you so much information. I want Ren to be happy, but more than that I want her to feel safe and comforted. Her last relationship damaged her."

Cole's nostrils immediately flared and he sat forward, his expression blank. "What do you mean by 'damaged'?"

"Her lover didn't give her what she needed. Worse, he made her second guess what she knew to be true. What she needed and wanted. He made her feel inferior. A slut and a whore who was too bold, too spirited and too confident. He tried to destroy that in her. He wanted a hapless doll to vent his authority. He didn't want a strong, vibrant woman and so he tried to make Ren something she wasn't."

"Son of a bitch," Cole bit out.

"Tell me, Madison, did you ever try to make Ren feel that way?"

"Hell no! What the fuck are you implying?"

Lucas smiled again. "Funny, that's what she herself told me. That you were never anything but cherishing, possessive and caring."

Cole's eyes narrowed. "What exactly are you getting to here?"

"You've already admitted your mistake. I'm merely driving the point home. But at the same time I can only be grateful that you walked away from her because I wouldn't have her now."

"If I have my way, you'll have her no longer," Cole said in a tight voice.

Lucas ignored the challenge. He wanted to make sure all of his conditions were outlined so Cole would have all the facts when he made his decision.

"There is another condition, one I take very seriously."

Cole gave a short nod to indicate Lucas should continue.

"There will be no other women during the time Ren is with you. I realize in some circles, it's accepted for a submissive to accept whatever her master chooses to do. Some men will take multiple women. I can't speak as to their motive or desires. I won't tolerate such disrespect of Ren."

Cole's brows drew together. "I have no interest in other women but I'm curious as to why you feel so strongly about it."

"I would not ever have her feel as though I needed more than she could give me. Again, in her last relationship, it was something the dickhead she was with did and it undermined her confidence. It took a while for her to recover her spark, and I'd never have it extinguished. Besides, if you need more than Ren can provide, she doesn't belong with you anyway."

"We agree on that much," Cole conceded. "I would never hurt her that way."

"I'm glad to know my intuition wasn't wrong about you."

Cole's brow wrinkled again but Lucas ignored it and got to his last condition.

"Ren must have a private place of her own in which to work. Her career is very important to her. It's part of her identity. She needs an area free of distractions where she can write and draw. I expect you to provide it and not encroach on those times when she chooses to work."

"What does she do?" Cole asked.

"She writes and illustrates children's books."

Cole's eyebrows went up. He looked surprised but he didn't give voice to it.

"I will of course provide Ren a place to work that is free of distractions."

Lucas nodded and then stood. The meeting was done. Cole would need time to consider Lucas's proposal. There was little point in rehashing the same points over again.

He turned to go but then at the doorway, he hesitated and twisted to look at Cole once more. "Don't take my generosity for what it isn't. I do this for Ren and only Ren. Don't mistake the gift as evidence that I'm giving her up. I won't *ever* give her up without a fight."

"Understood."

"Think about what I've offered. You have my number. Call me when you've made your decision and I'll make arrangements to bring Ren to you. I want it to be at your home. It's important for her to know that I'd never allow this to happen in her sanctuary. With me, and at her home with me, she is safe from all things, all hurts, everything that makes her uncomfortable. I would preserve that at all costs."

Cole nodded. "I'll be in touch."

And, Lucas realized as he rode the elevator back down, Cole *would* be in touch. He had the look of a very determined man. The time that Ren would spend with Cole would be the longest weeks of Lucas's life.

When he'd first made the decision to offer Cole the proposition, he hadn't imagined that he'd feel so . . . gutted. There simply wasn't another word to describe the ugly sensation snaking its way through his chest.

He could lose Ren. And it was the very last thing he wanted.

CHAPTER 9

Ren knew when Lucas told her to dress for a night at the club that she'd been working too hard. It was a signal she'd grown to recognize. Whenever Lucas thought she was pushing herself too hard, he'd take her to the club for an evening to blow off some steam, relax and enjoy one of her favorite activities.

She loved to dance. Loved to dress sexy and get down and dirty on the dance floor. And Lucas loved to watch her, so it was a win-win situation for her.

Tonight, perhaps more than ever, she needed that extra boost, so she dressed a little more daring than usual. Lucas hadn't told her not to wear underwear so she chose an extra short skirt that hugged the curves of her ass and looked glued to her body.

Her top was skimpy but not trashy looking, thanks to Lucas's impeccable taste and his bottomless wallet when it came to giving her the best of everything.

Her midriff was completely bared, as was her back. The top was secured by a tie around her neck and it hung loose over her breasts. Any movement at all would give those close to her a prime view of her nipples.

But since Lucas rarely left her side or let her venture too far when they went to one of his clubs, she didn't really have to worry about what others saw. She only cared what *he'd* be able to see and appreciate.

She was pondering her choices in shoes when Lucas walked into the bedroom, his hands shoved into his worn jeans, and as usual in bare feet. For a moment she let her gaze wander appreciatively over his well-toned body. But what drew her the most was the comfort she enjoyed from his warmth and the way he felt against her.

His eyebrows went up as he too sent his gaze seeking over her body. "Very sexy. Is this a test to see if I can make it out of the house without fucking you?"

She grinned, relaxing as some of the tension bled out of her. She'd been tense ever since her meeting with Cole, and she couldn't really explain why. She'd been invaded by this anxious sense of dread, like when she worried about something but didn't really know about what. It was as though an ominous, heavy cloud had settled over her.

Foregoing her usual reserve with Lucas, she went to him and put her arms around him, hugging him tightly against her. For a moment he seemed surprised and then he wrapped his arms around her and hugged her back.

He tucked her head underneath his chin and rubbed his hand up and down her bare back. "What were you contemplating so seriously when I came in?"

She smiled against his chest. "Nothing so earth shattering. I couldn't decide which shoes best suited this outfit."

His hand strayed over her ass and just barely below the curve of her buttocks to where the hem of her skirt rested. "What outfit?"

She laughed this time and pulled away, smiling up at him. He smiled back, clear affection in his eyes. She loved him this way. Calm and easygoing. Just as she loved him at his most intense.

"Do you wish me to change?"

His gaze drifted down her body, and she felt a surge of pleasure at the clear appreciation written on his face. "No. I like what you're wearing. The important question is whether *you* like it and if you feel as confident and sexy as you look."

It was hard not to feel that way when he looked at her like he was.

"Well, if I'm going sexy and daring, I'm going to go whole hog," she said as she pushed back into the large closet that housed all of the clothes and shoes Lucas had bought for her.

She came out a few seconds later with a pair of fire-engine red stilettos.

"I want a preview before we go out," Lucas growled.

"In that case, why don't you go get dressed. I'll be waiting when you get out," she said, lowering her voice to a wicked murmur.

He sent her a decidedly predatory look and then turned to go into his own closet.

Smiling, she sat on the edge of the bed and pulled on the sleek, expensive shoes. They gave her a nice height boost and with them on, she reached Lucas's nose.

She waited a moment until she heard Lucas returning and then she stood, angling her feet so she presented a sexy pose, her legs displayed to their best advantage.

He came to a full stop when he saw her. She shivered at the sudden fire in his eyes. Loved how he reacted, loved that she could incite such a reaction from this tightly controlled man.

"Do you have underwear on?"

She lowered her lashes provocatively and murmured a shy, "Yes."

She watched him from underneath her lashes, knowing he loved it when she played coy. As much as he revered the strong, confident woman she was, he was turned on when she decided to play the shy virgin.

"Show me."

Deciding that simply peeling up the tight-fitting skirt would be way too mundane, she eased backward, sliding onto the edge of the bed. She rested back on her palms and allowed her thighs to part so that he could see the hint of lacy lingerie.

In a flash, he was across the room standing between her knees. He shoved at the stretch material of her skirt until he rolled it past her hips, baring the daring black see-through lace of her panties.

She tried to control her smile as he quickly realized just what pair of panties she had on.

He made a sound that was a mixture of approval and crazed desire. Then he went for the fly of his slacks. He freed his cock and in a moment's time he was pressing through the slit of her panties and deep inside her pussy.

His fingers dug into her hips and his eyes bore ruthlessly into hers. He yanked her toward him and then hoisted her legs to curl around his waist.

"Careful," she murmured. "Wouldn't want to get messy on our way out to the club."

He thrust hard and deep, forcing a gasp from her. Then he leaned down and kissed her, the gentleness a direct contradiction to the force in which he possessed her.

"I'm going to come so deep inside you that there won't *be* a mess." His deep voice slid over her, dark and sensuous, like his touch. "Be a good girl and don't spill a drop. If you do, I'll have to punish you. Besides, I like the idea of you going to my club with my cum inside you."

"You're such a caveman," she teased.

He answered her with another punishing thrust. Then he wrapped his hand in her hair, pulling and angling her head so that he could graze his teeth along her jaw. "Damn right, I am."

She let out a soft, helpless whimper that she knew would excite him all the more. As expected, he became more punishing and soon the room was filled with the harsh sounds of raw fucking.

Her entire body shook as he pounded into her. He shoved aside the thin barrier of her top so that her jiggling breasts were visible.

He thumbed one dark nipple and stilled his thrusts for a moment. "I'd love to pierce your nipples. Perhaps that will be your next gift from me."

A delicious thrill rolled through her body. Lucas was generous in all things, but she loved especially when he bestowed gifts that *he* enjoyed. The idea of pleasing him with the erotic jewelry excited her.

He began to thrust again, but they were tight, controlled thrusts. Three more and he suddenly went stiff and she could feel the hot, slick sensation of his cum coating her passageway.

He stood there, still wedged tightly inside her as he stared down into her eyes.

"Wear the bright red lipstick. I want to look at you all night and fantasize about those red lips sucking my cock on the way home."

Her body hummed and she was desperate for release, but he hadn't given her permission and she knew it was likely he wouldn't.

As if reading her mind, he pulled out, his cock still very much erect and glistening with a mixture of her fluids and his.

"Get down on your knees and lick me clean. Don't get anything on my pants. I want you hungry and on edge all night. Think of me, Ren. Imagine what I'll do to you when we get home. Or maybe I won't wait. Maybe I'll take you right there in my club where anyone could happen on us. Would you like that?"

She went to her knees, hands locked behind her back. He held her chin and guided his cock toward her mouth. He slid inside and rocked gently back and forth until there was no trace of her fluids or his.

Still, he continued, his grip on her letting her know that he was in control. He fucked her mouth for several long minutes before finally he stepped away and tucked himself back into the confines of his pants.

He reached down to take her hand and carefully assisted her to her feet so she wouldn't trip in her heels. He arranged her skirt so that it once again covered her ass and then he fixed her top to lay over her breasts.

He pressed a quick kiss to her swollen lips. "Go finish getting ready. I'll wait downstairs for you."

CHAPTER 10

$\mathcal{L}$ucas drove them to the club in his silver Mercedes Roadster. He whipped into the parking space reserved just outside the private back entrance to the downtown building.

Ren was already anticipating the rush when the thump of the club music invaded her veins.

He got out of the car and she waited for him to circle around to open her door. He was laid back about a lot of things but not when it came to her. He had exacting expectations and whether they were in public or private, he saw to her every need.

He reached in to take her hand and assisted her out, holding her against him for a moment until he was sure she had her footing. It amused her because he bought her a ridiculous number of high heels. He loved them on her. Loved to watch her in them. But he was terrified she was going to fall and break her neck.

They were met by one of Lucas's bouncers as well as his club manager the moment they stepped toward the entrance.

Though Ren was clearly Lucas's submissive, the other two men treated her with deference and absolute respect. One of the club employees had once made the mistake of treating Ren as though she was a lot lower on the food chain or as if he had the right to command her as Lucas commanded her.

After Lucas had—quite forcibly—shown him the error of his ways, Lucas had fired him on the spot. It quickly became clear to not only the employees but to the club regulars that Lucas highly valued his woman and would tolerate no disrespect shown to her.

As a result, Ren was kowtowed to every bit as much as Lucas himself was. Perhaps more so. Many had realized that the path to pleasing Lucas lay in pleasing her. Lucas went out of his way to reward those who saw to her every need.

"Good evening, Mr. Holt. Miss Michaels."

Ren smiled up at the burly manager who had actually once been the head bouncer. "Hello, Duffy. How are things tonight?"

"Isn't that my line?" Lucas inquired dryly.

"Busy. Just the way we like it," Duffy returned. "Would you like your usual, sir?"

Lucas shook his head. "I'm going to take Ren around the club. See that my table is available and that a waitress is assigned to me."

"Should I accompany you?" Craig asked.

Lucas turned to the bouncer. "No. You can wait at my table."

Lucas wrapped a protective arm around her as they walked through the dark hallway, past the offices toward the doorway leading into the club. She could sense his displeasure but wasn't sure what had happened in the short period of time since they'd arrived.

Her question was soon answered and it both amused her and touched her.

"Where is the lighting for the hallway?" Lucas bit out to his manager. "I asked that this be addressed two weeks ago. What if Ren falls? It's too dark. She could trip on anything and never see it coming."

"The contractor will be out tomorrow," Duffy said hastily.

As they neared the doorway, the loud thump of bass and the roar of the crowd filtered through the thick, soundproof walls. Or at least as soundproof as they could get with the noise level through the roof.

Lucas reached for her hand and she twined her fingers through his, knowing he wanted her to stay close where he could protect her from anything.

She was happy to move closer into his warmth and strength as Duffy swung open the door and they walked into the cascade of flashing lights, raucous cheers and music blasting from all corners.

They entered close to the dance floor but Lucas led her to the stairs leading up the stadium-like platforms that housed tables on each row. At the top, situated directly in the middle with a prime view of the stage and dance floor, was Lucas's private table, glassed in on three sides. The only access was from the front, leading up from the dance floor, and to go inside the enclosure, you had to run a gauntlet of three security guards.

Lucas guided her away from his table, though, and over to where a group of men gathered, drinks in hand. They were talking it up with girls that passed their way, flirting madly and having a good time.

Ren recognized a few of them as regulars, men who knew Lucas and who Lucas often invited to his table.

As they approached, three broke away to acknowledge Lucas, promptly turning their backs on the women they'd been courting. Ren found such an action intriguing. A testament to the power Lucas wielded. But he commanded attention wherever he went. He wore such power as comfortably as other people wore shoes.

Lucas released her hand only long enough to lean forward so he could say something to one of the men. Ren was sure she knew his name but then she'd been introduced to the three of them at the same time and it was hard for her to remember who was who.

Daryl. She was pretty sure the taller man was Daryl. The shorter blond guy was Matt and the African American guy to Daryl's left was Jace.

She saw Daryl nod and gesture toward his friends. The next thing Ren knew, Lucas reached for her hand and pulled her forward. Jace then took her hand from Lucas, startling her. She glanced quickly at Lucas only to catch him nod to her that she was to accept this.

Lucas leaned in, cupped her cheek in a gentle gesture and bent his head so his mouth was close to her ear. "They're going to dance with you. Go with them. I trust them."

She wasn't unused to Lucas having to leave her to make the rounds or to conduct business. What surprised her was him allowing other men to dance with her, or even more, charging them with essentially taking care of her. Lucas wasn't one to trust others with what he valued. Not unless he was present and overseeing every aspect.

He kissed her cheek and then backed away, leaving her standing with the men. Jace flashed her a sexy smile and then gallantly gestured toward the stairs leading down to the dance floor.

She didn't glance back at Lucas as Jace guided her down the stairs. To do so would send the message that she didn't trust him. He wouldn't appreciate it and she'd die before ever allowing anyone to think she didn't have complete and utter faith in him.

Daryl came down on her other side and put a light hand to the small of her back while Matt walked behind them, effectively closing her off from anyone who might approach.

The music died for one split second while the DJ stirred the crowd into a frenzy. Jace leaned close to Ren where she could hear and said, "Lucas says you like to dance."

"I love it," she said with an exuberant smile.

Jace smiled back. "So do I. We'll have some fun. Sound good?"

She nodded and relaxed. He seemed perfectly nice, and if he wasn't, she didn't harbor any illusions that at least four bouncers weren't trained solely on her, and that as occupied as Lucas may be for the next little while, he wasn't watching as well.

Jace pulled her onto the crowded dance floor but he, Daryl and Matt quickly formed a triangle around her so that no one got too close. The music started again and the bass thrilled through her veins, making each muscle jump in time to the beat.

Lights flashed, the electric, energetic music slipped under her skin and she let it flow through her body to every part until she loosened up and let go.

The men moved in closer, pinning her in the middle of them. The crowd around them gyrated in time to the music but Ren had her own little piece of the dance floor and she was free to move without fear of crashing into anyone else.

Here nothing could touch her. Not worry. Not fear. Not insecurity. Not her past. There was nothing but her and the sensual pulse of music and movement.

She quickly lost her inhibitions. Forgot she didn't know these men. She sidled up to one, did a quick shimmy down his body. Quickly getting into the spirit, Jace held up his arms, tilted his body forward, and she met him in the middle, their bodies pressed together and moving in perfect synchronicity.

Warmth met her back and suddenly she was sandwiched between two hard bodies. They made no move to touch her or to put their hands on her, but their bodies cupped protectively to hers and she lost herself in the moment.

She put her hands up and turned to face Daryl. Jace slid up to her back, put his arms forward to block her in and they danced as a unit, smiling, writhing, laughing, her smile growing larger all the time.

Matt playfully pushed Daryl aside and crooked his finger wickedly at Ren. Not one to back down from a challenge, she sashayed forward, confident that her legs looked killer tonight. She was glad she chose the red shoes because they made her look and feel daring. Bold. Like a siren bent on seducing every male in her path.

She flipped her long hair back and let it slide over her shoulders then slowly worked her arms over her head, knowing that they'd get a glimpse of her breasts. They'd look. She knew that much. She also knew they wouldn't touch. Not if they valued their hands.

Matt was more daring than his two companions. When Ren got close enough, he grasped her hips and pulled her into his body so that his hips cradled hers. One hand remained on her hip while the other slid to the small of her back.

He held her tight against him and they danced while Daryl and Jace came in close, hands in the air, to shield them from everyone else.

They danced through several songs until sweat glimmered on her skin. The air was alive around her. Excitement was contagious.

She was having the time of her life. She'd needed tonight and Lucas had known it. He always knew it when she herself didn't even realize it. Her heart squeezed and unconsciously she searched him out in the crowded club.

She found him standing inside the enclosure of his table. He was behind the railing, his hands down, curled around the metal as he watched her dance. She could feel his gaze on her, knew he watched her every movement. There were people around him but she knew with no false modesty that they didn't exist. Nothing existed for him but her.

Feeling deliciously naughty, she turned so it wouldn't appear she was focused on Lucas and then she began to give him his own private show. Granted it was in front of hundreds of other people and anyone could see, but he would know it was for him only and that she didn't care about anyone else. Just him.

Jace and the others stood back a little, their expressions a mixture of "holy shit" and "I want some of that." Ren slid her hands down her body, drawing attention to her breasts, her hips and to the line of her legs.

She let them linger on the swells of her ass and then moved them back up to cup her breasts through the thin top. If she thought he could actually see that far, she'd give him a glimpse of nipple, but the only people who'd enjoy that particular spectacle were the men Lucas had charged to dance with her and she'd only tease them so far.

She rolled her hips, then her shoulders. She closed her eyes, tilted back her head and ran her hands through her hair and then back down her body as if she were in the throes of ecstasy.

So into her dance was she that she didn't realize that Jace, Daryl and Matt moved to the side. When she opened her eyes, Lucas was standing there, his eyes dark and possessive.

Wordlessly he stalked forward, curled his finger between her collar and the sensitive flesh of her throat and pulled her forward. It was a gesture she associated with possession. A reminder to her and to anyone looking who she belonged to.

He surrounded her, his body pressing hotly to hers and then he began to dance with her.

He wrapped his arm around her, cupped her ass and pressed her harder into his groin. They swayed and undulated in rhythm, their bodies so meshed together that it looked like they were fucking on the dance floor.

It had been a long time since he'd danced with her. He was a private person. Not much of an exhibitionist. He never minded that she loved to dance but most of the time he stood watch over her from a distance while she indulged in her love of music.

Tonight he owned her on the dance floor just like he owned her everywhere else. His brand was on her for the world to see.

As the music swelled, he pushed her downward and she swayed her hips as she slid down his body. When she reached his groin, he held her in place as he mimicked fucking her mouth.

Around them the crowd went wild at the erotic sight. His fingers fisted in her hair as he held her in place. The ridge of his cock was hard against her chin. He stared down at her, his eyes glittering with harsh arousal.

After a moment he pulled her roughly back up, turned her around and pulled her back against him until her ass was cradled to his groin. With one hand he pushed at her head, forcing her forward and then he slid the hand down her bare back, over the tattoo and then wrapped his fingers in her hair once more.

This time he pulled so that her head came up but she remained bent at the waist. His pelvis ground erotically against her ass, just like he was fucking her from behind.

The air grew thick around them. The mood had changed swiftly in the club. Other couples were being more daring. More sexual. It was an intense and beautifully erotic demonstration.

Lucas straightened her but kept her tightly pressed to him. His hand splayed over her rib cage but then his fingers delved lower, underneath the waistband of the tight skirt she wore.

She sucked in her breath as he slipped past her panties, found her wetness and his finger circled her clit.

By now she was beyond caring who watched. She was only aware of Lucas. How he commanded her body. How sensual she felt, cupped to his body as music flooded into their bodies, forcing them to move in a timeless rhythm.

She reached both arms up over her head and circled them back around his neck so that it arched her chest forward. To her surprise, Jace moved in close, slid his hands up her belly underneath her top to cup her breasts.

Her eyes widened and she held her breath, caught between the two men, one her lover, the other someone she'd merely danced with.

"Breathe," Lucas said in her ear. "He won't go further than I've instructed."

Immediately she gave in. Sensing that any protest she may have launched had passed, Jace rubbed his thumbs over her taut peaks while Lucas fingered the ultrasensitive flesh between her legs.

Daryl and Matt were on either side of Ren so that she was completely boxed in by the four men. Not much was visible to the others on the dance floor but no one could possibly doubt what Lucas and Jace were doing to her.

And she didn't give a flying fuck. She wanted to come. Here between these two badass men.

Lucas bent to nip sharply at her neck and then said loudly enough in her ear so she could hear, "Do you want his mouth on you, Ren?"

It was a shocking question, one she'd never imagine he'd actually ask. Lucas wasn't the type to ask. If he wanted Jace to touch her more intimately, he'd simply allow it. If he didn't, nothing she said or did would change his mind. Now she was unsure of how to answer.

"It isn't a trick," Lucas said. "Just answer the question."

His fingers stroked harder then slid lower to play at her entrance.

"Yes!" she choked out. "God, yes."

The warm chocolate of Jace's eyes caught fire. He looked like he'd been granted the keys to the kingdom. His big hands moved with surprising gentleness over her breasts and then he simply lifted her top, pushing it higher as he knelt in front of her.

Oh dear God, she couldn't believe this was happening in the middle of Lucas's club and that she didn't care. Lucas moved his hand to allow Jace access, and he gripped her hip, holding her solidly in place. As if she needed any urging to remain still for what was coming.

First Jace's mouth touched her belly, right over her navel ring. Followed by the rough edge of his tongue. It rasped over her delicate skin, eliciting a moan too low for anyone to hear. But Lucas felt it. She knew he did.

Jace licked a path straight up her midline until he reached the area right between her breasts. He kept those big hands cupped on either side of her breasts to shield as much of her from view as possible, but even with the other two men standing on either side of her and Jace going to lengths to hide her, there was no way they wouldn't be seen by the other club goers.

He drew away and then his mouth hovered just over her nipple. His hot breath danced across the puckered tip and she tensed in anticipation.

Finally his mouth closed hot and wet over her nipple and her knees nearly buckled. Lucas's grip tightened around her waist to support her and his hand slid back into her skirt, down to stroke gently over her clitoris once more.

Jace alternated teasing each nipple. He'd lick, nibble and suck in turns until she was begging Lucas to let her come. Lucas kept her on the edge, stroking until she was ready to explode and then stopping to pull her back, allowing Jace to continue fanning the flames with his wicked mouth.

"Do you want his fingers inside you?" Lucas asked against her ear.

This time she didn't even hesitate. She'd do anything at all to achieve release.

"Yes!"

She felt him nod in Jace's direction and suddenly one of Jace's hands slid up her leg, over her knee and to the inside of her thigh. He was up on his knees, his head level with her breasts. He brushed over the smooth lips of her pussy and then she felt Lucas use his fingers to spread them for the other man.

The action nearly had her orgasming on the spot.

She began to tremble. She shook from head to toe as Jace sucked her nipple strongly into his mouth again. His thumb found her entrance and plunged inside just as Lucas began fingering her clit again.

It was too much. The room spun around her in dizzy circles. The music was a distant roar. The lights twinkled like fairy dust, and she could no longer make sense of any of it.

Jace withdrew his thumb and then slid two blunt fingers inside her just as Lucas lightly pinched her clit between his thumb and forefinger.

"Come, Ren. Come all over his hand."

She needed no further urging. Her body bucked violently. Daryl and Matt pushed in closer, their bodies adding support so she didn't fall.

Jace's teeth grazed her nipple, each touch sending more spasms of delight straight to her pussy. While Lucas bit into her neck, Jace nipped sharply at one nipple, their fingers performing magic in the most sensitive places on her body.

She was no longer capable of standing on her own. She went limp against Lucas, trusting that as always, he'd never let her fall. He held her closely, kissing and licking gently at her neck while Jace worked her slowly down from her orgasm.

She lay there several long seconds, slumped in Lucas's arms, her breaths coming in ragged bursts. Then Lucas carefully straightened her clothing. Jace withdrew his hand from underneath her panties and arranged her skirt.

He stood to his full height again as the music and dancing continued on around them.

With Lucas's help, she got her feet underneath her again and stood, though she still leaned into Lucas.

"You may kiss him and offer your thanks," Lucas directed.

Ren walked into Jace's arms, leaned up on tiptoe with his help and kissed him on the lips. He swept his tongue over hers, tasting her, allowing her to briefly taste him before he pulled away.

"Thank you," Ren said so he could hear.

He chucked her affectionately on the cheek. "Any time, sugar."

Lucas walked her back to the stairs where they'd come down. Daryl, Matt and Jace walked back with them, surrounding them on all sides. At the stairs, two of the bouncers took over and the three men melted back into the crowd, gone before she could blink.

She continued up the steps with Lucas, still in a post-orgasmic fog. They drew the stares of many. Lucas had never been so bold with her, though they'd gotten a little frisky at Lucas's table before. But never something so open and public. It was . . . different. Not something she would have thought Lucas would do. In private? All bets were off. There was nothing she'd put beyond him whether it was one man or a dozen. Though it hadn't ever happened with her, she had no illusions about how far he was willing to take things.

Lucas saw her into her seat and then motioned for the waitress who had taken a nearby post.

"Water for Ren and I'll take a beer."

The waitress was back quickly but then she'd likely anticipated precisely what Lucas would order. Lucas didn't often deviate from his routine and his usual order only consisted of a variety of three drinks.

Ren drank thirstily of the water and leaned back, suddenly exhausted by the dancing and the mind-blowing orgasm. What she wouldn't give for a good snuggle and a comfortable bed.

Lucas reached over to curl his hand around her nape. He rubbed a thumb up and down the line of her neck as he continued to survey the goings on in the club.

As they sat and he rubbed her neck, her growing more lethargic and content by the minute, several people stopped by to speak with

Lucas. She tuned out the conversation and concentrated instead on his touch. She closed her eyes and absorbed the delicious sensation of his fingers, the heat of his hand, the comfort in knowing she belonged to him.

For an hour longer, she watched people come and go from Lucas's table. He talked easily with his customers, business associates and VIPs. He held court like a pro, never going to others but allowing them to come to him. Even the rich and famous came to him, their ego stroked that he allowed them to enter his inner circle.

Then he turned to her, lifted her hand to press a kiss to the back of her wrist and said, "Are you ready to go?"

She nodded, not bothering to defer to what he wanted. He'd asked and she wouldn't lie. She'd gotten what she came for and what he'd brought her for. Her mind was much freer of the weight it had borne for the last few days.

Chapter 11

Cole wasn't sure how he felt about his meeting with Lucas Holt.
He wanted to dislike the man. A damn lot. But it was hard when he
seemed so . . . decent.

He sighed and glanced at the clock. He was ill at ease. He was fucking nervous, and that pissed him off. He felt like he was preparing for
some kind of goddamn test that he didn't know the answers to.

Lucas was a cagey bastard, and he'd caught Cole completely and
utterly off guard with his proposal. It had been on the tip of Cole's
tongue to refuse. It enraged him on Ren's behalf. But then he remembered those damn rules. Or rather that there were no damn rules in the
lives that he, Lucas and Ren had chosen. Only those they made themselves.

And then, when his anger and surprise had abated, he knew that
there was no way in hell he could walk away from this kind of opportunity. He wasn't entirely certain what Lucas's motives were in offering

Ren to him on a silver platter, but what Cole did with the chance was what mattered.

He had another chance to make Ren love him. To make up to her all the pain he'd caused her. To show her the man he'd become.

He'd become more focused. Intense. He had a harder edge now and that might scare the shit out of her. He wasn't the same young man who adored her beyond reason and was a hesitant participant in their experimentation. He wasn't even sure he could be that man any longer.

It was a choice he agonized over. Show her the truth and take the chance that she'd never come back to him. Or lie to her and withhold the true part of himself forever.

Neither held any appeal but he knew he couldn't lie to her or himself. Lucas had warned him of the consequences of such an action. Ren would suffer no pretenses and he was fiercely glad of it. He wanted honesty between them.

He had two weeks. Two weeks to win back the woman he'd never stopped loving. And at the end of that time, he had to hope like hell that she'd choose him because he couldn't face losing her a second time. The first time had changed him irrevocably. This time would destroy him.

Ren sat between Lucas's knees as the limousine slid down the highway to God only knew where. Lucas had been cryptic on details and very explicit on how she was to dress and what she was and wasn't to wear.

She was on her knees, legs apart, the folds of her silk skirt fanned out on the floorboard. The top she wore had a plunging neckline that emphasized her full breasts and barely covered her nipples.

It was an outfit put together with access in mind. He wanted unfettered access to her.

He was distant though. And preoccupied. Whether it was business or something else entirely, she wasn't sure, but he seemed restless and cagey and she knew from experience that he was harder and rougher when he was in such a mood.

He slid his hand down the middle of her chest and then impatiently pushed aside the material covering her breasts. He thumbed her nipple idly, almost as if he couldn't quite decide what he wanted to do with her.

It was unusual for Lucas to show clear indecision and she wondered what could possibly be occupying his mind that he was so distracted.

Abruptly, he slid his finger between the band of her collar and her skin and yanked forward until she was leaning against him, her belly pressed to his crotch. He kissed her. Hard.

She felt . . . branded. Like he was proving all over again that she belonged to him. His teeth bit into her lip, drawing blood, and then he licked over the tender area, sweeping the blood away and onto his tongue.

She wanted to ask him what bothered him, but knew that particular boundary between them shouldn't be breached. He was private, and if he wanted her to know, he would tell her.

As he pulled away, he held her face in one hand, his grip firm as he stared into her eyes. He looked as though his control was barely leashed and that he might toss her down and take her roughly.

Her breath caught and held with anticipation. Her body tingled and came alive. Her clit pulsed and ached. Her breasts tightened, her nipples hardening.

"How well you know me," he murmured.

He stroked his hand over her cheek and then over the lip he'd nipped, soothing away the slight ache. His features hardened, and she shivered at the sudden infusion of darkness into his eyes.

"Get up on the seat. On your hands and knees."

She rose up on her knees, crawled over his left leg and onto the long seat he was slouched in. Her palms sank into the sumptuous leather and her knees pressed just at the seam between two sections of the seat.

She felt him move behind her. A cool rush skittered over her ass as he pushed her skirt to her waist and allowed it to bunch there.

"There are two things I want tonight," he said, the rasp of arousal deep in his voice. "My mark on your ass and my cum inside your body when we arrive."

She almost asked where they were going but held her tongue. He wouldn't have liked that slip. She shifted restlessly, aching for his hand against her bottom.

The slap, when it came, startled her and sent her forward. She braced herself against the seat and pushed back, begging silently for more. He loved when she did that.

He rubbed his palm over the burning spot to soothe the hurt and then administered another stinging blow to her other cheek. She moaned softly. With another man, that might have gotten her into trouble. But Lucas loved to hear her sounds of passion. He liked to know he pleased her even though her purpose was to please him.

He encouraged her uninhibited responses as long as it fell within the boundaries of obedience. If she enjoyed what she experienced, he expected her to express it. If she didn't enjoy it, she was also free to express that as well, but it may or may not cause it to end.

Lucas followed a simple rule. If it wasn't harmful—and by harmful, he meant causing her permanent physical or psychological damage—then she had no choice but to endure it. Afterward, he might invite her to tell him why she didn't like the experience and he would then consider whether he would ever make her suffer it again.

Cole hadn't been her only dominant lover. There had been a total of four in the last ten years since Cole. Lucas was her favorite, though.

He . . . He just got her. He understood her. He wasn't out to prove his masculinity or his power. He wasn't afraid to be wrong or to make mistakes, though she couldn't ever remember a time when he'd done anything she considered a mistake.

It probably sounded dramatic but she couldn't think of much she wouldn't do for Lucas. And it was because she trusted him. A component that had been lacking in her last relationship, and consequently it had been her shortest.

The next blow caught her unaware for the sheer brutality of it. The pain shocked her and suddenly Lucas's hand was wrapped in her hair and he yanked her back, forcing her head so that their gazes met.

"Am I boring you, Ren? Would you prefer to be somewhere else?"

Her mouth twisted in dismay because it was the last thing she wanted him to think. "I'm sorry, Lucas. I was thinking."

His hold loosened only slightly. "What were you thinking that was more important than me?"

"I was thinking of you," she said honestly. "I was comparing my relationship with you to the others I've had."

His hand gentled and he ran his fingers through her hair in a gentle pet. "Do you know what I love most about you, Ren?"

The question startled her. She'd expected his anger. Not this sudden . . . affection.

"You tell me the truth, no matter how awkward or potentially uncomfortable. It would be so easy to lie and say you drifted away or that you were thinking about where we're going. Why is that?" he finished softly.

Her brow wrinkled in confusion. His hand soothed over the subsiding burn where he'd marked her, stroking and caressing.

"Why do I not lie to you?"

"I suppose that's what I'm asking. I know that you're inherently an honest person, but even the most honest person will seek not to make herself vulnerable to another."

Her expression eased and she locked gazes with him. "Because I trust you not to use my vulnerability against me."

His eyes went warm with approval. He leaned down and softly pressed his lips to hers.

"Now tell me how our relationship compares to your previous ones."

She twitched against his palm, eager to feel the burn again. His hand stilled and then he pressed another kiss to her forehead in apology.

"I'm neglecting your need. When I'm finished administering the appropriate marks to your sweet ass and when I've availed myself of your body, then we'll finish this conversation."

She sighed her relief and gifted him with a smile.

"How hard and rough do you want it, Ren? I find I'm in a mood tonight. I'm not usually so indecisive but I go back and forth between wanting to allow my darker urges free or showering you with tenderness. I'm in an affectionate mood and then you smile at me like that and it only reinforces my desire to show you gentleness instead of power."

She raised her head and settled back on her heels, allowing her hair to spill down her back. He had one knee on the floorboard and she turned her head to the side so she could look at him.

"I am yours, Lucas. Do with me as you will. I will love whatever it is you choose to bestow on me and I'll take it without complaint."

He lifted his hand to cup her cheek. His eyes shimmered with dark promise. "I am very glad to hear those words. Especially tonight."

She cocked her head to the side, rubbing her cheek along his palm. She didn't ask him why. She simply waited for what he would tell her. Or not tell her.

"Tonight I'm going to give you to another."

She went completely still, shock rendering her unable to move or react. She stared back at him, but he too was waiting and in no hurry to further explain.

"Does that excite you?"

"I don't know. It's . . . surprising."

"Why would you find this surprising? I've discussed with you in the past that I find enjoyment in giving the woman I own to another man so that I can watch and enjoy."

She nodded. "It's just that you never have. In the beginning I expected it. But as more time went on, you seemed content not to share me with other men."

"Does it bother you that I seek to do so now?"

She frowned, unsure of how she felt. She'd considered such a thing just a short time ago and found that the idea excited her. The idea. There was a huge difference between what sexually excited her in theory and what actually aroused her in reality.

More than once, a kink that she was excited to try turned out to be something she didn't enjoy at all. Would this follow in the same vein?

Now she wondered if the night out at the club had been a mere taste of what was to come. Had he tested her to see how receptive she was to having another man's hands and mouth on her body?

And what had prompted him to take this step now? Was he bored with her? That thought sent panic and dismay racing along her spine. Had their time together come to an end? She shook the idea away because there was no way she could hold it together thinking such things.

"Ren," he prompted.

"It doesn't bother me that you would do it," she said slowly. "I'm unsure of whether I would enjoy it. The idea excites me, but it also frightens me. My trust in you is absolute but doesn't extend to another man."

He stroked her cheek again. "All very valid points. And if I told you the man in question was Cole Madison?"

Her eyes widened in shock. Her pulse bounded, firing so rapidly that for a moment she swayed, suddenly dizzy.

"Cole?" she whispered.

She closed her eyes and foregoing all discipline, she turned away from Lucas. He didn't reprimand her nor did he force her to look back at him. He slid back onto the seat behind her, silent, as he waited.

Then, "Take off your skirt, Ren."

Her eyes flew open and she blinked. Her fingers were curled into tight fists on the seat between her splayed thighs.

"You have precisely three seconds to do as I've told you or you will regret it."

The bite in his voice slid over her like a razor. She was numb with shock. And questions. She had so many questions.

Was this some bizarre test?

"One," he said quietly.

She jolted to awareness. Lucas never had to punish her for disobedience. It would be the height of disrespect were she not to perform his order.

She scrambled upward in the seat, pulling at her skirt until it pooled at her feet. She kicked it away, but she still didn't face him. She didn't want him to see how undone she was.

"Now the top."

She fumbled with the tie at her nape, loosening it so that it fell down her waist, uncovering her breasts.

He got up and moved to the back of the limo, to the seat that faced forward. The rasp of his zipper sounded loud in the dead silence. He lifted his hips to shove his jeans down over his hips, but he left them there, then pulled his cock over the band of his underwear and fisted it, pumping up and down, bringing the already hard length to even greater erection.

"Get on your hands and knees on the floor. Present your ass to me. Face the divider."

She rose, careful not to bump her head on the roof.

"Crawl to me," Lucas ordered.

She went down to the floor and then maneuvered on her hands and knees until she faced him. Then she turned to do as he'd told her and waited, ass pressed against the seat, his legs on either side of her hips.

He gripped her behind and then pushed her forward as he scooted to the edge of the seat. She started to walk her hands forward to give him more room, but he administered a sharp blow to her ass in reprimand.

She went still, palms dug into the floor, mouth trembling, her mind in chaos.

He reached underneath her legs, hooked his arms and yanked her up and back so that she was unbelievably spread, her body tilted downward and her feet hit the back of the seat.

Instead of thrusting into her, he reached down, positioned his cock at her entrance and then gripped her legs and pulled her onto him.

The position forced her elbows to bend and her cheek now rested on the floor. Her breasts were flattened against the rough carpet.

He slid his arms from underneath her and gripped her waist with both hands, moving down to anchor at her hips. He eased her forward and then yanked her back again, seating himself deeply inside her.

Each bump in the road, every slight dip, even the rougher surface of parts of the highway. She felt them all. One hand left her hip and he reached down to tug at her hair.

"Now, let's discuss a few things. Who do you belong to, Ren?"

She made sure she could be heard. "You."

He yanked her back again, taking her breath away. He was hard. Very hard. He felt so rigid inside her. Almost like she could feel the anger pulsing from him through his cock and into her body.

"If I choose to give you to another man, is it my right?"

"Yes."

"If I give you this time with a man who once meant something to you, you will be grateful and you will thank me. Furthermore, you will do everything he tells you. Are we understood?"

Her stomach clenched and her chest tightened. "Yes."

"It is for you I do this, and you will not shame me."

"Never," she whispered, broken over the mere thought of bringing shame to this man.

"If I have the driver pull over to the side of the road and tell you to fuck him, you'll do it."

"Yes, Lucas."

"If I tell you to allow him to do anything he likes with your beautiful body, you'll do it."

"Yes."

By now he was shoving roughly into her. He was no longer just pulling her onto his cock. He was meeting each pull with a powerful thrust. She closed her eyes and allowed the pleasure of his ruthless possession to wash through her.

She loved this above all else. Loved the rawness and brutality when he took her and spoke so explicitly to her. In that moment, part of her wished he *would* order the driver to pull over. The image of her bent over the back of the car, the driver pounding into her from behind while Lucas stood guard, satisfaction and approval glittering in his eyes, set her senses on fire.

If there had been any doubt as to whether she'd enjoy having Lucas watch while another man took her, it was gone. Now she imagined Cole pushing into her body. Cole commanding her. Cole's hands hard and rough on her skin. His cock punishing her. All while Lucas watched, silent and approving.

Her orgasm shimmered through her like ripples on the surface of a lake. Lucas stopped and leaned forward, forcing his weight on her, pressing her face harder into the floor.

"Oh no you don't," he said harshly. "We have several things to clear up, Ren. If you come, I'll bruise that pretty ass of yours so you can't sit for a week."

She groaned, knowing full well he'd do just that. She wanted to come. Needed to come, but having a sore ass for a week wasn't worth the immediate pleasure. She shut off the images of Cole that were bombarding her and focused instead on the sensation of Lucas uncomfortably wedged inside her pussy. The angle of his penetration was meant to be painful and not bring her pleasure.

Only when she had backed off the edge did he ease his hold and lean back to alleviate the pressure on her body. The burn inside her pussy eased and he stroked back and forth a few times until she was damp once more around him.

Without warning, he reached down and lifted her straight up, still buried deep inside her. He pulled her back, leaning so that she sat astride him, completely vulnerable, impaled on his rigid length.

And just as suddenly as he'd lifted her, he pushed her forward again until his cock came free and she stumbled off the seat.

"Lie down on your back," he directed. "And give me your legs."

She eased down onto the floor again and then inched herself toward him until he grasped her ankles. He jerked her forward, the carpet rough against her back. Then he pushed her legs back, curling her so that her weight was borne on her shoulders and her ass was presented to him.

He bent her legs double, which opened her even further to him. Then he gave her a satisfied smile.

"It seems to me if we're going to have a meaningful conversation, I at least want to be able to look at your face. My dick in your ass shouldn't provide distraction to a woman of your discipline."

CHAPTER 12

*R*en trembled in anticipation, her gaze focused solely on Lucas. She stared into his dark eyes as he rose over her and tucked his cock between her ass cheeks.

She was feeling vulnerable tonight. A little off kilter. It was a sensation she didn't like. As much as she loved all of Lucas's dark edges and embraced his willingness to push her as hard and as fast past that gray line of her limits, she was suddenly very unsure of herself.

Never had she felt so unsteady and so out of sorts. Instead of his ruthless dominance and possession, she wanted—no, she *needed*—his tenderness, a side, that while rarely shown or given, was as powerful, if not more so than his harder side.

Lucas froze, staring back at her, his eyes searching to her very depths. Slowly he unfolded her legs and pulled her gently toward him so her legs rested on either side of his hips. Then he simply reached forward, slid his hands underneath her shoulders and pulled her upward so she sat in his lap facing him.

Bewildered, she could only look on helplessly and wait for what was next. Had he seen what she'd tried so hard to keep from him? Had he plucked the thoughts right out of her head?

His palms glided up and down her back and she realized then he was indeed soothing her. Unexpected tears pricked her eyelids and then he enfolded her in his arms and held her close.

He didn't say a word. He didn't have to. He saw into her very heart. Every time. He always knew when he could push and when he couldn't. He'd seen it now and instead of punishing her for being out of sorts, he offered her the strength and comfort she so desperately craved.

"Why are you so upset, my Ren?" he asked several long minutes later.

She clung to him, her face buried in his neck. He pried her away from him and gently wiped the tears from her cheeks with his thumb.

She hated that she was so weak in front of him. That she'd cried all over him. She never cried. She was always so careful to only show him her strength and quiet determination. He'd seen her not at her best, but he'd never seen her so . . . distraught.

"I don't know," she said honestly. "I do and I don't. I'm so confused. I don't know what I want."

"That isn't like you. You're the most confident, self-assured woman I've ever known. You're comfortable in your skin. You always know precisely what you want and you've never been bashful about pursuing it. I've always admired that about you."

She laid her head back on his shoulder and wrapped her hand around the side of his neck, clutching at him, needing that contact. "You asked me what was different in our relationship or rather how our relationship differed from the others I've had. This, Lucas. *This* is what's different."

He stroked his hand through her hair. He pressed his lips to her forehead in the most gentle of kisses and then said, "Explain."

"You get me. *Really* get me. It's not all about you as a lot of people would assume a relationship where dominance is a factor would be about your needs and wants above all else."

"Your happiness is important to me," he said by way of agreement.

She sighed. "In all my other relationships, except one, it's been more about the man. Not always or all the time but mostly. In all but one, my partner never had my complete trust. In all but one, I was never . . . home. *You're* home to me, Lucas. I feel safe and cherished with you. I trust you."

He seemed pleased by her heartfelt declaration. He squeezed her warmly and she could feel the pleasure seeping through him. That made her happy. She wanted him to know how much he meant to her. How much his protection meant to her.

"You said except one. Do you mean Cole?"

She took in a deep breath. "Yes. I was happy with Cole. My relationship with him mimicked a lot of the things I value most about my relationship with you. Only ours is a more grown-up version of what I had with him. I like to think if only Cole and I had had time that we could have grown into something like what you and I have now."

"And yet the idea of me giving you to him distresses you," Lucas murmured.

"I'm scared," she admitted. "And confused. Maybe a little threatened, you know?"

He brushed his mouth over her temple, a simple gesture she felt all the way to her soul.

"Why, Lucas? Why are you doing it? I don't understand. I'm afraid to dig too deeply for the answer."

Before she hadn't been willing to ask, but now she had to know. Was it a test? She wasn't sure she could do this. He hadn't done it to hurt her. She'd never believe Lucas would be that cruel. Which meant he had a specific reason for sending her back into the arms of the man who'd broken her heart.

He pulled her back just enough that he could touch her jaw, cup her chin, rub his thumb gently across her lips. So comforting. So very real.

"You say you trust me."

She nodded without hesitation.

"Then trust me that this is what I feel is best for you. I think this is something you need. I would not do it if I thought it would hurt you. It may make you uncomfortable, but I think when all is said and done, this is for the best."

The calm in his voice soothed her frayed nerves. She did trust him. Implicitly. He'd never steered her wrong. He'd never done anything without her best interests at heart.

And the truth was that she *did* want to see Cole again. She'd imagined what it would be like to have him touch her as he'd once done. Wondered if he'd even want to. She hadn't been able to stop thinking about him since the night she and Lucas had gone to The House.

What had rattled her far more than her encounter with her first love was the guilt she'd felt for thinking of him ever since. Lucas was everything to her and yet she couldn't stop thinking about a man who shouldn't occupy her thoughts or her fantasies.

The fact that Lucas seemed to understand only made the guilt burn more brightly. That he'd gone as far as to make an arrangement with Cole because he thought it was something she needed made her want to curl into a ball of shame.

"Ren."

Lucas's soft admonishment had her looking up and tears gathered once more when she saw the understanding reflected in his eyes.

"Do you think I would be angry for you being human enough to feel emotion when confronted with someone you used to love? Do you think I would punish you for being honest enough with yourself and me to admit these feelings?"

He smoothed his hand down her cheek, wiping at the trail of moisture leaking down the side of her face.

"I'm angry at myself," she choked out. "You don't deserve this. I feel so disloyal."

He smiled then. "Do you get angry when I glance fondly at a former lover when she comes my way?"

She frowned and shook her head.

"Why is that?"

"Because I know you feel nothing more than a passing affection for her now."

Lucas nodded. "Exactly. Now, perhaps I do this so that it can be determined what exactly you feel for Cole Madison. I think it's important, don't you?"

Slowly she nodded, marveling at how logical and in control he was. She was a blubbering mess and he was a rock. Always her rock. She sighed and went into his arms again, rubbing her cheek against his chest.

"Thank you," she whispered. "For understanding me." *For knowing when to be gentle and when to be hard and forceful.* She left the last unspoken but he knew. He always knew.

Lucas reached up to lower the divider so he could speak to the driver. "You may take us to our destination now."

Judging by the length of time they'd been riding, Ren assumed that Lucas had given the direction to just drive.

After the divider slid back up, Lucas leaned down to retrieve her clothing that was strewn on the floor.

"Get dressed and straighten your appearance. I'm sure you'll want to look your best when you face your past."

He touched her cheek then ran a finger over her still quivering lips.

"Show no fear, Ren. Show him the woman I know so well. The woman you've become. You have nothing to be ashamed of. If you do nothing else, show him just how big of a mistake he made by walking away from you."

She smiled then and felt the warm brush of her confidence as it slid neatly back into place. Maybe Lucas was right. Maybe she did need to face Cole before she could move ahead to her future. A future she hoped with everything she had would include Lucas.

PART 2

cole

CHAPTER 13

$\mathcal{B}$y the time they slowed to turn into Cole's driveway, Ren had regained her composure—mostly—and repaired her makeup and straightened her clothing. If it weren't for her rapid pulse, she could fool herself into thinking this was just another exciting sexual venture for her and Lucas.

But it wasn't and no amount of telling herself would change the fact that for tonight, she was Cole Madison's.

Edgy excitement cut through the guilt and worry. Her body hummed with sharp arousal—and curiosity. Would she even respond to his commands now? Did he possess the knowledge to give her what she needed?

They slowed at the gate and her eyebrows rose when the driver had to stop and press the intercom button. She glanced out the window into the darkness but couldn't see the house from where they were parked.

A moment later, the gate slowly swung open and the limousine proceeded onto the grounds. The driveway was long and winding and only after several seconds did the house come into view.

It was beautiful. Light was cast onto the house from an array of ground lighting. The front was composed of stone instead of brick. Rustic and rugged looking. Exactly how she imagined Cole would have his house.

From what she could see of the grounds, they were exquisitely rendered and professionally maintained. Nothing seemed out of place.

The driver pulled to a stop in front of the circle drive of the house and before Lucas could open the door, Cole appeared at the top of the steps just outside the front entryway.

Ren scooted to the edge of the seat as Lucas got out in front of her. For a moment her view of Cole was blocked but then Lucas shifted to the side and extended his hand to help her out.

Cole was focused solely on her, his gaze locked. As her hand slid into Lucas's she prayed she wouldn't betray her nervousness by shaking.

No matter what Lucas had arranged, she was here as Lucas's possession and she would not bring shame to him by acting anything but calm and measured. Everything she did reflected on Lucas. She represented him in all things.

She stood gracefully as Lucas pulled her the remaining way out. The door closed behind her and she dimly heard Lucas give his driver instructions.

She ate Cole up with her gaze. He leaned against one of the columns decorating his front porch, hands in the pockets of his slacks. The pose was deceptively relaxed because she could see the tension in his eyes. She could feel it.

Dear God, this was real. She was walking up the sidewalk to Cole Madison's front door. She was here to belong to him for the evening. Maybe even the night. She had no idea of Lucas's plans. Only that she was to give herself unreservedly.

Butterflies scuttled around her stomach, but this time they weren't because of nerves. Excitement danced its way through her veins. Desire. Lust. All there at the idea of this man possessing her even for a short period of time.

Lucas assisted her up the steps and they stopped in front of Cole.

Cole tore his gaze from Ren as if loath to even acknowledge Lucas, but he stuck to protocol and addressed the man who owned her first.

"Lucas, I'm glad you and Ren could make it."

Lucas extended his hand and Cole shook it as the two men exchanged polite greetings.

Then Cole reached for her hand and Lucas released it. An electric charge singed over her skin as soon as Cole curled his fingers around hers. He pulled it up in a formal gesture and pressed a kiss to her knuckles.

"Ren, you look beautiful."

She blushed. Actually blushed, her face warm with pleasure. Cole slowly lowered her hand and then motioned toward the door.

"Please come in."

As soon as Ren stepped inside she noted the innate comfort that oozed from every corner. There was nothing cold or sterile about this house. It was warm and inviting. Decorated and furnished for comfort.

The couches and chairs were sumptuous, plush leather. The artwork wasn't modern, inexplicable renderings of God only knew what. Instead there was a rustic theme both in décor and color scheme that she loved.

It looked—and felt—like Cole. The Cole she remembered. The Cole he always wanted to be.

Sadness and regret welled inside her. Perhaps this would have been their home. Or maybe she needed to accept that they weren't meant to be.

For a moment she lost herself and nearly went to sit when Cole made a motion for Lucas to get comfortable. After a half step, she froze and went instead to the middle of the living room to await instruction.

Lucas had already told her. Tonight she was Cole's to command.

She glanced Lucas's way, just insecure enough to want his reassurance. He gave it with a slight nod. Approval flashed in his eyes, eyes that were usually closely guarded in front of others, but he knew how on edge she was.

Carefully she turned in Cole's direction and raised her gaze until she met his. The intensity in his expression sent shivers down her back. It was a delicious sensation of knowing she was hunted. There was no mistaking the naked desire in those brilliant blue eyes.

She caught her breath, suddenly nervous, giddy, *excited* to hear what his first command would be.

Cole stared at Ren, his chest so tight it threatened to split open. She was here. In his living room, his home, where she belonged. Where she'd always belonged.

She was here but she belonged to another man, and Cole was expected to perform in front of him so he could be judged. Deemed worthy of Ren. Hell, this sucked. He didn't want to share Ren with anyone. He wanted her where no one else could see her, where he could lavish her with attention. Spoil her endlessly.

Lucas's words flashed in his mind. She needed strength. She liked the hard edges. She craved them, needed them. Whatever happened between them for the rest of their time together, tonight he had to convince Lucas Holt that he could leave knowing Ren would be taken care of.

"Come to me," he said, not making a move toward her. It took a lot of discipline not to charge over, throw her over his shoulder and carry her off to his bedroom. Fuck Lucas Holt and his damn expectations.

But he forced himself to maintain the tight discipline he held in all other areas of his life. Apparently when it came to Ren, everything he knew deserted him. She stripped him bare.

Ren walked on soft feet the few steps to where he stood. She was so close he could smell her. Sweet, a little exotic and infinitely mysterious.

Their gazes caught and held. He could drown in those oddly colored green eyes of hers.

"Kiss me."

Her eyes widened. She was surprised by his command. But with little hesitation, she closed the remaining distance between them, pressed her body against his and leaned up to press her lips to his.

He inhaled deeply, overcome at the assault on his senses. Touch, smell, taste . . . Dear God, her taste.

He cupped her face in his hands and then slid his fingers back until they tangled in her hair. He held her captive, or maybe she held him in her thrall. Either way he wasn't about to hurry this moment.

He fed on her lips. Absorbed her sweetness. Their tongues brushed, flirted, retreated and then boldly advanced again.

For too long he'd merely dreamed of holding her again. Of being able to kiss her and know that she was his.

His lungs screaming for air, he dragged his mouth away and slowly released her. She stumbled a bit and he caught her arms, glancing down at the wickedly high heels she wore.

He frowned. "Take off your shoes before you hurt yourself."

There was faint amusement on her face as she slid the fuck-me shoes off and let them fall to the floor. As if he needed her wearing those shoes for him to want to fuck her . . . It was all he'd thought about for the last several days.

"You sound like Lucas," she murmured.

He scowled, not at all flattered by the comparison. She frowned a little in return, worry flashing in her eyes. Worry that she'd displeased him. He purposely steeled his features, angry that he'd allowed her to see his reaction.

"Take off your clothes. Piece by piece. Don't rush. You may lay them on the desk by the window."

Color rushed to her cheeks and she glanced downward. He found her shyness both endearing and heartbreaking. It hurt that the woman who used to undress so boldly before him was now self-conscious, as if he were a complete stranger.

He moved to her and her head yanked up, fear now crowding behind the nervousness. She licked her lips, poised to voice an apology for her hesitation. He could read her as surely as if she'd already said the words aloud.

He simply shook his head and then pulled her into his arms. He lowered her head so he could whisper in her ear. "Don't be afraid of me, Ren. It would kill me. I'll never hurt you. I would rather be alone with you so that we could rediscover each other in private, but this is Lucas's requirement and the only way I could have you."

She relaxed into his arms and rubbed her cheek along his shoulder, a motion so achingly familiar that it damn near gutted him.

Instead of having her carry out his command, he began to undress her himself. The last thing he wanted was for her to be on edge around him. Anything he could do to assuage her fears and uncertainty, he'd do.

He held his breath as he untied her top and let it fall away. She went to pull at her skirt, but he put his hand on hers. "No. Let me. I've decided I'd like to do it myself."

Her fingers shook as she let her hand fall to her side.

His knuckles graced the softness of her belly as he lowered his hand to catch at the waistband of the frilly skirt. Unsure of who he was teasing more, her or himself, he inched the material down until finally it billowed to the floor at her feet.

There she was, adorned only in lacy black lingerie, looking so sensual and utterly beautiful that he couldn't breathe. He didn't want to breathe. He just wanted to stare and drink her in until he was high on nothing but her.

She lifted her chin, and for the first time since he'd commanded her, she returned his gaze head on. She was as aroused as he was. Satisfaction was a savage thrill that coursed through his veins like a potent drug. She wanted him. There was no disguising the truth in eyes that never lied.

"Take off the panties. Just your panties," Cole whispered, barely about to speak around the knot in his throat.

Her thumbs tracked down until they caught in the thin string of the delicate lace. She did a little shimmy with her hips to ease the scrap of material down her legs and he nearly swallowed his tongue.

Soft, creamy skin. Smooth legs. Hips with just enough curve to be damn sexy and an enticing place for his hands to rest.

At the V of those perfect legs was a tiny triangle of trimmed, dark hair and it fired his imagination. Did she keep her lips smooth and bare as she had when they were together?

He'd never forget the first time she'd shyly presented her newly waxed flesh. He'd spent hours touching, licking and coaxing her to orgasm after orgasm.

From the corner of his eye, he saw Lucas move. Just shifting one leg over the other, but it brought reality crashing back. Total buzzkill.

He was expected to perform. To another man's standards. It made him want to bare his teeth and snarl like a predator issuing a challenge. If only it were that simple . . .

He turned away from Ren, leaving her standing in only her bra. He pulled a condom from his pocket, resentful of the need to use one. Lucas probably had her bareback on a daily basis. If Ren were Cole's he sure as hell wouldn't have anything between his dick and the pure sweetness of her flesh.

He lowered himself onto the armless leather chair and let his legs sprawl apart. Then he held the condom out to her and motioned her over.

She came without hesitation and stood before him, waiting his next instruction.

"Unzip me, suck me hard and then put the condom on."

Her eyes narrowed to half slits and they burned with sudden fire. He smiled secretly to himself. She still loved it when he talked crudely and explicitly to her.

She went gracefully to her knees, her hair falling forward over one shoulder. Her hands smoothed up his legs, a subtle tease, before she unbuttoned his fly and slowly lowered the zipper.

She pulled at his underwear, slipping the band over his rigid arousal until finally he was free. His dick popped out and into the warm clasp of her hand. As soon as she gripped him, he damn near passed out.

He'd told her to get him hard, but from the moment he'd stepped out of his front door to see her getting out of the limo, he'd been nothing more than a walking, talking erection.

She lowered her head and gently tucked him into her mouth. He moaned, not keeping his pleasure from her. She made a sound of appreciation around the head of his dick and then sucked him deeper.

"That's it," he murmured. "Good girl. That feels so good. Deeper. Now hold it. Yeah, just like that."

He felt her quiver around him, her soft sounds of pleasure spilling from her throat. She'd always loved when he was vocal during sex. Loved when he told her exactly what pleased him.

He pushed his fingers into her hair, pulling the strands back so he could see her cheeks puff out and then suck in around his cock. Her eyes were half closed, satisfaction glowing brightly in their depths.

He could hardly believe that she was here, between his knees, her mouth around him. It was a scene from his deepest held dreams, the ones he wouldn't admit to himself in the light of day but would look forward to each and every night.

It should irritate him or somehow make him feel much younger and less mature than his thirty-plus years that for all practical purposes he'd pined for this woman for ten years. But all he could think was that finally, finally she was here, with him, where she belonged.

He tightened his hold in her hair and then gently pulled through the strands so they spilled over his hand like a midnight sky.

"You decide when it's enough," he said in a low voice. "After you put the condom on, I want you to straddle me and take me inside you. If you aren't ready, tell me so that I can better prepare you."

He could hardly wait to have her in his arms. All of her. Her astride him, his dick embedded deeply in her body, his arms full of lush, beautiful woman.

She worked him in and out of her mouth several more seconds and then carefully eased her lips over the crown and then away, leaving his cock slick and shiny with her saliva.

She opened the condom and deftly rolled it down his rigid length and he stared at it, hating every inch of the latex as it sheathed him. Then she rose, standing before him in just that wicked sexy bra that barely covered the tops of her nipples.

He held out his hands to take hers and helped her position herself astride him. She settled onto her knees on either side of his hips and then reached down for his dick.

He shook his head and pushed her arm back up. "Put your hands on my shoulders and hold on."

He reached down to position his cock at her opening, rubbing up and down her slit to tease her. She let out a small sigh and briefly closed her eyes.

"Open your eyes," he said in the same measured tone he'd used with her thus far. "I want to see you when I slide into you, Ren. I want you to see me and know who it is inside you."

"I would know," she whispered.

He smiled.

He eased his hips up the tiniest bit so that the head of his cock was lodged just inside her. Then he met her gaze and issued his next command.

"Take me."

Her eyes widened, the pupils flaring. A shudder rolled through her and her fingers bit into his shoulders.

"That's right, Ren. I want you to fuck me. There'll be plenty of time for me to do the fucking. For now I want you to ride me."

She let out a small whimper as she began her downward slide. She opened around him and he let out a strangled moan as she fisted him in her hot, velvet glove.

He moved his hands to those delectable hips and reached around to cup her ass. Just the right amount of softness to the cheeks. Right shape. Firm and yet plush. Yeah, he was an ass man. He'd admit that. But her legs were a very close second. Especially in those sexy-as-hell shoes. He was determined to fuck her in those shoes at a later date. Just her shoes on and a smile.

He lifted, helping her to push upward until his dick was nearly free and then he lowered her back down until he was once again surrounded by hot, liquid silk.

That black lace bra was tantalizing him. Staring him in the face, the tops of her breasts plumped up over the demi cups almost baring her nipples. Almost. And that was what was killing him.

He put his arms around her and slid his hands up her back to the clasp of her bra. In a single motion he popped the hooks and the bra came free. He reached up, pulled her hands down from his shoulders long enough to free her of the bra, and then he stared greedily at the plump swells and her dark nipples that were so rigid that they'd puckered into tight little beads.

"Offer me your breasts," he said. "Cup them and guide them toward my mouth. I want to taste them."

She shuddered again and clamped down on his cock, sending a spasm of delight though his groin. Then she dropped her hands from his shoulders and cupped her full breasts in her palms. She stroked her nipples with the ends of her thumb and then leaned forward, offering him one, holding it teasingly close to his lips.

Instead of taking it in his mouth, he flicked out his tongue and licked the bud.

"The other now," he said huskily.

She moved so the other was there for him to take. This time he grazed the point with his teeth and nipped playfully until she made another sound that bordered on desperation.

"Ask me to suck them."

She swallowed but then said in a voice that was barely above a whisper, "Suck my nipples, Cole. Please."

"Louder. I can't hear you," Lucas said.

Ren's head snapped up and she turned in Lucas's direction, her eyes wide and guilty. Cole cursed the other man's intrusion but perhaps it had been intentional. A reminder of his presence.

He shot a withering stare in the other man's direction. He hadn't appreciated the interruption. As long as he could hear Ren, he didn't give a damn if Lucas could or not. She wasn't fucking Lucas. She was fucking Cole.

Then Lucas rose and walked toward the chair where Cole sat with Ren astride him.

"Tell me, Madison. Do you prefer her pussy or her ass for the next little while?"

CHAPTER 14

What Cole wanted to do was tell Lucas to fuck off. This hadn't been part of the agreement. As far as Cole understood, Lucas was supposed to observe. Nothing more. Then make a quiet exit leaving Ren to him for the next two weeks.

And it wasn't that Cole hadn't had a threesome here and there, but they were by far his less preferred method of sexual release. He just didn't share well. He could see the appeal. Had understood it when he'd joined Micah to have sex with Micah's submissive, Angelina. Angelina had been an exception for Cole.

But the idea of sharing Ren made him get all snarly and possessive and a whole host of other things he didn't really want to examine too closely.

Lucas met his gaze and calmly stared back at him. There was something in the other man's eyes that told Cole he needed to go along. And Lucas didn't push. He didn't insist. Nor did he try to take control and order Cole around. Well, because if he had, it would have been all over.

Cole would have thrown Lucas out and then taken Ren up to his bed where he would have kept her tied up for the next twenty years or so.

No, Lucas wasn't being pushy at all. But his expression told Cole not to challenge him on this.

Hell.

The idea of rolling over and going along just pissed him off.

Remembering also that Lucas had said Ren had exacting standards . . . Well, maybe this was some fucking test he had to pass in order for Ren to accept this whole thing.

In which case, he'd swallow a lot of bitter pills if it meant having Ren.

"Since I'm already balls deep in her pussy, I think I'll take her ass," Cole drawled. "What do you have in mind, exactly?"

"It will require you to get up close and personal with me and certain portions of my anatomy," Lucas said lazily. "Think you can handle that?"

"If I'm in Ren's ass, I don't really give a fuck what you're doing at the time," Cole returned through gritted teeth.

Hell, was Lucas a bisexual? Because if so, this was so not going to work out in the least. He'd seen plenty of cock. It didn't bother him. He could appreciate another man's body with the best of them. But he appreciated it best when it was fucking another woman's brains out and he could watch. Yeah, he appreciated that kind of cock. But it didn't mean he wanted it in any of *his* orifices.

Lucas looked amused, almost as if he was purposely fucking with Cole's head. Cole wasn't amused. He just wanted Lucas to leave already.

"Ren, get down on the floor, shoulders down and put your legs up on Cole's lap," Lucas ordered.

Cole's eyebrows went up because he wasn't getting a real good picture of how this position was going to work, but it still managed to intrigue the hell out of him.

Ren rose up, releasing his cock from her pussy. His cock flagged upward, trying its best to get back inside her.

Still straddling his lap, she reached for his hands and gripped them tight.

"Lower me down," she said.

Still not sure what exactly she was doing, he did as she asked and held her steady as she bent backwards and slid headfirst down to the floor until her shoulders met the carpet. Her back rested between his thighs against the chair, and her ass . . . Well, it was in perfect position. Now he was getting the idea.

Lucas took her legs and levered them back toward him, which only gave Cole an even better view of, not to mention access to, her tight little ass.

Lucas planted his feet on either side of Ren's waist and crowded in. He fumbled with his fly, releasing his cock with an impatient jerk. He was up and over Ren's opening, sliding home in one forceful thrust.

Holy shit but it looked hot.

Lucas silently handed him a tube of KY, and Cole wasted no time applying a liberal amount over his condom-covered erection. He levered himself up so that his cock was tucked to her tiny asshole but he hesitated, looking back up at Lucas.

They were both large men. She was a small woman. With Lucas already stuffed tight into her pussy, her ass was looking smaller all the time.

"I don't want to hurt her."

"Do you think even for a minute that I'd do anything to harm Ren?" Lucas asked calmly.

There was no anger. No ego. No hurt pride. Just a simple question that he obviously didn't expect an answer to.

Cole pressed downward, eyes closing at the exquisite sense of her flesh opening around him and tugging him deeper. Holy hell, she was tight.

His hands covered those plump ass cheeks. He gathered them in his palms, squeezed and massaged as he pushed harder.

After a moment where her body fought his invasion, she opened around him and he slid all the way in.

"Now fuck her," Lucas said.

"I don't take direction from you," Cole snarled.

"You do until I give her into your care," Lucas said quietly. "Now fuck her. Show her the hard edges now that she's seen the softer ones. Give her what she wants, Madison."

Wanting only to get rid of the other man as quickly as possible, Cole complied with the request. He began plunging into Ren's ass while Lucas rode her pussy with quick, ruthless strokes.

"She doesn't come," Lucas said as they moved in unison. "Not yet. Not until I've gone. Once we're finished, it'll be up to you to give her the pleasure she deserves."

Some of Cole's irritation eased away. He was beginning to realize that this was some ritual. One he didn't entirely understand but it was a rite of passage nonetheless. Lucas took his responsibility to Ren seriously. Even now he was easing her into Cole's command. How he could simply walk away mystified Cole, but then Cole himself had walked away once so he had no room to judge another man. Especially when he had Ren's best interests at heart.

For several long minutes, they pushed her relentlessly. They fucked her without mercy and she seemed to love every moment of it. She alternated between tight little whimpers, soft moans of pleasure and groans of frustration when they held her orgasm at bay.

Lucas's face grew more strained and then he rasped out to Cole, "Pull out."

Without contemplating why, Cole slid out of her ass.

"Hold her open," Lucas said.

Cole gripped her ass cheeks and spread them, so that her opening gaped, distended from his rough possession.

Then Lucas jerked out of her pussy and circled his cock with his hand, yanking in short, rapid motions.

Cum spurted onto her ass, most of it sliding into her opening. He directed two more streams and then slid quickly back into her pussy, thrusting as he continued to come inside her.

"Now fuck her," Lucas said hoarsely.

Cole understood that this was symbolic. Sort of a branding. Lucas marking her as his in the most intimate way he could before he released her into another man's keeping.

Oddly aroused and incredibly turned on by the thought of forcing another man's cum into her body with his cock, Cole positioned himself and then plunged deep, pushing the liquid deep inside her.

"Now you come," Lucas said as his thrusts slowed.

Cole needed no urging in that department. He was already so on edge that the slightest touch would send him spiraling into the abyss.

He ground his jaw tight and then slammed into her. Half a dozen punishing thrusts and he was coming and coming until he thought he'd blown the head of his dick right off.

"Pull her up but stay inside her while I say my good-byes," Lucas said quietly.

When Cole complied and pulled Ren to sit in his lap, his cock still wedged deep inside her ass, her eyes were wide with alarm. And panic.

She looked desperately at Lucas over her shoulder, and it was obvious he hadn't told her of his arrangement with Cole. Or at least not all of it. Cole swore under his breath.

Ren stared at Lucas, sure she hadn't heard him correctly. Say his good-byes? What did that mean exactly? She didn't dare move. Didn't dare leap from Cole's lap as she had the sudden urge to.

She waited. Dying a little more with each breath.

Lucas moved to her side then leaned forward and gathered her face in his palms. His touch was exquisitely gentle, his expression tender as he lowered his mouth to brush across her lips.

"You will obey Cole as you obey me. You will please Cole as you please me. In two weeks' time I'll return for you."

She closed her eyes against the sudden stab of pain. But he kissed each closed eyelid and whispered an order for her to look at him.

Her eyelids fluttered open and he stroked his thumb over one cheekbone. Carefully he undid the clasp of her platinum collar until it came loose and fell into his hand. Oh God, no, he wasn't. He couldn't!

She stared in shock as he pulled the collar from her neck. Fear and uncertainty clawed at her. It was worse than any whip or crop. She felt naked and so very vulnerable. Stripped. She no longer had a tangible sign of his ownership.

He turned to straighten his clothing and right his appearance.

Her heart tripped and turned over, thudding painfully against her chest wall. She held her breath until she felt light-headed.

Don't go.

She wanted to say it aloud but instead bit her lip until she tasted blood.

It was like reliving the day Cole walked away from her all over again. She hadn't realized how much she could still hurt as she watched Lucas walk away from her without so much as looking back.

Had he grown tired of her? Was this his way of ensuring she would be cared for? By giving her to a former lover who professed to still have feelings for her? Would Lucas even bother returning in two weeks as he'd promised or was it all a pretense to avoid an uncomfortable parting?

Only when he was gone from the room did a tear slip down her cheek. Her breaths squeezed painfully from her chest.

Cole cursed softly and his arms came around her body, pulling her against his chest. He held her close, his warmth enveloping her. He rested his cheek against the side of her head and then carefully eased himself from her body.

She flinched as he pulled out of her ass. Her desire had slipped away the moment Lucas had mentioned the word *good-bye*. She was frozen, caught in a wasteland. She didn't want to be having sex with Cole. She wanted to be with Lucas. She wanted *him* to be the one taking care of her and commanding her.

Gently, Cole turned her in his arms and then cradled her close, his hand smoothing over her hair. He didn't say anything. He simply held her, his chin resting on top of her head.

"I'm sorry," he said simply. "I never intended to cause you hurt."

No, she sensed he was as out of sorts as she was with Lucas's sudden departure. What she didn't know is if this was a predetermined arrangement or if Cole was just annoyed at how Lucas had handled it. Either way, she now belonged to another man for the next two weeks and deep down she feared that Lucas wouldn't be back for her. Ever.

CHAPTER 15

$\mathcal{N}$ ow that Lucas had departed, Ren felt awkwardness descend. She wasn't sure what she was supposed to do. How she was supposed to feel. She was a blunt, direct person, but right now, the very last thing she wanted was to discuss her feelings. She'd rather drink acid.

Already she could feel herself unraveling. The boundaries seemed to crumble. She hated this feeling. Hadn't felt this way sense she'd fled her last relationship and had been so desperate to reestablish her parameters. Her safety net.

Oh God, what if he didn't come back? What if he, like Cole, chose to just simply walk away?

And then Cole's voice. Sharp. Lean like a whip. Crisp. Cut into her scattered thoughts and snapped her to awareness.

"Get up."

She blinked but hastened to do his bidding.

"On your knees."

She sank to her knees and dropped her gaze to the floor.

"Look at me."

She lifted her chin enough that she could look into his eyes. He stared back at her. Hard. Determined.

"Who owns you now, Ren?"

"You do," she said quietly.

"Then let's establish a few things."

She was so grateful that tears swam in her eyes. Had he known just how much she'd needed this? She needed this direction. This focus. Needed the discipline. She needed him to be firm, because if he was gentle right now, she'd fall apart.

She wanted the security and the safety of his dominance. She desperately needed to reestablish the boundaries and know her place.

He stood, peeling the condom from his softening erection. He strode across the room, leaving her kneeling in front of the couch. After disposing of the condom, he tucked himself back into his pants and then stood there, his gaze trailing over Ren. It was as if he stroked her with his hand.

"Go to the middle of the room and kneel."

She rose and walked on unsteady legs to the center and then lowered herself back down onto the plush area rug. It occurred to her that he hadn't wanted her to kneel on the hardwood floor as she had been. Some of her panic and anxiety eased.

"For the next two weeks, you belong solely to me, Ren," Cole said in a quiet, firm voice that sent shivers down her spine.

There was steel in that voice. A dark promise that excited and reassured her at the same time.

"You will do as I command with no hesitation. Your body is mine. You are mine. Understood?"

"Yes," she whispered.

"You'll answer a few questions for me and then we'll discuss your accommodations here as well as my expectations."

She nodded her acceptance.

"Do you and Lucas use a safe word?"

"We did in the beginning."

"And not now?"

She shook her head. "I trust him. He knows me better than I know myself. I could still use it. I mean, it's not that he'd ignore it. It's just that I've never had to."

"You should choose one with me."

Her heart twisted. Her mind rebelled. Logically she understood and even embraced the need for one. Every time she'd started a new relationship, boundaries had always been set. A safe word had been established. Cole and Lucas had been the only two men she'd ever fully trusted, though, and something inside her balked at the idea that even now Cole would somehow hurt her.

She looked deeper, studying the firm set of his mouth and the intense blue of his eyes.

"It was an accident, Cole," she offered quietly. "I know you'd never hurt me."

He flinched. Then he recovered and his jaw tightened as if she'd angered him.

"You're a fool if you trust me so blindly. I'm not the same man, Ren. I'm a hell of a lot harder."

"Good."

His brow furrowed. He was taken aback by her response.

She lifted her chin. "I don't want easy. I've never wanted easy."

For a moment he didn't say anything. Then he closed the distance between them until he stood a mere foot away, staring down at her from his imposing height.

"Your safe word, Ren. Choose it now."

"*Lucas.*"

The word fell between them, and how appropriate the safe word was. It was a name she'd never invoke with Cole unless she was at her very limit. It was also the name of the man with whom she felt the safest with.

She saw his realization that if she did ever use her safe word that it would be the same as walking away—or rather running back to Lucas.

Cole's eyes gleamed in understanding and she swore she saw approval flash.

"Clever," he said, confirming her suspicions. "Very well. *Lucas* will be your safe word."

He touched her face, ran his thumb over her cheekbone and then let his hand fall away.

"You're more beautiful than ever. As beautiful as you were as a young girl, you've grown even more stunning as a woman."

Warmth surged through her veins at his sincerity and frank appraisal.

"You will spend every minute of the next two weeks with me. The only exception will be the times you work. In the morning, I'll show you to the space I've appropriated for your use. Lucas has said he'll arrange for the delivery of your things."

Instead of being happy at Lucas's forethought, she was only more convinced that he intended this to be their good-bye. Sadness crept into her chest until each breath ached.

"You won't use work to avoid me, however," Cole added softly. "You sleep with me. You eat with me. You go where I go. Understood?"

She nodded her compliance.

"Most important, Ren. You'll be honest with me in all things."

"I have no reason to lie."

"You may rise. It's late and you look tired and upset."

It appalled her that he could so clearly see through her after only a few moments of being with her. They hadn't been together in years. Back then, absolutely. Cole had always been adept at reading her moods, at knowing the moment something was wrong or if she simply wasn't feeling like herself.

Much like Lucas could now.

It had all started with Cole.

She rose to her feet but didn't move toward him. She stood, naked and vulnerable, her emotions and sense of loyalty divided and scattered like pieces to a puzzle.

And then he managed to catch her off guard again.

"Kiss me, Ren."

There was an odd catch in his voice. A thread of tenderness that underscored the command. It was the slight ache in his tone that cut to the very heart of her.

She moved to him, pressed close to his body and then she rose up on tiptoe to wind her arms around his neck. She could absolutely kiss him without touching him or holding him, but such a kiss would be impersonal. Cold. Without heart.

No matter that it had been so many years. Or that he'd hurt her unbearably by walking out of her life. She couldn't pretend he hadn't meant the world to her or that she still didn't battle her feelings for him.

Seeing him again had unsettled her. It had called to the front so much that she'd thought was buried for good. Lucas had known it. He'd seen it and acknowledged it even when Ren wouldn't.

He'd known what Cole had meant to her and what he might mean now and so he'd given her to a man she'd once loved—maybe still loved.

She pressed her lips to the firm line of Cole's mouth and sighed as the familiarity of the gesture brought old memories roaring back.

At first she worried that she'd done something wrong because he stood so still. She couldn't even feel him breathe. As she started to pull away to get his reaction, his arms came around her, and he hauled her against him.

One hand slid down over the curve of her behind to cup her cheek. The other hand tangled in her hair and cupped the back of her head, holding her in place as he plunged his tongue into her mouth.

"Ren."

Her name slipped from his lips, swallowed up by her, but she heard it, she felt it, all the way to her soul. It was the most tender of endearments. That one simple word, torn from his throat, told her more than a hundred others that he'd missed her. That he had ached for her, that he still ached for her.

"Hold me."

This time the request came from her. It wasn't an order. It was a soft plea, one she had no right to ask. He hadn't fully outlined his expectations of her, but it spilled out of her. Until she said it, she'd had no idea just how much she wanted it and needed it.

He issued no reprimand. No reminder of his authority or his control over her. Instead he simply swung her into his arms, holding her as if she were precious and fragile.

As he stared down into her eyes, he turned and walked from the living room. He mounted the stairs and she buried her face against his neck, inhaling his scent, allowing his warmth and strength to envelope her.

They entered a sprawling room that had to be the master suite. He flipped a switch with his elbow as he came through the door and the lamp in the corner flashed on, casting a dim glow over the room. Perfect. Not too bright but enough that they weren't shrouded in darkness.

When he got to the huge bed in the center of the room, he gently set her down on the plush mattress.

"Get comfortable," he said in a low voice. "As soon as I undress, I'll come to bed. And hold you as you've asked."

CHAPTER 16

Ken watched Cole disappear into the bathroom and then she slid down onto the bed, burrowing her head into one of the pillows.

She stared sightlessly across the room as she tried to process all that had happened tonight. Now that the initial hurt and confusion had passed, she was angry.

How could Lucas have done this to her? With no warning? Oh sure, he'd told her that she would be having sex with Cole minutes before they'd arrived at Cole's house, but he'd said nothing about *leaving* her with Cole.

She felt betrayed and that betrayal hurt more than she could have imagined. It briefly crossed her mind that she owed Lucas nothing, that his defection gave her no reason to obey his dictate that she remain with Cole for two weeks at which time Lucas may or may not return.

But at the same time, she couldn't make herself believe that Lucas had done this to hurt her. Whether he'd meant to or not, the result had been the same. But she couldn't help but think that he had only her best interests at heart.

She sighed and closed her eyes. After a year of feeling so . . . strong. Rebuilt. Secure and comfortable in her skin again. Now she felt adrift and she hated not knowing her path. She was a person who took great comfort in routine and ritual.

Her sense of self and her confidence had taken a beating in her last relationship. She'd left before irreparable damage was done, but it had still taken time for her to shake off the effects.

She didn't want to go back there. Ever. She was stronger than who that woman had been. But now, Lucas would test the strength she'd worked so hard to build.

The bed dipped and her eyes flew open. She'd been lost in her thoughts and hadn't even realized Cole had returned. Such inattention would only gain his censure.

But he didn't call her on it. Her merely slid his arms around her body and pulled her until her back was flush against his chest.

"You can talk to me, Ren."

She went still for a moment as his words washed over her. It was as if the last years melted away and they were young again. Inseparable. Set to conquer the world, hand in hand. Ren and Cole.

Oh God, she couldn't handle this without breaking down.

She turned in his arms and clutched at him as she buried her face in his chest. Hot tears spilled down her cheeks and onto his bare skin.

He locked her to him, holding her tightly, one leg thrown possessively over her as if shielding her from the world. It was a clear statement. Nothing can hurt you here. It was such a familiar gesture that it sent a fresh wave of pain through her heart.

"How could he do it?" she whispered.

Cole kissed her forehead as he trailed fingers through her hair.

"How could he just walk away? Especially when he knows how badly it hurt when you did the same?"

Cole tensed. His hand went still against her head and his chin that had rested against her forehead moved as he pulled away.

Then he sighed. "Ren, you can't expect me to defend the bastard. I've made it no secret that I want you."

She rose up on one elbow and stared into Cole's eyes. She wiped irritably at her tears, impatient and angry that she'd allowed him to see how devastated she was.

"Tell me this, Cole. Would you have ever given me to another man? Would you have ever brought me to another man's house and said here, she's yours, I'll be back in two weeks?"

"Come here," he said quietly, pulling her back to him.

He let his hand wander over her hip and down her leg before caressing his way back up to her shoulder.

"I can't profess to know what Lucas was thinking. I don't know the man. You know him a hell of a lot better. I can't muster the same outrage as you because I've gotten precisely what I want. You."

"Would you have ever done what he did?" she persisted.

"Hell no. But maybe I'm more of a selfish bastard than he is. Maybe he feels like he's doing what's best for you. I, on the other hand, would go to hell and back before I ever willingly gave you to another man. I let you go once, Ren. If you think I'm just going to stand back and let *you* walk away this time, you're mistaken. I'll fight with everything I have."

The determined words slipped into the tiny cracks in her heart like alcohol over a cut.

"He didn't fight for me," she whispered. "He just let me go. Like you did before."

"I'm not letting you go now, Ren. I'm here. Have you ever considered that Lucas is merely giving you space so that you can make a choice? It chaps my ass to give him any credit whatsoever, but I believe he just wants you to be happy. He damn sure didn't give you to me because he has any love for me."

Ren pulled her head back again and then reached up to touch Cole's face. She traced his bone structure and feathered her fingertip over his mouth.

"Yes, he gave me to you for two weeks. He knows I loved you. And he wants me to make a choice? Has it ever occurred to either of you that no matter who I chose, I would be devastated?"

Cole frowned.

"I feel manipulated, Cole. I feel like I'm being told that this should be easy. I've been with Lucas for a year. I trust him every bit as much as I trusted you when we were together. I loved you with all my heart. I was crushed when you left me. What Lucas and I have is undefinable. What you and I had was equally undefinable. I'm supposed to spend two weeks with you and then cheerfully choose between two men who've meant more to me than any other man I've ever had a relationship with?"

"I can't keep you here against your will," Cole said quietly. "I won't stop you if you walk out the door."

It wasn't what she'd expected him to say. Her shoulders sagged like deflated balloons. She rolled onto her back to stare at the ceiling. He'd put the ball in her court. It was true. She may cede all the power in the relationship to a man, but it was her choice.

"Make your decision, Ren. I'll give you tonight to deal with your upset. I'll expect your decision in the morning. If you choose to go, I'll make sure you get to where you want to go."

She reached up to touch her neck where the collar had rested for the last year. Her fingers trembled against her bare skin. "And if I stay?"

"If you stay, you'll submit to me. Without reservation. Without question. You'll be mine for the entire two weeks."

"And what then?"

He rolled onto his side so that he faced her. She glanced over to see the intensity reflected in those blue pools.

"Then you have a decision to make."

CHAPTER 17

*C*ole made no move toward her even though they slept in the same bed. He made no demands of her. In fact, he didn't so much as touch her.

After he'd told her she had a decision to make, he'd simply rolled over, turned off the lamp and then settled down to sleep. She, on the other hand, remained awake, staring into the darkness as she contemplated her circumstances.

She was completely befuddled by the turn of events. When Lucas had first told her that he was giving her to Cole, her emotions had been in a whirlwind.

Nothing had been right ever since that night at The House when Cole had walked back into her life.

It was hard to see past her hurt and betrayal, but after an entire night staring at the ceiling, she was beginning to realize what Lucas must have seen in her. And why he'd made the decision he made.

Lucas wasn't the type to demand attention. Or loyalty. If you were with him, yes, absolutely he expected your entire focus, your loyalty and obedience. But he wasn't going to make you do anything you weren't committed to.

He must have known what Cole's reappearance had done to her. Her distraction wouldn't have pleased him. What surprised her more was the way he'd handled it. With such gentleness and understanding.

Wasn't he angry? Was he afraid of losing her? Or was he resigned? Or did he even care about the outcome?

Or had he, like Ren feared, simply decided it was time for him to move on?

And if that was the case, why was she expending so much mental anguish over his defection?

Because you love him.

The admission frightened her. She hadn't allowed herself to love anyone since Cole. And it wasn't so much that Cole had ruined her for men for all time, blah blah. She'd been with several men since Cole. Men who had satisfied her. Men who hadn't even come close. The usual mixture of winners and losers in a woman's life.

It was just that no one had known her like Cole had. No one had managed to reach inside the very heart of her like Cole had. Not until Lucas. And she wasn't even sure he'd tried. He just did. He got her.

And if she loved Lucas, which she was now pretty certain she did, why had seeing Cole again put her into such a tailspin?

Because you love him too.

Or at least she loved the man Cole had been. She loved the memory of who he'd been and what he'd meant to her. Who was to say he was still that same man?

Who was to say he wasn't even better?

Tears of frustration bit at her eyelids. She'd expended more emotion in the last days than she had in years. She'd always been careful to keep herself firmly in check. Calm. Measured. She didn't like feeling distraught and out of control.

She understood—or at least thought she understood—Lucas's decision now. He wanted her to face her past. He wanted her to deal with the issue of Cole before she could move forward. With Lucas.

It was either that or he'd seized the opportunity to make sure Ren was cared for before moving on as he had in so many other relationships.

She wasn't sure what about Lucas made it impossible for him to commit to a longstanding relationship. He'd been up front with her from the beginning that their arrangement wasn't permanent, that it couldn't be.

But as time went on and he seemed content, she put it out of her mind that it was a temporary arrangement.

She'd let her guard down. She'd allowed herself to fall for a man she couldn't have.

Stupid.

She turned slightly to stare at the back of Cole's head as pale light softened the room through the curtains. Cole wanted her. She couldn't lie to herself that she didn't still have strong feelings for him. She did.

He'd laid it out plainly for her. He wanted her. He would fight for her. He'd never give her to another man as Lucas had.

He'd also offer her the kind of relationship she wanted and needed. Wouldn't he?

She had two weeks to find out. Two weeks in which to explore a relationship with Cole and to determine whether or not Lucas would come back for her.

And yeah, then she'd have a decision to make. A decision that already sent pain through her heart.

* * *

She felt him leave the bed. He was quiet so as not to awaken her, but then she still hadn't slept. Her back was to him and she briefly closed her eyes, not yet wanting him to know she was awake. When she heard him go into the bathroom she opened her eyes and took in a deep breath.

For the next two weeks she would be his. There would be no half measures. Not sorta kinda or in between. That kind of relationship or agreement would never fulfill her. She needed—she craved—full possession. The safety and security of a completely dominant lover.

She needed the structure and rigidity but she also needed a man who knew when not to push too hard. Lucas had been that man. But so had Cole.

She pushed herself up and slipped out of bed, her feet flexing when they hit the wood floor. There wasn't a rug or any carpet to soften her kneeling position, but it didn't matter. Her discomfort wasn't important. The message she would send to Cole was.

Complete obedience. Complete submission.

For two weeks, she was his to command.

After? She couldn't bear to think that far ahead. There was too much she didn't know, and she was afraid to speculate on the potential outcome.

She walked naked around to the foot of the bed and then faced the door to the bathroom. She sank gracefully to her knees, rested her hands palms up on the tops of her legs and settled her gaze forward, waiting for Cole to return.

He couldn't possibly misunderstand the significance of the gesture.

Several long minutes later, she nearly closed her eyes when she heard the door open. Butterflies danced in her belly, but she forced her chin up so she could meet his gaze the moment he saw her.

He frowned.

Not exactly what she'd expected.

"Jesus, Ren. Your knees. How long have you been kneeling like this?"

He strode forward, reached down and gently pulled her to her feet. She wobbled a little unsteadily, taken aback by his reaction.

He guided her back to the bed and eased her down on the edge. He had a towel wrapped around his waist and his hair was still damp from his shower. A single bead of water trailed down his side and she had the insane urge to run her tongue over it.

To her further shock, he went to one knee in front of her so they were on eye level. Every part of her rejected the sight of him kneeling in front of her. She stared at him with no idea of what to say or how to react.

He touched her cheek and sighed. "I appreciate the sentiment. I understand it. I'm relieved as hell. Don't get me wrong, the sight of you on your knees blows me away. But I don't want you in pain, Ren. I have hardwood floors in the bedroom. It can't be comfortable for you."

"I wanted you to know," she began quietly.

He nodded. "I know you did. It's me, remember? I think I went a little weak in the knees when I opened the door and there you were. It took me back to a much better time. When we were young and together, testing something new and powerful. I was so damn grateful that you didn't get up and walk out while I was in the shower. Do you know how hard it was for me not to run out to see if you were still there? To calmly go through the motions of a shower and shaving all the while my gut was in a knot because I was afraid you wouldn't stay?"

"I'll stay. I'm yours."

He cupped her cheek then leaned forward, brushing his lips across hers. First just a tender brush. Then he came back, fusing his mouth to hers. Her lips parted on a sigh and he slid his tongue over hers until she tasted the mint of his toothpaste.

As he pulled away, he murmured, "Oh yes, Ren. You're mine. You'll never doubt that for a moment."

Then he rose and discarded the towel around his waist. He was such a beautiful man. He'd lost the lean softness of youth and in its stead was a muscled, rougher man that made her mouth water.

His cock was rigid, flared up toward his navel from a nest of lighter brown hair, almost blond like the rest of him.

"Go get a condom from the nightstand and put it on me," he said in a terse, barely restrained voice.

She scooted off the bed and hurried to do his bidding. She wanted him inside her again. Last night had felt . . . practiced. Almost as if they had been putting on a show for Lucas's benefit, and maybe Cole had.

Today, there was no one but Cole and Ren. No Lucas. No pretenses or awkwardness.

She tore open a condom and returned to sit in front of Cole. His erection was on level with her mouth, but he didn't appear to have any intention of having her pleasure him with her lips and tongue.

With shaking fingers, she rolled the latex over his rigid length. Automatically her gaze found his as she awaited his next directive.

"Lay back, spread your thighs and bend your knees so the bottoms of your feet are flat on the mattress. Then spread yourself and hold on to your knees."

She leaned back, clutching at her knees as her soles dug into the mattress. The position opened herself completely to him. She was vulnerable but so very excited.

He ran the tip of his finger from her clitoris to her opening and then slid it inside to the knuckle. She shuddered violently, her hips arching off the mattress in response.

"Keep yourself open," he bit out when her hold on her knees loosened.

She reasserted her hold and then sucked in her breath when he lowered his head between her splayed thighs. Oh God.

He pressed the most tender of kisses to her opening and then lazily slid his tongue upward until it rolled over her clitoris.

Her fingers dug into her knees and it was a battle to maintain her position when her entire body was screaming in pleasure.

He licked her again, making long, sensual swipes with his tongue. The roughness over such tender and sensitive skin drove her to madness. She twitched from head to toe and was one breath way from coming completely unglued.

But he was in no hurry and he seemed content to stroke her with his tongue and suck lazily at her quivering flesh. He rimmed her entrance and then slid his tongue in, tasting her from the inside out.

Pressure. All she needed was just a little pressure in just the right place and she'd explode in the mother of all orgasms. But he seemed to know exactly how close she was to meltdown because he continued with gentle, featherlike strokes and caresses. He flicked his tongue expertly over and around her clit, never putting quite enough force behind the movements to send her the rest of the way over the edge.

But how he drove her mad. He was good. So very good at making her feel exquisite, mind-numbing pleasure. He was patient too. Never tiring as he coaxed her ever closer to the ultimate sexual peak.

But then he'd always been this way. Possessive and demanding, absolutely, but generous and loving as well. Even when it was all about him, somehow he always managed to put her first. She'd always adored him for that.

"You taste just as good as I remember," he said huskily as he pulled away.

She stared at him through passion-glazed eyes, unable to move. Her entire body was liquid. He'd reduced her to a boneless, quivering mass of desire.

He took a step back and then positioned himself at her opening. He stared down at her, those blue eyes so unbelievably beautiful. "Look at me. Only at me."

She locked her gaze with his just as he pushed inside her. Her breath caught and then came out in a gasp at his sudden possession.

"Mine, Ren."

He pushed deeper until his hips were flush against the backs of her thighs and he held himself there.

"Who do you belong to?"

"You," she replied softly.

"Who takes care of you?"

"You."

"Say my name."

"Cole," she said obediently.

"Who owns you, commands you, takes care of you, sees to your every need?"

"You do, Cole. I'm yours."

He thrust hard for several moments, his face straining as he slammed into her. It was a pure act of ownership. He was branding her. Putting his stamp on her. It was a display of sheer dominance.

Then as suddenly as he had taken her, he slowed and his thrusts became gentler. He leaned forward and slid his hands up her waist, causing her arms to fall to the bed. Her knees fell forward and her legs relaxed and he pulled her close to him until their bodies were tightly meshed and he was deep inside her, his hips undulating in a sensuous rhythm.

"And who's going to cherish you and protect you and lavish you with all the affection you deserve?" he said against her mouth.

Her heart twinged and emotion knotted her throat. She kissed him back, feverishly, not answering the question for several long seconds. Then she finally pulled away and stared straight into those mesmerizing blue eyes.

"You are," she whispered.

"Damn right I am," he growled as he surged forward again.

He was big and powerful. He pinned her to the mattress, his weight easily making her captive to his demands. But he made her feel . . . safe. Desired. Wanted. And yes, cherished.

She should have felt apprehensive and unsure, as she had each time she'd slept with a man for the first time after embarking on a new relationship. But with Cole, it was like coming home. It was reconnecting with something she'd long been denied.

She knew that he'd never hurt her no matter what he thought or what blame and guilt he carried.

Trust wasn't something she gave easily. It was hard won and she rationed it carefully. No, she knew he'd never hurt her physically. But emotionally?

He'd once broken her heart and she didn't know that she could withstand another blow like she'd endured the day he walked out of her life.

Only now, it could well be her doing the walking away and it didn't make her feel the slightest bit better or empowered.

It scared her to death.

He kissed her with savagery that seemed pint up to now and was suddenly released in a violent storm. As if he'd kept his control so tightly leashed for all this time.

His hunger was palpable. He consumed her. Desire consumed them both.

Lucas may have marked her the evening before but Cole was possessing her body and soul as if he could drive away everyone else in the world but him.

"Come for me, Ren. Show me your passion. Show me the girl I once knew. Show me she's still there, the Ren I loved with everything I had."

Tears were tiny daggers to her eyes. Each word pricked her soul.

Even now, so many years later, he could cut to her very core with his words.

Her orgasm fluttered over her, light and delicate, a direct contradiction to the force in which he was restaking his claim. His body drove ruthlessly into hers, but his eyes . . . His eyes spoke a different message. They were gentle and loving. Intense. Burning straight through the barriers she'd constructed over the years.

It spread lazily through her veins, flooding her with sweet, endless pleasure. Sweet. Soft. Stroking over her body like a honey-dipped feather.

She sighed and tightened around him. Her palms stroked over his firm muscles and taut flesh and then she hugged him to her, buried her nose against his neck and inhaled his scent.

He was the very best part of her past. Of a girl bridging the gap between child and woman.

And now, if he had his way, he'd be very much a part of her future. A future she'd always envisioned having with him.

"That's my girl," he murmured as he stroked her down from her orgasm. "Now it's my turn."

He raised himself off her enough so that she was forced to meet his gaze. Then he began thrusting rhythmically. Harder. Until the slap of his hips meeting her flesh echoed over the room.

"Look at me," he said harshly when she would have closed her eyes and dreamily drifted away.

Her eyes flew open again and she stared at the firm line of his jaw. The fire and determination in his eyes.

He screamed possession without saying a word. His body owned her. Over and over he took until she moaned softly, unsure of whether she wanted mercy or wanted none.

"Every part of you . . . mine. Your body is mine. Your ass is mine. Your breasts are mine. Your pussy is mine and I'll possess it whenever

I like for however long I like. Your mouth is mine to take. Say it, Ren. Say it while I come inside you. Tell me you're mine and make me believe it."

She reached up for him, looped her arms around his neck and pulled him down. "I'm yours, Cole. All of me. Every part. I'm yours to do with as you wish."

And for now it was the absolute truth.

CHAPTER 18

$\mathcal{R}$en lay curled in Cole's lap on the overstuffed couch in his sunroom. It was a beautiful room, full of windows bursting with light from the side and above. The room was almost completely glassed in and the view of his garden was magnificent.

It reminded her of a children's book. A fantasy garden that hid secret pathways. Enchanted and magical.

It was clear that this house was Cole's refuge. Built to exacting standards. Ultimate comfort and privacy in mind. Here nothing could encroach and that gave her an added measure of security and comfort.

He took another strawberry and held it to her mouth. She took a bite, the sweet fruit delectable on her tongue. Cole had arranged for an entire buffet in the sunroom and had fed her by hand whatever she wanted.

She felt pampered and ridiculously spoiled and now she was content to lie in his arms.

He'd kicked up his feet and stretched lengthwise on the couch so his back was to the arm. She was draped over him and every once in a while he reached for something to feed her. His other hand stayed in her hair and he absently stroked through it and down her arm almost as if it was impossible for him to stop touching her.

"I think this would be perfect for your office," he said. "Do you think you can work here or do you prefer something not so open?"

It shouldn't have surprised her that he would have arranged for her to have space to work. Lucas would have seen to it.

"It's perfect." And it was. Where better to create her own children's tales than in a setting that looked straight out of one?

"I'll have all your things brought here and arranged to your liking."

She frowned. "I don't have my stuff yet."

"He had everything sent over this morning," Cole said quietly.

"Oh."

Silence descended and she tried so very hard not to read anything into the fact that Lucas had made no effort to see her. She wouldn't allow it to hurt her because she had no idea the motive or lack of one and she refused to speculate.

"Do you remember when we used to do this on the weekends?"

Cole's question brought her sharply out of her thoughts and sent her mind seeking in a completely different direction. Maybe it had been intentional. But it was effective because her mind wandered back to days spent just like this. She sprawled across Cole's body, both of them content to just be.

Her smile was wistful and a little bittersweet. "Yes, I remember. We had such good times."

He kissed her forehead. "Yes, we did."

She angled her head so she could stare up at him. "How can we just fall back into this, Cole? We don't even know each other anymore. It's been ten years since we were together. This has all happened so fast that I'm having a hard time putting it all together. Is it a game? Are we having a fling for old time's sake? I feel like I need to know what the expectations are. I mean, Lucas gave me to you. I get that. The three of us are adhering to rules that most other people don't have any knowledge of and yet they're important to all of us. Or at least they are to me. I need to know where I stand with you. Take away the rules, the agreement, the fact for the next two weeks I am for all practical purposes your property and just tell me what this is."

"You don't ask much," he said dryly.

He stroked his fingers through her hair, kissed her tenderly on the forehead again and then expelled his breath in a long sigh.

"I made a mistake, Ren. I've always known it. Walking away from you was the worst decision I've ever made. I hurt you and I hurt myself. We were so young and I was so worried that I was taking you over. I should have trusted in your strength. I should have had more faith in myself but I loved you so much, it killed me to think of hurting you, of what I did to you or *could* do to you in the future."

She leaned away to rest against the back of the sofa so that she could see his face.

"But the need in me wouldn't go away. It shamed me because I thought that anything that had brought someone I loved pain was an . . . abomination. It wasn't until later that I realized that it wasn't the practice of dominance and submission that was wrong. It was my handling of it and my ignorance. It was me who placed you in a position of danger. You were mine to protect and cherish and I failed you on every level."

"No," she whispered, shaking her head.

He touched her face, stroked his fingers down her cheek as his gaze devoured her. Almost as if he couldn't quite believe that she was here and would disappear at any moment.

"After you, I refused to participate in any practice that I didn't extensively study and devote long hours to mastering. We wondered when we began if it was curiosity or a deep-seeded need within us. For me it was a need and now I realize it was the same for you. How perfect we were for each other," he said ruefully. "Even more so than we ever imagined. But the truth of the matter was, I needed time to mature and grow and time to gain the knowledge necessary to provide a safe environment for you."

"Did you have other relationships? Like ours?" she asked, though she dreaded the answer. It was stupid and hypocritical. She'd certainly had relationships. She hadn't been celibate but somehow it hurt her to think of Cole cherishing another woman as deeply as he'd cherished her.

"Not like ours," he denied. "Nothing like ours. My . . . Well, you can't even call them relationships. They were encounters. And they were all very clinical. There were women who intrigued me. Whom I was attracted to, but the ones I was perhaps the most attracted to belonged to other men. Maybe subconsciously I felt safe in letting myself feel something for them because I knew I never had a chance with them."

Her brow furrowed in confusion. "Why wouldn't you have wanted a chance?"

His gaze settled on her. Deep and serious. "Because they weren't you."

Her breath caught and she felt light-headed.

"Ren, I loved you. I know you didn't think so. Especially when I walked out on you. But for me there's never been another woman who made me feel like you did. There were a few who came close and maybe if they hadn't belonged to other men I would have enjoyed being with them."

He caught her hand and pulled it to his mouth to kiss her palm. "I've been very successful in life. I've achieved all the goals I've set out to achieve. It's brought me a measure of happiness. But there's always been something missing and when I looked up in that restaurant and saw you for the first time in all these years, it all fell into place for me. It was like being hit by lightning. I can't even begin to explain how it felt."

She stared back at him in complete befuddlement. Her stomach knotted and she could barely squeeze air into her lungs.

"I looked at you and knew what was missing in my life. What I *wanted* in my life. I've never stopped loving you, Ren. I can't make it any simpler than that."

She swallowed but the knot didn't go away. She had no idea what to say. How to feel. How could she make herself so very vulnerable when she was setting herself up for hurt no matter how this played out in the end?

Cole framed her face and leaned forward to kiss her lightly on the lips. "I've been brutally honest with you for one reason and one reason only. Because I want you to know from the start where I stand so that no matter what happens this week, no matter how hard I push you, no matter how far I take you out of your comfort zone, you know one thing if you know nothing else. You'll know I love you and that I'd never do anything to hurt you again."

He released her face but his gaze held her captive. "You can belong to any number of men. You can be possessed. You can be a possession. You can submit. You can be dominated. But none of that necessarily means you are loved and cherished above all else. You'll know that with me, Ren. You'll never doubt it for even a moment if I can help it."

Tears gathered in her eyes. "Oh Cole." She leaned forward until her forehead touched his and he swam in her vision as she tried to hold back the flood of emotion. "I've missed you so much."

He tangled his fingers in her hair and held her close as their breaths mingled. "I've missed you too, darling."

"It's all so fast," she murmured.

He nodded. "It is. We'll slow down. I never thought it would be easy. You can't imagine what it felt like to see you and know you belonged to another man. Really belong. I knew what that collar signaled and I knew that I'd have to fight for you. But there was no way in hell I was going to walk away again."

She snuggled into his arms and laid her head on his shoulder. He was so strong and comforting. Warm. She needed that strength.

"I won't be easy," he warned.

She shivered at the dark promise in his voice.

"This time we have together will give you the opportunity to see who I really am."

She glanced up into his eyes. "And you'll see that I'm not weak. That I need your strength and the rigidity of a dominant relationship. It's not just what I want, Cole. It's what I need. It's what I have to have."

He nodded. "I understand. I'll give that to you, Ren. I'll give you everything."

Contentment slid over her, loosening some of the tension in her muscles. She went limp against him as he continued to stroke her body, his touch tender and soothing.

"Now tell me about this career of yours," he said against her hair. "Rennie Michaels? Children's author extraordinaire?"

She laughed lightly. "It started as an escape. A way to deal with my unhappiness. My unfulfillment I suppose you could say. I would drift away, telling stories in my head and one day I decided to write them down. And then I began to draw the scenes, adding words to the pictures that danced around my mind. The second day I was with Lucas, after he moved me in with him, he came across my drawings and one of the books I'd put together myself. He insisted I submit it and so I did. To be honest I think he helped. He had connections. Before I knew it I had an agent and then an offer. They fast tracked that first book because it was already completed and little to no revisions were necessary. It released a few months ago and I'm working on the third in the series right now. The second will be released in four more months."

"I'm proud of you."

Her cheeks bloomed with heat and she smiled. "I love it. Sometimes I get too wrapped up in it, but I enjoy it. I have a purpose now. Job wise, I mean. Before I worked in marketing. I got my degree after you and I split up. But it's so stressful and against my true personality. It was exhausting to make myself be this person I wasn't and I finally quit trying. I owe a lot of that to Lucas. He was content to just let me . . . be."

She glanced anxiously at Cole, already regretting that she'd brought up Lucas twice. It wasn't that she was intentionally throwing Lucas in Cole's face nor was she trying to make Cole jealous or make him feel threatened. The simple truth was Lucas had everything to do with the woman she was now. The woman she'd become over the last year.

She would have gotten there on her own eventually but Lucas had been a rock-solid source of support. She'd always owe him that.

"It sounds like Lucas recognized what a very special woman you were from the moment he saw you," Cole said in a low voice.

Ren nodded, relieved that he didn't take offense.

"What about your last relationship? Lucas said the man you were with hurt you."

Ren could feel how stiff Cole went the moment he brought up the subject. There was a darkness to his eyes that told her how very dangerous he could be when provoked.

She swallowed and sighed. "A lot of it was my own fault."

Cole scowled.

"No, really it was. I mean, it wasn't my fault he was a dickhead, but it was my fault that I stayed as long as I did and that I settled for something I knew would never make me happy or fulfill me. That's on me."

"What did he do?" Cole gritted out.

"He wanted to change me. He had very set ideas—stereotypical ideas—of how a dominant submissive relationship should work. To be honest he'd watched too many porn flicks or read too many bad novels on the subject. Quite frankly he was a joke. He wanted to be king of the castle and for me to kiss his feet. His idea of dominance was abuse and disrespect. He felt powerful when he was humiliating me."

Cole's nostrils flared and rage built like a storm in his eyes. His grip tightened on her and just as quickly he began to rub his hand up and down her arm in a comforting motion that she was unsure that he was even cognizant of.

"That son of a bitch," Cole hissed. "The little bastard. So he got his rocks off acting like an abusive asshole."

Ren shrugged. "Basically, yeah. My fault. I mean, that I took it so long. I was at a crossroads and my problem wasn't so much that I thought I wanted him. I knew I didn't. My problem was that I didn't know *what* I wanted and so I was afraid."

He gathered her tightly in his arms and pressed his lips to her temple. "I'm so sorry you had to endure that. I'm glad you found Lucas. It sounds like he was a much better man."

"He was—is," she returned quietly. "In a lot of ways he saved me. From myself. He refused to let me settle."

"It hurts me that someone hurt you. I'd like to kill the little son of a bitch. When a woman submits to a man, it's the most precious gift she can give. Herself. Unreservedly. The man has to respect and honor that gift above all else. Even if he respects nothing else in the world, he must respect the woman in his care. It's his sworn duty to protect, honor and cherish his submissive. To take care of her and provide a safe haven. Someone who would put his own needs above his woman's is no man."

She pushed herself up and rearranged herself so that she sat astride him on the couch, her knees resting on either side of him. She stared down into his eyes, touched beyond words at his vehement declaration.

"Do you know, when you say those things, I don't believe they are just words," she said. "You mean them."

"Damn right I do," he said with a frown.

For the first time, she looked to the next two weeks without a twinge of sadness and uncertainty. Anticipation licked through her veins, and more powerful than the anticipation, was yearning.

She didn't just need what Cole would give her. She wanted it and him. She'd never stopped loving or wanting him. At times she'd thought that she was still caught up in a youthful fantasy and that the memories would never translate to reality.

But here he was in front of her. Strong. Demanding. Unyielding. Dominant, so very dominant. Hard and yet unbelievably tender.

He was everything she wanted and needed and everything she'd missed for the last ten years. Cole wasn't as good as or the same as that young man she'd known when she was just a girl.

He was way better.

CHAPTER 19

They napped and lounged in the sunroom. At some point, two men carried in the boxes containing Ren's writing and art supplies, but Cole motioned for them to be quiet. Ren still slept soundly on his chest and he had no desire to wake her and let go of the moment.

There weren't words to describe his contentment. His absolute satisfaction in holding her in his arms. It overwhelmed him and brought back so much of the past years when he'd searched in vain for what he'd been missing from the moment he walked out of her life.

He was fortunate and so very grateful that she hadn't chosen to walk away from him. That she'd decided to stay and give him—them—a chance.

When the men had finished unpacking the boxes to Cole's satisfaction, he waved them away and then gently shook Ren awake.

Her eyes came open and she looked disoriented for the briefest of moments before she smiled and snuggled a little deeper into his arms.

"I have plans for us this afternoon if you're up for going out."

She raised her head and pushed away the heavy silk of her hair. "Of course. I've been lazy the entire day."

He smiled and touched her cheek. "If you have then so have I. I quite enjoyed our day together so far. But you have need of clothing and I thought we could enjoy dinner with friends. I'd like you to meet them in a more relaxed setting."

Her eyebrows scrunched together. "Cole, I have more clothes than I know what to do with. Unless . . . Did Lucas not send anything over with my writing stuff?"

Cole took a measured breath. "He did. I sent them back."

She cocked her head, obviously confused, but she didn't question him. An action he approved of.

"You're mine now, Ren," he said in a soft voice. "It's my responsibility to provide for you. To care for you. To ensure all your needs are met while you're in my keeping. I won't have another man do those things for you."

She nodded her understanding.

"So I thought perhaps we could go shopping. I have a distinct desire to outfit you in clothing that complements your natural beauty. Then we'll meet two couples that I'm friends with for dinner. You've met Damon and Serena already but you haven't yet met Micah and his wife, Angelina."

She pursed her lips and her eyes grew thoughtful for a moment. He could see the question hovering but she made no effort to voice it.

"Ask your question, Ren."

"It's really none of my business," she said ruefully. "Just a thought that occurred and I'm not even certain why I want to know."

"Ask it."

"These women. Serena and Angelina. You spoke of being attracted to and of being . . . intimate . . . with women that belonged to other men. Are they . . ." She took a deep breath. "Are they the women you spoke of?"

Cole went soft at how small her voice sounded. She was trying so hard to pretend only a passing interest but he remembered what Lucas had told him of her previous relationship and the promise he'd exacted from Cole about having other women. As if he could even bring himself to look at another woman with Ren at his side.

"Look at me," he said in a tender voice. "First, you're it for me, Ren. All I want. The only woman I need. I have no desire—*feel* no desire— for another woman when I have perfection staring me in the face."

"Oh," she breathed, her eyes rounding and then sparkling with delight.

"Now to answer your question because I'll never be anything but honest with you. I have touched Serena. Intimately. But not in the way you'd think. Damon is very, very possessive of her. He doesn't share. He trusts me and I spend a lot of time at his club, and so he would often have me prepare Serena. For him. For his attentions. It was part of his process. He's very methodical in all things. That's as far as things ever went with Serena. And I never had any desire to take things further. They are dear friends. She and Damon both."

Ren nodded her understanding, relief lightening her eyes.

He touched her and then shifted so he could sit up to hold her because he considered that the next might not be as easy to hear.

"Angelina . . . she was different and in order to tell you the difference, I need to go back and tell you of my role at The House. A role that I basically made for myself and one I was content with."

She nodded again but the frown was back.

Unable to resist, he leaned forward and pulled her down into a long, heated kiss. She melted instantly, so sweet and unresisting. He could honestly spend all day doing nothing more than touching her. The next two weeks were going to be hard because all he wanted to do was lock himself in a room with her and make love to her until neither of them could take anymore.

But what he had to do was show her his life. How her life with him could be. He couldn't afford a single misstep. Not when his entire future rode on convincing her that he could be the man she needed.

"Now, about Angelina. She belongs to Micah. Completely and utterly belongs to him. He's so crazy in love with her. He'd do anything and everything to make her happy."

Ren sighed. "That so wonderful."

He could hear the wistful note in her voice and he wanted so badly to tell her that she could have that. She could have it and more because if she stayed with him, not a day would go by that he wouldn't show her how very precious she was to him. Had always been.

"Micah is also . . . hard. Darker I guess you could say. Angelina fits him well because her desires and needs are every bit as dark as his. He's fierce and demanding but he loves her so damn much."

"He likes her to be with other men," Ren guessed.

"Yes and no. You see, it's kind of complicated, his and Angelina's past, which is why he fought her for so long. He was once married to a woman he loved very much but he shared her with Angelina's brother, his best friend. They both loved her. She was with them both."

Ren frowned and cocked her head. "Then how?"

"I know. It all sounds like some kind of soap opera, right? Hannah, his wife, and David, his best friend, were killed in a car accident. Only it wasn't really an accident. They were murdered by a man who was obsessed with Angelina, who at the time was far too young and David was extremely protective of her."

"Oh my God. That's horrible!"

Cole nodded. "So Micah leaves Miami, comes here. He's grief-stricken. It took him a good while to get over what happened. And then comes Angelina who had been in love with him the entire time.

So you can imagine all the conflicting emotions that Micah was feeling when confronted by this gorgeous, now grown-up, Latina bombshell."

"He didn't take it well, I'm guessing," Ren murmured.

She leaned forward now, seemingly absorbed by the somewhat twisted story. Okay so it was a lot twisted looking back.

"He pushed her pretty hard," Cole said. "He didn't believe that she knew what it was he really needed and wanted. He didn't believe that she knew what she was getting into."

Ren snorted. "Typical know-it-all male. Always knows better than the female what she wants or needs."

He eyed her balefully. "Anyway, if I can continue, I'll get to my point."

"Ah yes, what was the point of this conversation? I've quite forgotten."

He smacked the side of her ass. "Disrespectful baggage. I'll have to punish you for that later."

The shiver that stole over her body delighted him. And stirred his blood like crazy. He couldn't wait to have her spread out before him. Helpless. Dependent solely on him and his mercy. Provided he had any.

"Now, the thing is, back to my role at The House, because this kind of ties in. I did a lot of preparing. I touched. But mostly observed. I never had actual intercourse with the women there. I was tempted a few times but it wasn't the right situation. I liked being at the club. I enjoyed the lifestyle. But mostly I was an outsider looking in. Until Angelina."

Ren battled her frown. She tried not to allow him to see her reaction. She went still and he could feel the battle she waged with herself. It was obvious she still carried the scars from her previous relationship and it pissed him the fuck off that some bastard had actually cheated on her. Her! Who the hell in their right mind would even look at another woman when they had Ren at their feet. A willing submissive. Eager to do his bidding, to please him. She was so beautiful inside and out and he hated this son of a bitch for making her doubt that inner beauty.

That this asshole had paraded these women in front of Ren—hell he'd probably fucked them in front of her—all the while sending her the message that she wasn't good enough, that nothing she could do would please him.

If he did nothing else in these two weeks, he'd show her that no other woman existed for him except her. She would know without a doubt that while she may submit to him and give him the most precious gift a woman can give to a man, in reality, she wielded absolute power over him.

"So you had sex with Angelina. Was she your first? I mean, from The House?" Ren asked.

"Well, yes and no. Micah invited me over. He trusted me. There were things he wanted that he didn't feel comfortable doing himself."

Ren's eyebrows raised and he could see the interest gleam in her eyes.

"Hot wax," Cole explained. "He didn't want to hurt Angelina and I have experience with the practice. Micah did not. He may have tested her limits and maybe even tried to push her away and to prove that she couldn't take what he would demand from her, but he would have died before hurting her."

Ren donned a thoughtful, musing look. "I think I might like this Angelina. Except the part about her having sex with you."

He chuckled. "There were other men present. Two others, to be exact."

Her eyes widened again. "So she had sex with all of you?"

Cole studied her reaction closely. She seemed intrigued and he wasn't sure how to take that. He wasn't big on sharing. It was one thing he had in common with Damon. Before Angelina, he'd never even participated in a threesome. He was too damn possessive to share a woman he cared about with another man. But he could understand the appeal better now.

He finally nodded. "Yes, it was something that turned her on. We made sure she enjoyed herself. There was one other time, and perhaps I enjoyed this encounter more. It was more . . . intimate."

Ren shifted her position so she could lean back against the couch with her feet over his belly and dangling off the couch. "This is a fascinating conversation. I'm so intrigued by all of it. So there was another time. With just you, Micah and Angelina?"

He nodded. "Yes. Micah invited me to The House. At the time he and Angelina were staying there. She had some asshole stalking her and Micah wanted to keep her safe. For the first time, I understood the appeal in sharing a woman with another man. The first encounter, with the other men, was more clinical for me. I was there to perform certain services. This time he wanted to watch. He wanted to watch me dominate his woman. His possession. I'd never considered how arousing it would be."

"So the other night when Lucas . . . when he intervened. Did you like it then?"

He grimaced. "Yes and no. I hated that he inserted himself. But then I understood why. And well, if I'm honest, it was fucking hot. I loved seeing you between us. I can't even begin to explain why. Maybe it's best if I don't analyze it. All I know is that it was a hell of a turn on."

"It's the first time he's ever shared me with someone else," she admitted softly.

"Did it upset you?"

She sighed and pulled her hair behind her head and held it there in a ponytail before letting it go again. He watched her closely because he sensed . . . It wasn't disappointment exactly. But he'd seen the curiosity and even perhaps desire that had flashed when he'd spoken of Angelina having had sex with multiple men. If he had to guess, it was a desire that perhaps Ren had entertained but that Lucas had never provided for her.

"Lucas . . . Well, here's the thing with Lucas. He's hard. I'm sure you know this, and well, I wouldn't be with him if he wasn't providing me exactly what I need in a relationship. He's unapologetic. Don't get me wrong. I know without a doubt he'd never do anything at all that would harm me. But I belong to him. Not just in a sense of being his. Even for a dominant submissive relationship, he's hardcore. I'm his. I'm his property. He does what he damn well wants with me when he wants unless it would cause me physical harm or emotional distress."

Cole nodded. "I get that."

"So, one of his kinks, like you said about Micah, is that he enjoys watching another man dominate, and I mean completely dominate, his woman. Sometimes he just likes to watch while another man completely owns his woman. Other times he likes to direct. And by that I mean he watches but he orchestrates every thing that happens. He tells the man what to do, how to do it, how hard to spank or flog, how hard to fuck. Whether to fuck her ass, her pussy or her mouth. I know he enjoys this and has practiced it with his other submissives."

"But not with you," Cole guessed.

She shook her head. "I've expected it. And maybe a part of me has even anticipated it. I think it's the unknown and that it's all kinds of forbidden and edgy." Then she laughed. "Okay, that sounds ridiculous. Like having a threesome is edgier than the absolute lifestyle I live with Lucas . . . and now with you," she added softly.

"I've wondered if it would be something I would enjoy, and then the other night when he took me to his club—"

She broke off and her cheeks colored slightly. Cole raised his eyebrows. "What happened at the club?"

"Well, he's always so possessive of me. Like, look but don't touch. That sort of thing. He's very picky about who he allows near me. Especially at the club. But he sent me off to dance with these three guys, which was surprising enough. But then he comes out and dances with me, and, well, it was different. He's not much of an exhibitionist, but he was fake fucking my mouth, he had me bent over like he was fucking me from behind. And then . . ."

"Oh you can't stop now," Cole said dryly. "Not when it's getting good."

"He allowed one of the men to touch me. With his mouth. He sucked at my breasts. And then he touched me. He slid his fingers inside me."

"Did you like it?"

"Yeah," she breathed. "It was hot. Exciting. I felt so naughty and wicked. And now I think maybe it was just a precursor or a warm-up because he knew he was going to give me to you."

Cole frowned. He didn't like the idea of Lucas letting random guys feel her up just to get her ready for him.

"So last night, when Lucas and I both were inside you. Was that the first time you experienced that?"

Her pupils dilated and she nodded. Her skin had flushed and she was warmer than she had been just a moment ago.

"You liked it."

He knew she had, but he wanted to hear it from her.

"Yes, I did," she whispered. "I can't even explain it. It was so . . . powerful. Completely different than the night in the club. I didn't know that other man. And while it had this edgy, forbidden feel to it, I still clung to Lucas because I felt safe with him. Last night, I was between two men I trust. I felt completely safe with both of you. I knew neither of you would ever hurt me. It was . . . freeing. I don't think I've ever felt more powerful and yet I was completely and utterly powerless and vulnerable. I *loved* it."

He pulled her down to kiss her again, as he'd done so frequently over the last hours. He simply couldn't get enough of her. He loved reminding himself that she was here, in his arms. She was his.

"You'll always be safe with me, Ren. Even when I'm pushing you. When I'm hard and demanding, and I can be both, no doubt. I love that you're open with me about what you like. What turns you on. And what makes you feel safe. I'll never willingly or purposely do anything that ever makes you feel afraid, insecure or inferior. And I'll damn sure never do anything to humiliate you. If you don't feel comfortable going to dinner with Angelina because she's someone I've fucked, then we'll absolutely stay home. But know this: I fucked her. Did I like her? Did I respect her? Absolutely. I'm not an asshole. But I fucked her because it felt good, it turned me on and it was what she and Micah wanted. I didn't make love to her and therein lies the difference."

Ren smiled and leaned down to kiss him and then she curled her arms around his neck and hugged tightly. When she finally pulled back, she wore a mischievous smile.

"I do hope this doesn't mean that you're going to spend the whole two weeks 'making love' to me."

He sent her a smoldering look that should have worried her. And maybe it did by the sudden increase in her respirations.

"Oh no, Ren," he said in a soft voice. "I'm going to make love to you, absolutely. But I'm also going to fuck you so long and so hard that you'll beg me for mercy. And if you're a good girl, I just might decide to have a little."

He knew he'd said exactly the right thing because her eyes caught fire and she stirred like a wild thing in his arms. He remembered all that Lucas had said in their meeting and as much as it galled him to receive advice from another man—especially a man who had such a strong hold on Ren—he also knew that Lucas was exactly right.

Ren didn't want or need a man who'd coddle or pamper her endlessly. She needed a dominant man who wouldn't give an inch and who would take her to the very edge of her boundaries and then pull her back with a gentle hand.

And hell yes, he could be that man. He *was* that man. Ren may not know it yet. But in a few days' time, any doubt she may have would be gone. He'd damn well make sure of that.

CHAPTER 20

Shopping with Cole was a whole new experience for Ren. It wasn't as if she hadn't shopped with him in the past, but they'd had a decidedly smaller budget back in the day. They'd bought things like jeans, tennis shoes and seen budget films at the dollar cinema. They may have walked by an exclusive retail shop, but that was the extent of any name-brand shopping for them.

This time, Cole seemed determined to cater to her every desire and not only that but he was involved in every single purchase. He studied each outfit, had her try on every pair of shoes and then he simply made his selections based on what he thought looked the best on her.

As for her part, she hadn't a single complaint. His tastes were as impeccable as Lucas's. He knew precisely what complemented her figure, her hair, her coloring and he seemed to love any top that showed off her tattoo.

She also discovered his love of ultrafeminine lingerie. He loved her in soft colors. Pinks, peaches, lavenders. Lucas usually leaned more toward black and darker, more sultry colors. Cole liked . . . girlie.

He was also wickedly evil. He'd requested she try on a particular set of lingerie complete with the hot pink stilettos he'd picked out himself. Ren called them Barbie shoes. Cole merely informed her she looked hot in them.

His eyes glittered in approval as she stood before him, clad in pale pink lace panties and a matching bra and wearing those killer fuck-me shoes.

Okay and well, she had to admit, she felt like a total bombshell with the way he devoured her with his gaze.

"Tonight I'm going to fuck you in nothing more than those shoes," he said in a growly voice. "I'm going to hold on to the heels and spread you wide while I ride you long and hard."

Oh hell. A shudder worked up her body. Her knees shook and she nearly went down in those heels. Cole was on his feet and caught her to him but chuckled at how flustered she appeared. He knew exactly his effect on her. He delighted in it.

"I could fuck you right here, Ren. The saleslady won't interrupt. She's perfectly happy to give us all the time and privacy we want."

"It's not her I'm worried about," Ren muttered, not willing to admit just how turned on she was by the idea of him fucking her right in the dressing room. Or maybe even turn her over his knee and mark her bottom in her pretty new underwear. Or maybe he would make her suck his cock on her knees while he sat so indolently in that chair where he'd watched her model.

Her imagination had taken her on a delicious trip through all the possibilities.

"What I wouldn't give to see what's going on in that pretty head of yours right now," Cole murmured. "Care to share?"

She shook her head vehemently and actually blushed. She hadn't felt like a little girl in so very long and now she was actually blushing like a preteen with her first crush.

"No way I want someone to walk in on us!" she whispered.

Cole smiled.

That smile made her immediately suspicious and her eyes narrowed as his smile only grew more arrogant. He crooked his finger, his eyes daring her to refuse.

She took the few steps to close the distance, her pulse racing. He touched her jaw and then leaned down so he was a mere breath from her mouth.

Oh but he was delicious. He looked delicious and smelled so yummy she wanted to lick him from top to bottom and everywhere in between. He oozed sexuality from every pore. He was the type of man who she'd pick out of a crowd every single time. Aloof. Confident. A little arrogant. Bold. And absolutely, mouth-wateringly gorgeous.

"The store is closed, my darling. There is only you and me and a very happy saleslady who was only too thrilled to close the store for us to have a very private shopping excursion. And I guarantee she won't appear until I've summoned her."

"In that case," she murmured.

"Care to share what devious thoughts you were having?"

She grinned. "I am ever obedient."

"Mmm, yes you are. Now I must consider what I want my darling submissive to do."

She lowered her eyes demurely and then took a step back just so he could see her in those decadent heels and the frothy pink lingerie that he did seem to love so. She was so excited she nearly went up on tiptoe in her eagerness to see what he would exact from her.

His eyes immediately went dark with approval. The power that rolled off him was a tangible wave that wrapped around her and lured her seductively in.

Oh yes, she was his. She would do whatever he commanded. She would please him as he'd never been pleased. It was a sudden, fierce need that came from deep within. From her soul. It was a craving as strong as any desire she'd ever experienced. She wanted to be his, wanted his strength and his dominance. Right here, right now, among the beautiful outfits he was showering her with. She wanted him to assert his dominance and his ownership.

When his hands dropped to his belt, her knees threatened to give out. Slowly and methodically, he undid the buckle and pulled at the leather until it came free of his slacks.

She had no idea what he planned to do with that belt but she hoped. Oh God, she hoped. She could literally feel the hot kiss of leather on her ass and she nearly swooned with want.

"Go to the mirror," he ordered.

His voice was all business and yet layered with a gruff darkness that was so very seductive.

She honest to God wasn't sure if she could take the three steps to the mirror.

She put one foot hesitantly in front of the other, grateful when she remained steady.

"Face it and put your hands up over your head, palms pressed to the glass, then push out so there is space between your body and the mirror."

She did as he commanded. Pressed her palms to the full-length mirror and then took one step back.

"Spread your legs and look at yourself."

She raised startled eyes to view herself, surprised at how aroused and how . . . drugged . . . she looked. Already she was well on her way to a place only he could take her. She embraced it. Welcomed it. Craved it with every inch of her body.

He slid his hand over the curve of her behind. Caressed the cheeks, one and then the other. He toyed with the thin strip that covered the cleft of her ass and then smoothed his hand over the plump flesh again.

"Such a beautiful ass, Ren. Perfectly shaped. So deliciously fuckable. But equally delicious? My mark on those pretty, dusky cheeks."

Without warning he issued a sharp slap with his hand. It rocked her forward and she closed her eyes as the bite of pain was quickly replaced with the warm haze of pleasure.

"Open your eyes, Ren. I want you to watch yourself while I use my belt on your ass. I want you to see how beautiful you are. And then you're going to watch me fuck you from behind while you keep your hands against the glass. If you move them. Even an inch. I'll punish you."

Her eyes widened. They hadn't discussed punishment. She wasn't even sure what he considered punishment. Lucas rarely ever punished her. There was no need. She took her obedience very seriously. It was a matter of respect and she'd never disrespect Lucas or Cole.

Cole smiled back at her. "You won't move your hands, Ren. I know you."

No, she wouldn't move them. No matter what he did. No matter what he made her endure. No matter how much he drove her wild with mind-blowing pleasure. She'd obey and she wouldn't move her hands.

"Face forward."

Her gaze returned to her own reflection and she saw the excitement and anticipation glowing in her eyes. Behind her, he moved and then looked directly at her, ensuring she was doing as he'd commanded.

She flexed her fingers against the glass just as the leather snapped across her ass. She jumped, flinching against the sudden fire. Just as quickly a whispery moan escaped her lips and her eyes turned all soft and glowy as pleasure hummed through her veins.

"Don't look away," he said hoarsely. "See how beautiful and wild you look. See what I see."

She stared back at the woman in the mirror. She *was* beautiful. Her eyes flashed. Her neck arched. Her hair flowed over her shoulders and she looked seductive, sensual and vibrant.

The belt snapped against her flesh again and it was all she could do to keep her eyes open as bliss descended. Each blow was an erotic mix of edgy, fiery pain and decadent ecstasy.

He wasn't easy. He didn't wimp out. He didn't pretend to spank her and throw little pats her way. She would have been deeply disappointed and thoroughly unsatisfied. This was what she needed. That edge. The thin line between what she could and couldn't take. She wanted it pushed. She wanted to strain her very limits every single time. She wanted him to take her there and then pull her back with a loving hand. Just like Lucas.

"How many can you take, Ren?"

She blinked, perplexed by the question. It wasn't one she should answer. Through her haze, she knew the right answer.

"As many as you choose to give me."

Satisfaction carved a line through his features. His mouth firmed and his eyes glinted in approval.

"Your ass is so pretty. It has a nice rosy blush that complements your lingerie quite nicely. The only thing better than the marks from my belt will be the fingerprints I leave when I hold you down and fuck you."

She shivered and her palms slid the barest of inches, suddenly slick against the smooth glass. She was quick to reposition herself, ready for the next lash.

It came like fire. Quick. Searing. Suddenly one after the other. He forewent the methodical striping that he'd begun and peppered a line over her entire ass until her entire backside throbbed and burned.

Then the belt slid from his hand and landed on the floor, the metal buckle clinking on the polished tile. He gripped her ass in both palms, massaging roughly over her burning flesh.

Impatiently, he ripped the thin lace of the panties and they fell down one leg to hang at her knee. He pushed upward on her buttocks, baring the entrance to her pussy, drawing it so tight she knew it would be almost impossible for him to get inside her easily.

She didn't want easy. She wanted an animalistic taking.

He unzipped his slacks but left them on. His cock protruded through the fly and he rolled a condom on before returning his hands to her ass.

He slapped the cheeks to bring back the burn. He continued to administer stinging swats until she moaned and twisted restlessly in his hold.

Then he was inside her. Quick. Brutal. Shocking.

But so very good.

She leaned her forehead against the glass, overwhelmed by the ferocity of his possession. He was so thick and huge within her. She'd been damp, but she hadn't been completely prepared. She loved how snugly she fit around him. Loved the delicious friction of his too-large erection in her tight opening.

"You're resisting me, Ren," Cole said as his fingers dug more tightly into her ass.

He gave another hard push and she gasped when he only gained an inch. Then he pulled out, his cock rippling over swollen, engorged flesh. She nearly orgasmed on the spot and had to use all her restraint not to let go.

"Open for me. Take me all the way," he ordered.

Then he surged forward, until his hips slapped against her hips. His entry was rough, delicious, painful, intensely pleasurable. A whole host of conflicting sensations that had her incoherent.

Her mind went blank. She couldn't even conjure the simplest of thoughts. All she was aware of was Cole's possession. Him inside her. And how very right it felt.

Her face was flushed. Eyes heavy and drugged. Her lips were swollen and yet he hadn't kissed her. Had she bitten them in reaction to the mind-numbing bliss she was experiencing?

Her hair was tousled and sexy around her face. She looked like a wild creature wrestled and subdued. She arched her neck and moaned when he rammed into her again.

Then suddenly he pulled out and wrapped his arm around her waist. She was lifted into the air and he carried her across the room to where one of the armchairs was positioned.

He pushed her roughly down and ordered her to grip the arms of the chair with her hands. Then he lifted the bottom half of her body up so that her weight was supported by her hands gripping the arms. He spread her and then thrust back into her.

"I needed deeper," he rasped. "I can take you deeper this way. Keep your head down. Arch your ass. Open yourself to me, baby, Ah hell, that's it. Love it when I'm deep inside you."

The words slid over her flesh like the finest silk.

He fucked her ruthlessly, taking his pleasure and driving her further and further to madness. After a moment, he picked her up again, like she weighed nothing, and positioned her on the large ottoman on her hands and knees. And then he fucked her from behind for five long minutes.

His stamina amazed her. He was a machine. A beautiful, ruthless machine designed to bring her maximum pleasure.

He wrapped his hand in her hair, twisted and then pulled her head back, angling it so she was forced to meet his fierce gaze. His eyes glittered. Animalistic? Oh yeah, she'd gotten her wish. This was no gentle wooing. No swoony love-making session. This was as guttural as it got.

He was fucking her, owning her, giving her no doubt that he owned every inch of her body and that he could do what he damn well pleased with her.

"Come, Ren. You have exactly ten seconds to take your pleasure before I take mine."

To reinforce his command he pulled harder on her hair and began fucking in long, rapid strokes that shook her entire body.

Her vision blurred. Heat fanned out over her body until sweat broke out on her forehead. Tension. So much tension. He drove into her body, hammering with speed and force that made her breathless.

And then his other hand went to her neck. Just a simple, gentle caress. He ran his fingers over her shoulder and then down to her breast to tenderly brush over her nipple.

The contrast between the savagery of his possession and the one hand in her hair holding her so tightly and the other hand caressing her so sweetly completely undid her.

Her orgasm flashed over her, brutal in its intensity. So . . . powerful. She couldn't breathe. She could only take what he continued to give her as wave after wave of excruciating pleasure consumed her.

She didn't want it to end. Not just the orgasm, but the experience of being so consumed by this man. She wanted him to keep touching her. To keep that contact between them and the intimate connection made so much stronger by trust.

Did she trust him? Definitely she did. And maybe that made her a fool, but she saw no deception in him. All she saw was genuine regret and a soul-deep desire to make up for past mistakes.

Even when she'd felt betrayed by him, she'd known he would never hurt her. Never.

His thrusts slowed and he became gentler as her skin prickled with post-orgasmic sensitivity. Then he pulled out and walked around in front of her, yanking impatiently at the condom.

"Open your mouth."

Her lips obediently parted and he placed the tip of his cock on her bottom lip and began to work his hand back and forth.

"Put your tongue out. That's it," he said when she complied.

He closed his eyes and groaned, gave one more pull and the first jet of semen shot into her mouth. He continued to guide the hot liquid onto her tongue and then he slid into her mouth, warm and rigid and emptied the last of his release into the back of her throat.

For the longest time he remained there, his cock deep in her mouth as he stroked her hair with loving caresses. Then finally he pulled away and brushed his thumb over her swollen lips.

He tucked himself back into his slacks then bent to retrieve the belt he'd dropped on the floor. Her ass tingled all over again as she relived each and every stroke of the leather.

"Get dressed," he said softly. "I'll have the saleslady collect our purchases and send me the bill."

CHAPTER 21

*R*en was nervous and she wished she wasn't. With Lucas she didn't worry because . . . She frowned a moment, feeling disloyal for the thoughts crossing her mind. But it wasn't like she could turn off an entire year of an intense, close connection to a man she trusted implicitly.

When she was with Lucas, she didn't fear new situations. She knew with absolute certainty that he would take care of her, make sure she was comfortable and that any fears or nervousness she might experience would be soothed.

With Lucas, she felt confident and at peace both with herself and her role in his life.

Now she was going with Cole to meet his friends and the fact that she was on edge was pretty damn ridiculous. She'd even met Damon and his wife already, though not under the best of circumstances.

But she'd only been with Cole two days. She'd only been back in his life such a short time. Though she did trust him, she hadn't yet reached the same level of confidence as she had with Lucas. No, Cole wouldn't hurt her physically, but he'd hurt her emotionally. He'd devastated her and he had the power to do so again no matter how much she wished no man held such power over her.

And well, there was the fact that Cole had been intimate in varying degrees with both women who would be present. If that didn't make things awkward, she didn't know what would.

She put on a pink dress that fit her like a dream with just a little swish at her mid-thigh. Enough to make her feel a little sassy and the color set off the dramatic midnight black of her hair and her creamy skin tone.

The hot pink fuck-me shoes were the natural choice, but when put together with the dress, it made her feel like a tart. The Barbie shoes would wait for another night when she didn't care one way or another what others thought of her.

Instead she went with strappy silver sandals with a clear heel and just enough bling to make her feet sparkle. What girl could resist sparkly shoes? If there was such a woman, it wasn't her.

She brushed out her hair, applied pink lip gloss and then went in search of Cole. He was waiting at the bottom of the stairs and whistled appreciatively as she descended.

His smile brought back so many memories. He looked . . . happy. And younger. Much like the young man she'd known ten years ago. Only now he was much more larger than life, older, wiser and so damn gorgeous and confident that she went weak in the knees around him.

What would their lives be like now if he hadn't walked away? Would they have stayed together? Would they be happy even now?

As she got to the last step, he reached up to take her hand and assist her down. He pulled her in close, breathed in the scent of her hair, just like he always used to do, and then he nudged her chin up so he could take her mouth.

And she said take, because that's precisely what he did. He didn't kiss her exactly, although that was what happened. But it was the way he kissed her. It was a reminder—a forceful, unmistakable reminder—of his possession. That he considered her his. But at the same time, it wasn't a sterile, clinical gesture.

It was . . . sweet. Breathtaking.

Warmth spread through her veins until her pulse throbbed and her chest squeezed for air. All her lip gloss would be gone but she didn't give a damn.

What woman didn't want to be kissed this way? Tender. Yet strong, dominant, reassuring. That was the word she was trying to think of. *Reassuring.*

His touch held a wealth of reassurance. It told her *I'll never let anything touch you. I'll take care of you. You're mine.*

When he pulled away, their gazes locked and he seemed content to simply stare at her. He touched her cheek with his finger and traced a gentle line over the contours of her face.

"You're beautiful, Ren. You've always been beautiful but there is something mesmerizing about you now. Time has been very good to you. You look . . . content. Confident. And I can't tell you how sexy I find confidence on a woman. You look like a woman with nothing to prove and it makes me want to possess you all the more."

Her cheeks tightened with pleasure at the compliment but also at the sincerity that warmed his eyes. She self-consciously tucked a strand of hair behind her ear and he chuckled softly, tracing the path of her hand with his own.

"You always did do that when I complimented you. It's still as adorable now as it was then."

To cover the fact that she had no idea how to respond, she broke away and performed a sassy twirl and then held up her hands. "Do I look all right? Not going to embarrass you in front of your friends?"

He frowned and then caught her hand. "Never."

He tucked her into his side and started for the front door. Parked outside was a steel gray Aston Martin. She lifted one eyebrow as he opened her door for her and she slid into the luxurious leather seat.

When Cole slid in next to her and started the engine, she quickly buckled herself but stared over as he pulled out of the drive.

"How did you make your fortune, Cole? Not that I ever doubted you wouldn't become a success, but when we parted, you were still rais-ing cash for your first business venture. At the time, no one wanted to deal with you because you were so young and you didn't yet have a business degree. Did you ever finish school?"

Cole grinned, pulled out on the highway and gunned the engine. "Nope. You better than anyone knows that school frustrated me. I didn't like the regimen, the discipline and above all the patience. I never subscribed to the whole do A and then B and eventually get a job doing C."

She sighed. "Unlike me, who craved the routines and schedules and the comfort of knowing I'd be employable after graduation. Even if I did never end up using my degree. So you made it all on your own?"

"I bought into a partnership because I was never able to raise enough capital to go out on my own. After two years, I bought out my partners, spent another year streamlining the business until it was turning a healthy profit and then I sold it for a very nice sum of money. Enough to live on and begin a new venture."

"And what do you like to venture in?" she asked.

"Damon and I partner on a lot of projects now. I have a keen inter-est in timber, chips and bio fuels."

She wrinkled her nose. "It all sounds like Greek to me. You invest in potato chips?"

He laughed and reached over to tug at her hair. "No, smartass. Wood chips. To make paper out of. I supply paper mills with chips. I also own a sawmill and am partnered with Damon on another. But I also fund a lot of development and I turn over real estate."

"So you're in the business of making money," she teased.

Cole snorted. "Aren't we all?"

She shrugged. "I suppose. I guess you're just particularly good at it."

He nodded and didn't offer any false modesty, which she found even more drool-worthy. She hated a man who didn't own his success. Or made silly excuses or blamed luck. Cole knew he was good. He may not walk around bragging about it but he wasn't about to not take credit for it either.

"So tell me something," she said after clearing her throat. "About tonight."

He turned to quickly glance at her, one eyebrow lifted. "You aren't worried about tonight, are you? We don't have to go. Just say the word. I'll arrange for us to have a nice dinner together just you and I."

She smiled, touched by his concern. "No, that isn't what I mean. I'm just wondering how this is supposed to play out. I mean, am I going as your . . ." She formed the word carefully, not wanting to sound offended or like she thought he was being disrespectful to her. " . . . submissive. I mean, I know you said both Damon and Micah are like these big dominant males with women who are completely submissive to them, and I just wasn't sure what my role is tonight. I just don't want to embarrass you or do or say the wrong thing."

To her utter shock, his expression went grim and then he swerved onto the shoulder before pulling to an abrupt halt. Then he turned in the seat to face her.

"What you are, is someone very important to me. These are my friends. Very good friends. It's no different than any other group of friends who get together and have dinner, have a few drinks, laugh and have good conversation. Yes, Serena and Angelina are submissive. They also happen to be very much in love with their husbands, and conversely they are adored beyond reason by their men. If you want to know if they know anything about our relationship, the answer is no. However, they are well acquainted with my proclivities, if that word doesn't offend you, so they are very likely to guess or at least speculate on your role in my life."

"I'm sorry," she offered softly. "I'm still just a bit off kilter with all of this. Three days ago I was with a completely different man. A whole different set of rules. You have to know, this isn't typical of me. I prefer long-standing, intimate relationships with a foundation of trust. I'm not into bed hopping or partnering up on a whim. I'm still a little bewildered by how quickly I became the property of another man."

He touched her chin, forcing her gaze back upward. "Not just another man, Ren. Me. There's a difference. You were mine first. And don't apologize for wanting information before walking into a new situation. I should have done a better job of explaining it to you. I'd never ever want you to feel uncomfortable, embarrassed or uneasy. I'm not some asshole who has to flash around his submissive on a leash in order to prove I'm some kind of man. I don't need those kinds of statements in order for the world to know you're mine. The only people who need to know it are you and me. Everyone else? I could give a fuck about."

She smiled because now more than ever he sounded just like the Cole she'd always known. No, he'd never given much credence to what others thought. It was likely what had made him the success that he'd become.

He smoothed his palm over her face, brushing aside a strand of hair. "Does it bother you, Ren? For them to know you're mine?"

There, behind the confidence and the blunt words, was a thin layer of worry. Not exactly insecurity but perhaps disappointment.

She leaned up, cupped her hand over his strong jaw and then pressed her lips to his. "No," she whispered. "It doesn't bother me at all.

I find I just don't want to disappoint you in any way. I've never wanted to disappoint you. That doesn't go away. Not in ten years."

He kissed her back. Thrust his hand into her hair and held her to his mouth. His tongue brushed across her lips, tasting, retreating and then boldly advancing again.

He rested his forehead against hers, still holding her to him as he quietly caught his breath.

"No, Ren. You've never disappointed me. It was me who let you down. All I want is for you to be yourself and be happy. I love the real Ren. And I'd never want you to be anyone else."

She swallowed hard. Her heart twisted, robbing her of breath. This was all she'd ever wanted, wasn't it?

A year ago, she would have said yes, unequivocally. To have Cole back, to have him here, saying the words he was saying. To have another chance to make the past right.

But that was before Lucas. Even as her heart soaked up every piece of Cole, there was still a part that clung stubbornly to Lucas. Maybe it would go away in time. Maybe it wouldn't.

If Lucas came for her tomorrow, would she be able to tell him no? Was it easier for her to cling to Cole and to accept this fire between them because she feared that Lucas had left her just as Cole had left before?

She didn't like the possible answers to those questions. She didn't like that if Lucas was standing in front of her right now, she didn't know what way she'd go. How could she?

The coward in her hoped that Lucas had moved on because it meant she wouldn't have a choice to make. She was deeply shamed by that part of her. But the idea of having to choose between two men she cared deeply for had the potential to completely break her.

She shook off the dark thoughts and refocused on the present. If she could put Lucas away in a neat little box, she was happy—extremely so—with Cole. No, they hadn't been together long. Maybe it wouldn't even work out. But for now . . . For now? She was content. A little excited. Hopeful. Who knew what the next two weeks would bring?

Cole kissed her nose and then pulled back, repositioning himself in his seat. He reached over to squeeze her hand and then drove back onto the highway.

A few minutes later, they pulled up to a gated driveway and Cole rolled down his window to speak into the small intercom box. The gate began to open and Cole accelerated up the winding drive and around a corner to a beautiful home.

It was larger than Cole's and while the landscaping was exquisite, it didn't feel as homey or personal to her as Cole's house had. But for her, Cole's home fit him, or at least her image of him.

Cole parked behind another vehicle and Ren waited as he walked around to get her door. He reached down for her hand and pulled her up to stand beside him.

"I meant it, you know," he murmured.

She lifted her brows questioningly.

"You're beautiful."

She smiled and relaxed. He twined his fingers with hers and started for the door, keeping her beside him the whole way.

Like Lucas, he just had a way of ensuring she felt comfortable.

She closed her eyes. Enough about Lucas. She had to stop with the mental comparisons. It wasn't fair to either man, but it sure as hell wasn't fair to Cole, who was doing everything in his power to make her happy.

A tall, imposing man answered the door. Ren's brow crinkled and she glanced warily at Cole. The guy looked like a bouncer. A higher-class version, but someone into personal security for sure.

Cole just grinned. "How are you, Sam? Is Serena keeping you on your toes these days?"

Sam grimaced and then stepped aside to gesture Cole and her inside.

"Mr. and Mrs. Roche await you in the sitting room. Would you like something to drink? And your lady?"

"This is Ren," Cole said. "Ren, this is Sam, Damon's jack-of-all-trades."

Ren smiled while Sam gravely shook her hand.

"Would you like a drink?" Cole asked her. "Damon stocks very good wine. Well, and everything else. Chances are, if you want it, he has it."

"I like white wine. I'm not picky."

Cole nodded. "Make that two."

Sam disappeared and Cole took Ren's hand again and led her further into the house. It was opulently furnished but nothing was gaudy. Damon, and perhaps Serena, had excellent taste. The artwork was beautiful. The furniture was tasteful and elegant. The entire house had a look of refinement that was hard to achieve on purpose.

But it still made her vaguely uncomfortable. Almost like she was in a place she could look but not touch. Already she felt the urge to tense up, put on a fake mask and never let these people see inside.

They walked into a spacious sitting room, although it looked like a regular living room to Ren. But perhaps when people had this many rooms in a house, they felt the need to name them all something different.

Damon and Serena were sitting on one of the sofas and another couple sat on the loveseat diagonal to the sofa. The woman was small and curvy, with beautiful caramel-colored skin that told of her Hispanic heritage and long dark brown hair. Her eyes were dark as well, a perfect match to the dark- haired, dark-eyed man who sat next to her.

Both couples rose when Cole entered the room with Ren. Ren hung back automatically even though Cole bore her forward with him.

"Cole, so glad you and Ren could make it," Damon said warmly. "It's very nice to see you again, Ren."

Ren smiled back until her jaw felt frozen. Serena stood at Damon's side and offered Ren a genuine smile as well.

"Come with me, Ren. I'll introduce you to Micah and Angelina and then we girls can let the guys do their thing."

Damon rolled his eyes but let go of her hand. Serena reached for Ren's wrist and guided her in Micah and Angelina's direction.

"Micah, Angelina, this is Ren Michaels. Ren, these are dear friends of ours, Micah and Angelina Hudson. Their daughter, Nia, is at the sitter's tonight."

"It's a pleasure, Ren," Micah said, his husky, deep voice washing over her. It had that thread of authority she so craved, one guaranteed to make her sit up and pay attention. He too was a man confident of his dominance.

"Hi, Ren," Angelina offered sweetly, her shy smile delighting Ren.

"Okay, let go of Angelina so we girls can go sit. There's only so long a pregnant woman should have to stand, and my feet are screaming," Serena said impatiently.

Micah cracked a grin. "Sure thing, doll. I know when I've been given my marching orders."

He leaned down to kiss Angelina and then stepped around the women and ambled over to where Cole stood with Damon. Not two seconds later, Sam appeared with wine for Cole and Ren.

After Ren took her glass, Serena motioned her and Angelina toward the couch. "Let's go sit."

Angelina grinned and leaned toward Ren. "She's cranky. Don't mind her."

"I heard that," Serena grumbled. She eased back onto the couch and sighed so loud that the men threw amused looks over their shoulders.

Ren perched on the loveseat across from Angelina and Serena, still unsure of what to make of these women.

"She and the others were all about cracking jokes about me when I was a waddling house," Angelina continued with a smug smile. "It's not so fun for Serena now that the shoe's on the other foot."

Serena glared at Angelina. "Shut up."

"Who are the others?" Ren asked curiously.

"Our other friends. Girlfriends," Serena explained. "There's Faith, Julie and now Lyric, and of course Angelina and I."

Despite not really wanting to get into sensitive subject matter, Ren was fascinated by Serena being pregnant and how it played into her relationship—the type of relationship—she and Damon had. She knew enough from Cole to know that Damon was the dominant force twenty-four seven, in and out of bed. And yet when Damon looked at his wife, his eyes were soft with love. When he touched her, there was such gentleness and caring. Damon was the type of man Ren herself most longed for and had found with both Cole and Lucas. The other men in her life? Not so much.

"You look preoccupied," Serena said, interrupting her thoughts. "Is something wrong?"

Ren smiled slightly. "I was being nosy and trying to decide whether to be rude and ask you a question."

Both Angelina and Serena lifted their eyebrows. "Oh do tell," Angelina said. "I think I definitely want to hear this."

Ren's cheeks warmed and her courage faltered. "It's none of my business."

Serena shrugged. "I'll let you know if it dips too far into the off-limits territory."

Ren sucked in her breath. "I just wondered, with you pregnant now and a baby entering the picture. How did it change your relationship?

And before you think I'm some freak with too much curiosity for her own good, it's just that I've often weighed my desire for a family—children—with the type of relationship I need and I can't reconcile the two. But you . . . you seem to have it all. I think I envy you."

Serena's eyes softened and she and Angelina exchanged secret smiles.

"I was worried at first. The decision to have a child wasn't made lightly by either of us. But in a lot of ways it heightens our relationship. It's hard to explain. I've always loved Damon's dominance and his protectiveness when it comes to me and how he cherishes me and takes care of me. But it's even more pronounced now that I'm pregnant with his baby. It's been truly wonderful."

Angelina nodded her agreement. "It was the same with me and Micah. He was just so gaga over the idea of me being pregnant with his child. He wouldn't let me lift a finger. He wasn't any less dominant, but his dominance was exerted in other ways."

"It's not that things didn't change," Serena continued. "They did. I mean, it's not like he's going to bust out with a flogger or something when I'm as big as a house with swollen ankles and hormonal swings from hell. He still demands my obedience and my respect but he's less demanding of me physically if that makes sense. But no less emotionally."

"No, it makes perfect sense," Ren murmured. "I think it must be wonderful to have that."

"You should have seen Cole that night in the restaurant," Serena said in a low voice. "When he saw you again. I've never seen him like that. He was so determined to find you."

Ren smiled. "Yes, he was."

"As much as I hate to interrupt you ladies, dinner is being served," Damon said as he came to stand beside Serena. He lowered his hand and gently pulled his wife up beside him.

Ren stood and edged toward Cole. His hand slid over her shoulder and he squeezed reassuringly. Just that simple gesture warmed her to her toes. He wrapped his arm around her waist and stood there holding her to him while he waited for the others to precede them out of the living room.

"Everything okay?" he murmured in her ear as they turned to follow.

She nodded and then laced her hand with his, liking the comfort of his touch. He kept his fingers twined with hers as they entered the dining room and then he ushered her into her seat before taking the one next to her.

Dinner conversation was light and she relaxed more as the evening wore on. Cole's friends were good people. Down to earth. Damon obviously had more money than God, but he wasn't pretentious, seemed to have no ego, but he wore confidence as surely as Cole did.

Micah wasn't as affluent as the other two men but he fit in well with the others. He too oozed confidence. His expression, his demeanor, it all spoke of a strong man who knew exactly what he wanted and apologized to no one.

In the company of so many gorgeous, alpha males, Ren was lightheaded. She was well acquainted with the entire spectrum of dominant men. There were those who played at being dominant, those who tried to be dominant and then there were those who just were. It didn't take effort or practice. It came to them as naturally as breathing. They had nothing to prove, no ego to be stroked. They liked what they liked and adored the women in their care.

These three were such men.

She was suddenly eager to return home with Cole so she could enjoy his every whim. It heated her blood to imagine what he would want from her, what he would exact or how he'd seek to gain his pleasure from her.

And then she imagined herself round and big with his child. How much more adoring would he be? He already was so mindful of her well-being. Her throat tightened at the wistful thoughts. Having his baby was a lovely fantasy.

She shook her head. Seeing Serena had made her fanciful. She was still far too young to worry about having babies. She hadn't even managed to land in a stable relationship yet. But one day . . .

"I hope you're thinking of me."

Cole's soft murmur caressed her ear and she started guiltily. When she realized only he had noticed her inattention to the current conversation she relaxed and leaned into his side.

"I was," she admitted. "I was thinking of later tonight. When I'm yours to command. I was imagining what you would want."

His gaze smoldered and the blue in his eyes burned like a flame. And then he simply stood, helped her gracefully to her feet and said in Damon's direction, "Thank you for dinner, Damon." He nodded at Serena. "And you, Serena. It was lovely. I'll be taking Ren home now. I'm afraid the evening has been tiring for her."

Amusement gleamed in Micah's eyes as his gaze drifted from Cole to Ren. It took all of Ren's control not to blush.

"See you later, man," Micah called.

"It was nice to meet you both," Ren said to Serena and Angelina. "I hope to see you again sometime."

"Oh, I think you can count on it," Angelina said with a grin.

Cole's hand tightened around her arm and she found herself being propelled toward the doorway where Sam waited.

"Good night," Sam said politely as he showed them out.

Cole muttered a good night and then hurriedly pushed Ren into the car. When he slid into the driver's seat a moment later, his hands shook as he put the keys into the ignition.

He turned to look at her as he accelerated down the drive. "I hope you're up for what I have in mind, darling. It was sheer hell sitting next to you all night when you were looking so damn sexy in that dress. And then to know you were thinking of me and what I would do to you later . . ."

She smiled, well satisfied with the promise in his eyes. "I'm up for it."

CHAPTER 22

*T*he ride home was tense and silent. Every inch of Ren's skin was alive and aware. Her senses were hyperreactive. Every look he threw her way. Each time he moved. It all served to heighten the anticipation of when they'd arrive home and she'd see just how ruthless he could be.

She sensed it in him tonight. How close to the edge he skated. As if to now he'd leashed that part of himself he most wanted to let loose.

She couldn't wait.

How magnificent would it be to feel the full force of all that power. To know that she was safe and protected by his strength.

She shivered as they pulled into his drive. It was hard to breathe. Each respiration was short, rapid and so light that at times she thought maybe she held them in.

"Get out," he said in a terse voice.

Her hand shaking, she fumbled with the handle before finally pushing the door open. She stepped out and he was there instantly, so close she could smell him, could feel the warmth emanating from his tense body.

"Go inside, undress. Wear only the pink heels I just purchased for you. Wait for me in the bedroom, on your knees, ready to receive me. You have five minutes."

She didn't hesitate. Turning, she hurried inside, her pulse thumping with enough force as to unsettle her. She had to force herself to go slow up the stairs or risk falling.

Once in his bedroom, she stripped down to nothing and then ducked into her closet for the pink shoes. She slid her feet into them and caught a glimpse of herself in the full-length mirror on the back of the closet door.

She looked deliciously wanton. Her hair was tousled and spilled over her shoulders and down her back. Her nipples were dark and taut to the point of aching. And the fuck-me shoes made her purr with approval. *Oh Cole, are you in for a treat.*

She smiled because she wasn't one for false modesty. She looked good. She was in shape. And she liked her body.

She slid her hands over her hips and then up her waist to cup her breasts. Cole thought her beautiful and he said it in a way that made her believe she absolutely was. He liked her confidence but she'd realized quickly that her confidence was at its highest with him and Lucas.

She fully believed that one of the reasons some of her past relationships hadn't worked and that one man in particular had worked so hard to break her down was because he and others like him had been threatened by her confidence. Some men didn't deal well with a capable, confident woman and their instinct was to do everything in their power to destroy them.

Conversely, there were men like Lucas and Cole who reveled in a strong, self-assured woman. Yes, they were dominant, but they celebrated strength in their women. Even as they controlled, protected and cherished them.

It was a contradiction not understood by many. How could a man bent on completely dominating a woman possibly appreciate strength and self-sufficiency?

Ren had seen men from the full spectrum. Some played at dominance. Some were abusive in their absolute control. Some had no interest in the woman's happiness, only their own. To some it was a game and nothing more. But then there were men like Cole and Lucas. Men who appreciated beauty. Celebrated it in many forms. And recognized that it came from a much deeper place than flesh.

These were men who had deep respect for the women in their keeping and in return they garnered Ren's respect. It wasn't something she offered lightly. Neither was her trust. Both had to be earned.

Looking at it that way, she realized she couldn't lose. No matter which way she chose or which way was chosen for her, if Lucas had indeed walked away from her. She was fortunate. More fortunate than most, because she'd found not only one man she could trust absolutely, but two.

Peace settled over her like a warm, comforting hug. Peace, like everything else, was fleeting. Tomorrow she might be back to worrying or agonizing, but just for now she could let go and live in the moment. Because she might not ever get today back and tomorrow never offered any guarantees.

She smiled, nodded to herself in the mirror. She had a man to please and in doing so, please herself. She turned and retraced her steps back into the bedroom, stepped onto the thick rug Cole had put down the morning after she'd stayed on her knees on the hardwood floor waiting for him.

He hadn't said a word, but the message was loud and clear. He would have her do nothing that brought her discomfort.

She went to her knees, briefly closed her eyes and took in a deep, calming breath. Then just as quickly as calm had descended, she heard his footsteps on the stairs.

Her pulse leapt to life and pounded beneath her skin. Her breathing sped up and got more shallow. Anticipation licked up her spine, sending chill bumps scattering across her back.

And then he walked into the bedroom, stopped and let his gaze rove appreciatively over her body.

He filled the room. The very air around her changed and went thick and heavy. He moved like a dream. There was authority in the way he carried himself. No hesitance. His gaze never left her, but neither did he show any hint of reaction.

He walked around her, loosening the buttons of his shirt. She kept her gaze straight ahead and remained still as he took his time undressing. After a moment he went into the bathroom and it seemed an eternity until he returned.

He was down to his jeans and she couldn't help but stare at the lean muscle of his chest and rib cage. His shoulders were broad, and his arms rippled with muscle. A smattering of light brown, almost blond hair gathered at the hollow of his chest and then meandered in a straight line to his navel.

It was hell to wait when she wanted nothing more than to get to her feet and take what she wanted. And he looked to be in no hurry.

He crossed the room and opened an oak armoire. A moment later, he closed the door and she could see him holding coiled rope. A lot of rope. She swallowed and sucked in air through her nose.

He came to stand in front of her, holding the rope and then he slowly began unwinding it.

"Stand," he commanded. "Legs apart, gaze forward, arms at your sides."

Hoping she didn't pitch forward, she awkwardly got to her feet, making sure she didn't teeter in the heels.

Satisfaction darkened his eyes and she soaked up his approval.

"I love a woman in bondage," he said, his voice low and husky and so enthralling she found herself leaning in his direction. "There is something so compelling about a woman bound and helpless, dependent on me for pleasure, for mercy, for everything."

He was killing her. She closed her eyes and moaned softly, unable to quell the need that rose sharp within her.

"I'm going to cover you in rope, Ren. Only your breasts will be bare. Your pussy, your ass, your mouth. All of the things that please me the most and that I'll avail myself of for my own pleasure."

She swallowed again and lowered her head slightly in a show of submission.

He slid his fingers underneath her chin and prodded her upward once more. "Never look down, Ren. You may submit to me. You may obey me. But never, ever, will you look down like you're lesser. Eyes and chin up always. Show me the proud, spirited woman who *chooses* to give me the gift of her submission."

Tears burned her lids and she fought to keep them from falling. She met his gaze with fierce gratitude. For understanding her. For accepting her and for wanting her to be strong.

He leaned forward and pressed his lips to hers. Just a whisper. Like a salute to the woman she was. His acknowledgment of who she was.

He began winding the rope around her body in intricate patterns. It was soft against her skin and he was careful that it didn't abrade her flesh anywhere. The rope was pliable and would do no damage to her body.

Underneath her breasts and then over, drawing attention to the plump swells and presenting them to their best advantage. Between and over her legs, under and over her shoulders.

"I'm going to lay you on the bed to finish," he said as he paused.

Gently, he lifted her and put her on her side on the bed. Immediately he curled her legs behind her, bending them at the knees before securing the rope around her thighs and ankles to keep her legs tightly bound together. When he was done, he rolled her onto her belly and brought her hands behind her back and secured them to her waist.

She was rendered immobile. The only part of her body she could move was her head. She was trussed hand and foot and positioned in such a way that she was absolutely helpless.

His hand smoothed over her ass in a gesture meant to comfort. "I'm going to suspend you from the ceiling. There is enough rope that it won't cut into you and will easily bear your weight, but if anything hurts you at any time, I want you to tell me."

She nodded.

His hands moved over her body, securing more rope and then he stepped back and pushed a button on the wall by the bed.

She gasped when she was lifted off the bed and began moving toward the foot and then over the floor. She dangled several feet above the carpet she'd knelt on and at first the sensation was dizzying.

Cole was there, immediately, his hand cupping her cheek and caressing until she gained her bearings.

"Do you know what I love most about this position? Besides the fact that you're incredibly arresting wrapped in my rope, suspended in my bedroom. You're open and vulnerable. I can have you in any way I want as many times as I want for as long as I want. And I'm going to have you, Ren."

He walked around behind her and trailed a finger down the cleft of her ass, down to her pussy. He circled her entrance, pushed in to the knuckle once before withdrawing and fingering her clit.

Then he spun her slowly around so that he was standing at her mouth. He reached down, grasped her jaw, holding her in place, a clear sign of what he intended to do.

He let her go and she heard the rasp of his zipper. Then he turned her head to the side so that he had a better angle of entry into her mouth. Her hair hung down, trailing toward the floor. He caressed her cheek, petting and touching even as he prodded her mouth open.

"I'm going to fuck your mouth, Ren. There's a difference. I could demand that you suck me off but what I want is for you to remain perfectly still while I fuck you long and hard and use your mouth just like I would use your pussy."

His words incited dark fire deep within her soul. Those words, those dark promises called to a need buried so deep inside her that it was an essential, living, breathing part of her. It wasn't just what she needed or wanted. It was who she was and she embraced it with every part of her.

He gripped the back of her head and guided his cock to her mouth. As soon as her lips parted, he shoved deep. Rough, hard, to the very back of her throat.

Her reflex was to gag but she battled with every ounce of her strength, forcing herself to relax and let him use her as he wanted. The very last thing she wanted was to fight him. She wanted this. Wanted him. All the shadows, the hard edges, the parts that he hid from everyone else.

She swung carelessly with the ropes as he pulled her to meet his thrusts. He slid over her tongue, his taste filling her mouth. She made wet sucking sounds as he ground against her chin, sounds he seemed to enjoy.

His hold on her was ruthless and yet there was tenderness in his fingers. Or maybe she imagined it. There was nothing gentle about his possession of her. He fucked her every bit as hard as he'd hinted.

She forced air through her nostrils and they flared when he lodged himself in the back of her throat and remained there several long seconds. But he always seemed to know precisely when she'd had enough and was at her limit. He eased back, granting her the freedom to breathe and to swallow and steady herself.

Then he was back inside her mouth. Stroking. Thrusting. Fucking. All too soon he angled her head further back and tilted her mouth upwards as he pulled at his erection.

Hot semen splattered over her mouth and cheek but most he guided past her lips, over her tongue, filling her mouth. Then he slid back inside, slower, longer strokes now, forcing her to swallow his release.

When he pulled away, she was breathless, his taste on her tongue, her body burning for more.

He wiped the semen from her lips with his thumb and then walked away. A second later, she was lowered onto the plush rug below her on the floor. He turned her on her side so she wasn't facedown and then he walked quietly away, leaving her bound, awaiting his attentions.

CHAPTER 23

$\mathcal{T}$he room was quiet. She had no idea where he'd went or even how long he'd been gone. She awaited the discomfort that would surely come from being bound in such a position, but in truth, she was comfortable on the soft rug.

What made her tense wasn't discomfort. It was anticipation of when he'd return and how he'd take his pleasure this time.

When the footsteps sounded on the hardwood floor, a thrill rushed through her blood and hummed through her veins. Her body jerked a moment as she rose once more into the air and was suspended from the ceiling.

She spun in a slow, lazy circle before he put his hand on her leg to stop her progress.

"I wish you could see yourself as I see you."

The first words slid over her skin like silk.

"Beautiful. Vulnerable. Open. Mine."

The last word sent a tremble through her muscles.

His.

She loved the way it sounded. Loved the primal savagery that accompanied such a possessive statement. She was his possession. His woman. His to do with as he liked. Such power made her throat clutch.

He stepped between her splayed thighs. She was bound in such a way that her pussy was bared, thighs spread wide and legs doubled back and tied so she was unable to move even an inch.

He smoothed one hand over the curve of her ass, squeezing and caressing the plump flesh.

"Relax."

The order was terse. He expected obedience. He was a patient man, but when he issued a command, he wanted immediate results.

She forced every muscle in her body to go limp.

She felt the probe of a large, blunt tip at her anal opening. She stretched around it before he pulled away and eased the pathway with lubricant. Then he pushed forward again and she tensed out of reflex.

He immediately stepped back and before she could even imagine what he meant to do, fire cracked over her ass, taking her breath away.

A crop. Just one pop, but it was enough to remind her of the consequences of inattention, no matter how brief.

Again she forced herself to relax and he began again, working the tip of the plug into her behind. He was gentle and in no hurry. He took his time until she was adequately stretched enough to push in the remainder of the plug.

She flinched and reared up, inadvertently causing herself to swing outward. Cole caught her, but instead of issuing another reprimand, he leaned down and kissed the center of her back.

"Shhh, darling. It will pass. Breathe and try to relax. Give it some time. I won't rush you."

His words more than anything calmed her and made her stop fighting the burn of the plug's invasion. It was a large plug, larger than any she'd used in the past. But then he wasn't a small man and if he planned to use her in that way, she'd need as much preparation as possible if he wasn't going to hurt her in the process.

Sometimes she wanted the pain. She wanted to be taken without regard or consideration of her comfort. She wanted to be used, wanted to provide the ultimate pleasure for the man who owned her. But tonight, more than most, she felt more vulnerable, and while she wanted the hard, ruthless edges, she knew her limits weren't quite as capable of being pushed as they normally were.

The gentleness mixed in with his dominance was what she most needed and wanted right now. He seemed so in tune with her emotions. Lucas had always told her a good dominant knew his submissive better than she knew even herself. He was right, and he and Cole both certainly seem to anticipate her needs before she was even able to articulate them to herself.

"All right now?" Cole asked as he caressed the small of her back.

She nodded, watching her hair bob below her as she hung from the ropes Cole had so intricately wrapped her in.

He stepped closer, running both hands over her ass before moving them lower to the backs of her thighs at the very top above where the rope was coiled around her legs. His fingers dug into her flesh and then she felt the hard probe of his cock.

In an instant he yanked her back at the same time he pushed forward. He was balls deep into her pussy, and she let out a hoarse yell at the shock of his invasion.

She was small, so much smaller now with the plug stuffed into her ass. Cole wasn't a small man, but he felt enormous now inside her, stretching her, forcing her to accommodate him.

With her suspended by the ropes, he was able to move her freely, pulling her to meet every thrust. Then he held her immobile and began driving into her until her entire body shook with the force of his possession.

He curled his fingers around the ropes crossing her back and held on as he plunged into her over and over. Then he caught the ends of her hair and pulled until her head came up. He wrapped his fingers in the strands and continued to power into her.

She moaned when his hand drifted over the top of the plug buried in her ass. He toyed with the end, sending wicked sensations through her body. Then he began to ease it out, all the while making long, hard strokes with his cock.

Sweat broke out on her forehead and she bit her bottom lip to prevent herself from tumbling into oblivion. She wanted release. Needed to come so badly that she was afraid at the slightest touch, she'd break apart.

Then the plug slipped free and just as quickly, Cole withdrew from her pussy and then slid deep into her ass.

"Come, Ren," he said in a harsh voice that told her just how close he was to his own release.

But she'd already begun to unravel the moment the bite of pain mixed with the heady pleasure of his possession had overtaken her. Her orgasm wasn't a soft, ebbing tide but rather it was a tsunami that crashed over her at light speed.

She had no awareness other than sharp, unrelenting pleasure that seemed to become more explosive with each passing second.

The loud smack of flesh meeting flesh and her own staggered gasps filled her ears until it was all a roar she couldn't distinguish.

The next thing she became aware of was being held in Cole's arms. The rope was gone and he was gently rocking her back and forth, her head tucked beneath his chin.

He kissed her in between whispers, though she had no idea what he was saying. His hands slipped up and down her body, caressing and soothing. They were on the bed and it bewildered her that so much time had passed without her knowledge.

Without even realizing it, she wound her arms around Cole's neck and turned her face further into his neck. He shifted her in his arms so she'd be more comfortable and then held her just as tightly.

"I missed you," she whispered.

He stroked her hair and for a moment he didn't speak. When he did, his voice cracked just a bit. Almost as if he'd had to take the time to compose himself to answer.

"I missed you too, darling Ren. So very much. I can't tell you how much joy it brings me to have you back in my arms."

She kissed his neck, inhaled his masculine scent, let it surround her and dance through her nostrils.

"I can't let you go again," he said in a voice so low she almost couldn't hear him. "I won't let you go."

CHAPTER 24

$\mathcal{C}$ole was awake early, as was his habit, but this morning he didn't hurry to get out of bed. Today he awoke to a warm, soft body draped across his chest. Ren was sprawled over him, one leg curled over his and inserted between his knees. One arm was flung over his belly and her cheek rested against his chest.

He had his arms full of everything he'd ever wanted and he had no desire to end the moment. So he lay there, his arm wrapped around her body, stroking through her hair, listening to her breathe.

And he realized he'd never been happier than right here, right now. A month ago he would have said he was content. Satisfied. Or maybe it was that he was resigned.

He'd thought of Ren less and less as the years wore on. She had been relegated to his past. A part of a painful mistake he was forced to admit he'd made. Only when he'd seen her again, had he realized just how much he missed her presence in his life. How much he wanted her back. There was no possible way he could see someone ten years later and have that kind of reaction to if he wasn't still seriously hung up on her.

Ten years was a damn long time. A lifetime for most. People did a hell of a lot of changing in a decade. He'd certainly changed. So had Ren. And yet in many ways they hadn't.

The saying went that you couldn't go back, but he could damn well go forward. With her.

He tilted his head down so he could kiss her forehead. She stirred and stretched sleepily before snuggling deeper into his embrace. He kissed her again simply because he couldn't resist.

Her eyelids fluttered open and she settled her unfocused gaze on him.

"Mornin'," she murmured.

"Morning."

He wanted to turn her over and slide into the satiny clasp of her body. Wanted it more than he wanted to breathe. But he'd been rough on her the night before. He'd taken her many times and had used her hard. She was likely tender and he in no way wanted to cause her discomfort.

She pushed up on one elbow, her hair falling like a curtain onto his shoulder and over his chest. "I need to work this morning," she said almost apologetically.

"Of course. I won't interfere in your writing. I'll come get you for lunch. Lucas said you have a bad habit of forgetting to eat."

This time she didn't seem to mind the mention of the other man in her life. He hoped in time she would become numb to hearing Lucas's name.

She twisted her lips into a rueful smile. "Unfortunately he's right. I tend to get caught up in things and let time get away from me. I've fallen asleep at my desk more than once."

"Well, you have a few hours of work time before I haul you out for lunch."

She grinned and leaned down to kiss him. "Deal."

It felt odd to walk into the spacious room Cole had allocated as her work area. She was used to the study Lucas had set up for her. She was comfortable there. Knew where everything was. The furniture suited her. She even loved her desk.

Cole had certainly gone the extra mile to make her comfortable and he'd been exceedingly generous, but it was still new and unfamiliar.

Someone had unpacked all her things and had even arranged them, or had at least attempted the task. She began rearranging, needing the comfort of knowing things were where they should be and in order.

The first hour she spent putting her art supplies in order. By then she was itching to start creating so she settled at the desk and pulled out the leather-bound journal that had the first draft of her writing and her sketches.

Her process was likely more complicated than most, but it suited her and it gave her a measure of comfort. She always did preliminary sketches and the rough draft writing in the journal. When she was satisfied that she had things as she wanted, she then made hard copies that she'd eventually turn in to her publisher.

For each book she bought a different journal. She loved the feel of paper bound in leather. The pages had been faux weathered to give it a worn, aged look. And the cover was leather so worn and soft that she loved to caress it with her fingertips.

She was a very tactile person. She loved touch. Needed it. Lucas— and now Cole—gave her what she needed. They were openly affec-

tionate with her. They seemed to need to touch her as much as she
needed to be touched. Not every man she'd been with had been cognizant of her needs or perhaps they simply didn't care to meet them.

But she found she suffered when she was denied close, personal
contact. Which was contradictory given how closely she guarded her
personal space and only trusted a few to get close enough to ever
touch her.

She loved comfortable things, though. Shoes, furniture, journals.
She surrounded herself with things that felt good and appealed to her
senses.

But above all she needed and desired structure and routine.

She caressed the cover of the journal before opening it to the last
page where she'd drawn the last sketch. Her pencils were in a cup to
her right, colors in order of light to dark. As she reached for one to
touch up a few lines in the picture, her cell phone signaled an incoming text.

Excitement surged through her. Lucas wasn't much on texting. He
much preferred direct communication, but she'd hoped that he'd at
least contact her during the two weeks she was with Cole. Surely he
would at least make sure she was happy.

She dug her phone out of the pocket of her jeans and opened
the text. It was from her friend Savonna. She tried not to allow disappointment to eat at her. She shouldn't even be thinking about Lucas.

Saw Lucas at club last night. Where were U?

For a long moment, Ren stared at the text, battling her reaction
to it. Then, slowly, she blanked the screen and put the phone aside,
not replying to the question. What could she say anyway? *Lucas is
moving on so he hooked me up with another guy.* Yeah, like that wasn't
twisted.

It took all of her discipline not to text back and ask Savonna if Lucas had been there with another woman. The simple truth was there were some questions you didn't want to know the answer to.

She picked up her pencil. A soft lavender she'd intended to touch up the morning sky over the lake in one of her drawings. It shook in her hand and doubt crowded into her mind despite her best effort not to dwell on Lucas.

Give yourself a break, Ren. No one in the world would be over a break up in a few days, no matter that they had this gorgeous, hunky, beautiful man to turn to.

But still she wished there was a switch that she could just flip and turn it all off. The doubt, the fear, the worry and the sadness.

The pencil dropped from clumsy fingers onto the open journal and the drawing of two young children sitting on a dock, feet in the water, watching as the sun rose higher in the sky.

Idly she turned back the pages, going back through the story, studying each of the drawings and the simple story of childhood in all its innocence.

Tears gathered as realization hit her. Maybe it had been in her subconscious all along but she'd never seen it until now. This was so much the story of her and Cole. Happier days. The sweetness of first love and the sadness that accompanied that first good-bye.

Even before she'd seen Cole again, she'd channeled those memories into this book. Perhaps it was her way of letting go. Only now he was back in her life. Why couldn't she have met him again a year ago when she was coming off her relationship with Grant? There were no obstacles, no barriers, nothing at all to get in the way of their reunion.

She dropped her head as she slowly and carefully closed the journal. There would be no work done today. Instead she reached for her artist pad, opened it to a blank page and then chose the black charcoal pencil from the jar.

*   *   *

Cole checked his watch and then turned in the direction of the sunroom. He'd waited as long as possible. He hadn't wanted to part with Ren even for a few hours to give her time to work. He'd busied himself with phone calls and catching up on e-mail, but his concentration was shot.

After sending an e-mail to the wrong person, he'd given up trying to go through the motions of work at all.

He paused at the doorway, watching as Ren bent over, pencil in hand, her face creased with concentration. Her bottom lip was sucked between her teeth and she scraped absently with her top teeth as she stared down at her creation.

She was dressed in nothing more fancy than a faded pair of blue jeans and a cropped white tank that bared a portion of her back where her tattoo snaked up her spine.

But the contrast of her dusky skin against the white of her shirt coupled with the jet black tresses of her hair made him want to peel her clothing right off her so he could run his hands and mouth over that beautiful flesh.

It was a hell of a note when a man's life changed in the space of a few moments over a chance meeting. He wasn't one to fight the inevitable, and he knew without a doubt that Ren was a big part of his future. The only part that mattered.

Nothing else in life had come easy to him. No reason this should either.

"Ren."

He waited a moment and then realized she hadn't heard him. She was hunched over her drawing, her hand moving in quick, jerky motions.

He walked toward her, curious as to what she was laboring so hard over. As he neared, he could see that the drawing was black and white and was of a woman sitting on a rock staring out to sea. On the right, immersed in an incoming wave was what appeared to be a sea serpent with long, jagged teeth. It should appear menacing, but there was simple beauty in the creature.

To the left, a dragon with wings outstretched was coming in to land atop a rolling wave. Both creatures were focused on the woman and yet she stared beyond them both, almost as if she wasn't aware of their existence.

"Interesting," he said over her shoulder.

She bolted upward, jerking around in her seat. Pencils scattered in every direction and the paper drifted to the floor.

"Sorry. I didn't mean to startle you. I called to you from the door but you didn't hear me."

For a moment she looked bewildered and then she surveyed the mess with a grimace.

"I'll get them. Just sit for a minute," he said.

He bent quickly to gather up the pencils, but when he went to put them back in the cup she wrested them from his hand and began sorting the colors, frowning in concentration as she manipulated them.

He studied her for a few seconds and then knelt to carefully pick up the drawing. When he rose, she took the paper and smoothed it over her desk, her fingers running lightly over the woman in the picture.

"Hey, are you okay?" he asked gently.

She tilted her head to look back up at him and smiled, her eyes a little clearer than they'd been a minute ago. "Yes, of course. I just get caught up in what I'm doing. I'm not the most aware person in the world. I didn't mean to seem ungrateful for the help. I just like things a certain way."

He smiled back at her. "You always did."

She frowned pensively a moment. "I guess I did, didn't I?"

Privately, Cole had always thought that she had borderline OCD. She wasn't extreme but she did like things a certain way, in a certain order and she was always happiest when she was settled in a routine that she didn't deviate from.

He'd known this about her early on and he had his own theories about why, but they'd been just that. Theories.

Her parents had been strict but at the same time, they were flighty, unorganized people. Morally, they were strict and they kept a very tight leash on Ren, seeking to protect her from "moral corruption."

But in every other aspect of their lives, they'd lacked discipline and structure. There were no rules in the house. It was never tidy. They were habitually late for everything, a fact that pained Ren, who liked to be early and if she was late, she'd just as likely not even go.

It was another reason that Cole had been so afraid that he'd taken over Ren's life and made her into something she wasn't. He'd provided structure and discipline to a young girl who desperately wanted and needed both. He'd always been secretly afraid that she'd wake up one day and decide that he was just a crutch and nothing more.

Just another of the many mistakes he'd made as a young man. Why fate was giving him a second chance, he didn't know, but he wasn't looking a gift horse in the mouth.

"You ready for lunch? Thought we'd go for something casual."

"Define *casual*."

"As in what you're wearing is just fine and it's all purpose so you're guaranteed to find something you'll like on the menu."

She smiled and hopped down from her stool. "Sounds good to me."

He drew her into his arms, just wanting to hold her for a minute. She seemed a little . . . fragile. Maybe just a bit off today. There was something in her eyes that gave him pause.

She wrapped her slim arms around his waist and laid her head against his chest. She squeezed tight and he returned her affectionate hug, brushing his lips over the top of her glossy hair.

I love you. I've always loved you.

He wanted to say it so badly. The words burned his lips, but he held them back because it didn't feel like the right time. He wasn't sure when the right time was, but it wasn't now.

He'd said it in a casual way before. Had said it in the past tense. Even mentioned that he loved the real Ren. But he hadn't told her with all the depth of the emotion behind the statement. Maybe he wasn't even sure himself. But the longer he spent with her, even though they'd only been together a few days, the more urgent the need to tell her.

She was warm and soft in his arms. Perfect. Not a fantasy. She was here. Real. And so perfect she made his gut ache.

"Come on, darling. Let's go eat. It's a beautiful day out. A little chilly so let's grab your jacket."

She drew away and then leaned up on tiptoe to kiss him. "Thank you."

He threw her a puzzled look. "For what?"

She smiled a little sadly, her beautiful, soulful eyes finding his. "For being just right for me."

CHAPTER 25

The weather was absolutely perfect. Just a hint of a nip in the air. Bright blue skies without a cloud in sight. No haze over the city. Dead leaves skittered across the paved drive as Cole ushered Ren out to the car. He loved that sound. Loved the smell of burning leaves even more.

Maybe tonight he and Ren could have a bonfire and sit out and watch the stars. Just the thought brought him back to nights back home in Tennessee. More than once, he'd taken Ren to the lake, built a fire, spread out a blanket and she'd lay her head on his lap while they counted fireflies.

He'd never considered himself a nostalgic person, but he found himself thinking more and more about the past without the negative filter. They'd had some good times. Really good times. For too long he hadn't been able to get beyond his own mistakes to remember the best of his time with Ren.

He drove to Cattleman's, a restaurant that was a regular haunt of his group of friends, Ren's hand tucked securely into his the entire way.

It was a rustic-looking steak house that was a local favorite and the food was actually really good. And today he wanted Ren to relax. Casual environment. Laid back. He didn't care as long as he got to spend time with her.

He zipped into the parking lot, got out and went around to open Ren's door. As soon as she was out, he slid his arm around her waist, holding her solidly against him as they walked toward the restaurant entrance.

She flipped her head back, closed her eyes and inhaled deeply. Then she smiled and it lit up her whole face. "You're right. It is absolutely beautiful today. I'm so glad I'm not spending it inside working."

He dropped a kiss on her forehead. "No chance of that. I can't be away from you for more than a couple of hours."

They stepped inside and Cole waved to the bartender who jerked his thumb toward the back of the restaurant.

"Ah, good, my table is open," Cole said as he guided her back.

Ren raised her eyebrows. "Your own table?"

"Well, sort of. I kind of share it with a few friends. Whoever happens to be in gets first dibs. It's a little quieter. Out of the way and we get excellent service."

"Sounds like you're all spoiled," she said with a grin.

He pulled out a chair for her and smacked her on the ass just before she sat. "You have no room to talk about anyone being spoiled."

"That's true," she acknowledged as he took the seat across from her. "I'm not ashamed to admit I love being spoiled."

"And I'm not ashamed to admit that I love spoiling you," he added.

Her face flushed with delight and her eyes lit up. Yeah, it was good to get her out. He wasn't entirely certain what had made her so melancholy earlier in the morning, but she seemed to have come around now.

"Now, what would you like to eat?"

She studied the menu and then sent him a soft smile. "You choose. You know what I like."

He motioned for the waiter and ordered two steaks, medium, two salads and a side order of onion rings. At the mention of the onion rings, Ren's head popped up and her eyes widened in surprise and then she grinned.

"Oh man, it's been a long time since I've had onion rings. I'm surprised you remember."

"There isn't much I've forgotten about our time together, Ren," he said softly. "There were parts I didn't choose to remember, but being back with you has made me realize just how good we were together."

She reached across the table to cover his hand with her own and she squeezed, surprising him with the affectionate gesture. "We were, weren't we?"

He leaned forward, picking up her hand and raising it to his mouth so he could kiss the soft inside of her palm. "And as good as we were then, we're even better now."

"If I was having this conversation with anyone else but you, I'd think I'd lost my mind. The idea of even contemplating these things with a man I've only been with for a few days is just . . . Well, it's crazy."

He smiled because he understood her befuddlement. "But we haven't only been together a few days and I'm not just any man."

She nodded. "Exactly. Still, it just seems so . . . fast. And maybe too good to be true."

He chuckled lightly. "Still the straightforward Ren I've always known."

She shrugged. "I don't know how to be anyone else. Maybe I've tried in the past, but that never seems to work out, you know? I've already decided that if I have to be someone else with a man, then I don't need to be there."

"And I've always maintained you were an extremely intelligent woman. But darling, it's not too good to be true. It's good, yes. But it's real."

"I know," she whispered.

"So tell me how you came to be in Houston," he said as he sat back in his chair. He had a much better view of her now and he liked looking at her. Liked knowing that at least for now she was his. His woman. His possession.

"Lucas," she said by way of explanation. "We met in Vegas. He has a club here and maintains a residence here."

Okay maybe that wasn't the best question but now he'd opened that particular can of worms and hell, the man was a large part of her life and the reason that Ren was sitting in front of Cole now. He couldn't be ignored even if it was what Cole most wanted.

"Then how'd you end up in Vegas?"

She made a face. "My last relationship. I sound like such a disaster, don't I? Like I can't make any decisions on my own and drift from man to man, following wherever they lead."

The disgust in her voice was heavy and she shook her head even as she spoke.

"I didn't live in Vegas. I was there with Grant for a pleasure trip."

"Grant being the asshole you were involved with prior to Lucas," Cole confirmed.

She nodded. "I met Grant in Los Angeles. I hadn't been involved seriously with another man in two years. I dated but nothing heavy and definitely nothing that would lead to a full-time dominant submissive relationship."

Cole sat forward a bit. "Okay, let me ask because now I'm curious. When you say full time. What do you mean exactly?"

She sighed. "I don't trust easily, which probably sounds like bullshit to you. I probably come across as this naïve moron who trusts any man who seems authoritative in the least."

"That's not what I think at all."

"I've had five relationships that I would call full-time, serious relationships where I readily gave up control to a man. Two of the five were you and Lucas. That leaves three in . . . hmmm . . . the last nine years since I've been with Lucas for the last year. Of the five, I'd say I only fully, unequivocally trusted you and Lucas. I'm not saying the two other than Grant were awful. They weren't."

Cole watched her closely, the consternation in her eyes and how fidgety she'd suddenly become. It was apparent she wasn't comfortable discussing her past, but it was important to him to know what had happened in the ten years after he'd left her.

"But in between those steady relationships, I visited clubs, let off some steam, did a few scenes but I always hated it afterward because it felt so fake and put on."

He stiffened as he imagined her in some dark ass dungeon club with a bunch of wannabe dudes in way too much leather and wielding whips and chains. Christ. Over his dead body would she ever venture into another one. The mere idea of what could have happened to her set his teeth on edge and made him weak in the knees.

She waved a hand airily. "Anyway, back to Vegas and how I got there. I was living in Los Angeles when I met Grant. I'd had a falling out with my parents after my last relationship because they dropped in unexpectedly to visit me. I lived in Nashville at the time. Let's just say they saw more than a girl ever wants her parents to see. They were horrified. They called the cops and it was a huge mess to sort out and I was embarrassed as hell. Mom and Dad were mortified. I was mortified. The guy I was with was pissed because he spent the night at the police station while I explained to the cops that I was in a consensual relationship and I wasn't being abused."

"Jesus," Cole muttered. He could well imagine how that had gone down with her parents.

"I needed a clean break and some distance. Mom and Dad, after their initial horror, were pissed and disapproving and that's the mild word for it. I was basically told I was unwelcome in their home as long as I chose to live a life of sin and that if I didn't change my ways, I was going straight to hell."

"Nice," Cole bit out.

She shrugged. "You know how they are, Cole. You better than any-one know how set they are in their opinions. The first time they ever saw my tattoo I thought my mom was going to blow a gasket. She actu-ally called and made an appointment to have it removed."

"Still, that couldn't have been easy for you even knowing or ex-pecting their condemnation," he said quietly.

She went silent for a moment. "No, it wasn't. At first I thought I'd just give them some time. Make a clean break. Let emotions die down and then I'd contact them again."

"Did you?"

"No. I got out to L.A. and I could use the excuse that I was busy or that I was involved with my own life, but the simple truth is I was scared—I'm still scared—that if I contact them again or actually go see them, that I'll get that door slammed in my face and I'm not sure I could handle that. Thinking or assuming that it'll happen is far differ-ent from the cold reality of seeing it."

"I understand," Cole said. "Still, maybe . . ."

She nodded. "Yeah, I know. I keep saying maybe. Maybe one day. Perhaps one day I will. But then I got involved with Grant and maybe in the back of my mind I thought that they were right about me because I was so miserable with him and nothing was right about my relationship with him. I just couldn't face their judgment because a small part of me wondered if they'd been right about me all along and I had sprung from some mutant gene pool."

Cole scowled, feeling the hot edge of anger tear through him. "And do you still feel that way?"

"No. It's the way I felt then, but you have to understand I was a wreck and I over-dramatized everything. So to get back to the point of all this, Grant wanted to go out to Vegas for a weekend. I didn't really want to go anywhere with him but I was still clinging to the idea that I owed him my loyalty and my obedience. I was stupid, but there you have it. I went and it was the worst weekend of my life."

Cole's eyebrow went up. He wanted to press. He wanted to know in exacting detail precisely what happened and he didn't want anything left out. Lucas had covered part of it, but it had been vague. Ren had hinted at the things that Grant had done but Cole wanted hard facts because then he wanted to go kick the ever-loving shit out of the asshole.

"What did he do to you, Ren," he asked softly.

They were interrupted by the waiter bringing their food. Ren looked relieved, but Cole wasn't going to let it drop. He was a patient man, and this was key information.

He waited until she'd received her food and the waiter disappeared. "Ren?" he prompted.

She set her fork down and her lips turned down into an unhappy moue. "This is so embarrassing. It sounds like something out of a frat party instead of a thirty-something man with a reasonable amount of intelligence."

Cole pursed his lips. "I'd say you're being generous on the intelligence factor, but continue."

"He wanted to demonstrate his authority over me in a very public way. He was cruel and he humiliated me at every turn. If that wasn't enough, he also wanted to have a veritable orgy in his hotel room. An orgy he wanted me to participate in. I'm as kinky as the next person but my tastes just don't run to women. He fucked their brains out but I had no desire to join in. All the while he taunted me with how much of a woman they were and how much better they were at following instructions, blah blah. Well duh, he was paying them a hell of a lot of money."

"Son of a bitch," Cole bit out. "Did he hurt you, Ren? Physically, I mean?"

She shook her head. "I can take care of myself, though that's probably hard for you to believe. I was appalled at myself for putting up with his shit for as long as I did. I don't even know why I did. He was there, he was comfortable—for a while—and I didn't feel quite so alone when I was with him. At first anyway. After a while I think I felt even lonelier when I was with him simply because I knew the relationship was a disaster."

She waved her hand again and shook her head. "Anyway, to make a long story short, I packed my shit and got my own hotel room. The next night I went to a club because I love music and I love to dance and I just wanted to lose myself for a while. I didn't want to have to think or feel. The very last thing I wanted was to hook up with another guy, but I met Lucas and I'm still not sure what happened exactly. He took me home with him and I've been with him ever since."

There was a hell of a lot she was glossing over. He let her eat and he concentrated on his own food for a while before he gently turned the conversation back to Lucas.

Ren sighed. "I used him. At first, I mean. He knew it. I knew it. He didn't seem to mind and I was honest with him. But he helped me pick up the pieces and he gave me back something that I'd been missing since the whole incident with Mom and Dad in Nashville. He gave me back myself. My confidence. My sense of identity and he let me know it was okay to be me and he refused to let me apologize for who I was or what I wanted."

He wanted to hate the bastard. He really did. But damn it, he'd taken care of Ren when she needed it the most. How could he hold that against Lucas? If it weren't for Lucas she might still be out in L.A. or Vegas or stuck in some horrible relationship with some bastard who didn't treat her like the treasure she was.

The thought made him ill. The idea that he owed Lucas a hell of a lot of gratitude made him more ill at ease. He wasn't even going to get into what he owed Lucas for these two weeks because he was going to be a complete bastard and fight for Ren with everything he had.

"The really bad thing was that before Grant and before that mess with Mom and Dad, I was perfectly comfortable in my skin. So it wasn't like I didn't know how to be okay with who I was or that I lacked self-confidence. I just lost it for a while and I had to find it again. In some ways I think I would have been more forgiving if I'd always been inse-cure and uncertain."

The self-condemnation in her voice made him ache. "You're being too hard on yourself, darling. You didn't lose yourself for long and de-spite what you may tell yourself, there is no way you'll ever make me believe that you wouldn't have eventually gotten it all back without Lucas. I'm sure he helped and I'm glad he was there at a time you needed him. But I know you. You may have had a setback but no way would you have remained that shell of yourself for long."

Her smile was more crooked this time. She perched her elbow on the table and cupped her chin in her palm as she stared over at him.

"You're very good for my ego, Cole Madison."

"And you're just good for me, Ren Michaels."

Her mischievous grin was back and her cheek dimpled as her smile broadened. Some of the fire was back in her eyes and they twinkled with silent laughter.

"Let's go do something fun."

"Like?"

Her grin deepened. "Oh, I don't know. You're pretty handy with rope."

He threw back his head and laughed. "Let's get out of here. I'm sure I'll think of something we can do."

She frowned as he rose from his chair. "What about the check?"

He held out his hand to help her up. "On my tab."

She wiped her hands and then slipped her fingers around his, allowing him to pull her to her feet. He kept hold as they made their way to the front. At the door he stopped long enough to help her into her light jacket and then they stepped outside.

He started ahead of her when she suddenly pounced on him from behind. She scaled his back and wrapped her arms around his neck, giggling close to his ear.

In retaliation, he spun her around until she laughed and begged him to stop before she upchucked her lunch. He gripped her underneath her knees, hoisted her higher and took off toward the car.

She bounced and laughed the entire way and he grinned, letting her happiness wash over him like the sun. They probably looked like idiots, but he didn't give a damn. He'd give just about anything to hear her laugh so freely.

They were nearly to his car when a silver Mercedes pulled into the parking spot in front of them. Cole halted in his tracks when Lucas stepped out of the car. His cool gaze slid over Cole and Ren and then he looked beyond them toward the restaurant entrance.

Ren went completely still. So silent he couldn't even hear her breathe.

Without a word, Lucas walked past them. No acknowledgment. Not a single word of greeting. Ren's intake of breath was sharp in Cole's ear. Her distress radiated in waves and Cole bit back a string of curses before they could escape his lips.

Chapter 26

For the space of a moment, Ren's gaze locked with Lucas's. She went still against Cole and her heart leapt into her throat. Then Lucas looked past her. No acknowledgment. She could have been a stranger on the street.

He walked by. She turned but he didn't look back. Coldness crept through her body until she was numb with it. She let herself slide from Cole's back and would have ended up on her knees on the hard, cracked pavement of the parking lot if Cole hadn't caught her.

"Come, Ren," Cole said, his voice quiet and soothing in her ear. But firm. She didn't even think of disobeying as he gently helped her to her feet and guided her toward his car.

She looked back again, though she hated the weakness that made her do it. Lucas had disappeared into the restaurant. What was he doing here? They'd never come here together. She'd never been here even once until today when Cole had brought her for lunch.

How could he look through her like she was nothing?

She hastily wiped her burning eyes, determined that she wouldn't let Cole see what her encounter—or non-encounter—with Lucas had done to her. Then she nearly laughed because there was no hiding her devastation.

"How could he?" she choked out as Cole closed his door, sealing them into the interior of his car. "Oh God, Cole, how could he just walk by me like that?"

Cole had no answer. He merely started the engine and backed out of his space before roaring out of the lot. The drive home was silent and tense. Cole stared straight ahead, his jaw tight. He looked . . . angry. At her?

Her reaction had not only been undisciplined and disloyal—to Cole—but it had also been a slap in his face. She couldn't blame him if he wanted nothing more to do with her.

She turned to stare out the window as she felt the betraying slide of tears down her cheeks. Even as she wiped them with her palm, more dampness replaced what she took away.

She hated herself for caring. She had Cole. Cole who adored her. Cole who would do anything to make her happy. And yet she'd allowed Lucas to hurt her and in doing so, she'd betrayed her agreement with Cole.

Caught between two men. Belonging to both and yet to neither. It was the most horrible place she could ever imagine.

When they arrived back at Cole's house, she opened her door as soon as the car stopped and fled toward the house. She couldn't bear to face Cole. Couldn't bear the disappointment in his eyes—or the anger.

At first she wasn't sure where she should go. She had no real identity in this big house, as roomy and as comfortable as it was. It was Cole's home. Not hers. But her belongings were in Cole's bedroom. In his closet.

She hurried up the stairs and burst into his bedroom, her misery growing with each passing second. She was almost to the closet when she realized that nothing here was hers.

She backed to the bed and sank onto the edge. Her head went down and she closed her eyes. Cole had bought everything she wore. He'd refused the things that Lucas had purchased for her. Hadn't wanted another man providing for her during his time of ownership.

All that was hers was her writing and art supplies.

She wrapped her arms around herself and hugged, trying to ward off the bone-deep chill. It shouldn't matter. She kept telling herself it shouldn't. But it did and no amount of lying to herself would change that fact.

She loved Lucas. She loved Cole.

She tensed when she heard Cole enter the room. She kept her eyes tightly shut and her head bowed because she couldn't face his judgment.

Silence descended. So heavy and weighted that it felt oppressive. And then.

"Look at me, goddamn it."

Her head snapped up and she met the full fury of his gaze. Oh God, she couldn't do this. She couldn't.

"Don't you dare look away from me," he said when she started to lower her head again.

His eyes blazed. A fiery blue that sent a shockwave through her numbness.

"I've been too soft. Lucas was right. That's not what you need. No coddling. On your knees, Ren. Don't make me tell you twice."

She scrambled off the bed, bewildered and clumsy as she went to her knees on the carpet at the foot of his bed.

"Who owns you?" he snapped.

"You," she uttered softly.

"I can't hear you."

"You," she said louder.

"Who protects you?"

"You."

"Who takes care of you?"

"You."

"Who loves you, Ren?"

Her mouth opened but nothing came out. Her eyes swam with those damn tears again and a sob knotted in her throat.

"Look at me," he barked.

Slowly she raised her tearful gaze back to him but what she saw shocked her. There was no anger. Not at her. His eyes burned bright with . . . love. And understanding.

His lips were drawn into a thin, determined line. It amazed her that he could be so furious and yet look at her with such tenderness.

"Did you honest to God think I'd be angry with you for being human?" he asked hoarsely. "That I'd punish you because that son of a bitch hurt you? Goddamn it, Ren. What must you think of me?"

She had no response. What could she say? Her hands shook. Her entire body trembled.

Slowly he went to his knees in front of her, until they were eye level. Then he simply opened his arms and she launched herself forward, wrapping herself around him as tightly as she could.

For several long minutes he stroked her hair and simply held her while she sobbed into his neck. She hated doing this. Hated that she was breaking apart in front of Cole. But she also realized there wasn't another man—apart from Lucas—that she'd ever trusted enough to be this vulnerable in front of.

Exhausted by the spent energy and emotion, she lay limply against Cole until finally he pulled her gently away. He stroked his finger down one damp cheek. And then he asked her again in a low, husky voice.

"Who loves you, Ren?"

"You," she whispered.

Satisfaction glinted in his eyes. Then he rose, pulling her with him. The authority was back in his demeanor and expression. He gave her a look that brooked no argument.

"Pack a bag for several days. Make sure you have swimwear and suitable clothing for much warmer weather. If there's anything you're missing, let me know and I'll send out for it."

Her brow furrowed. "Where are we going?"

He lifted one eyebrow at her daring and she was reminded once again that Cole was never a man to cross. Ever.

"Do as I said. Provide me a list of anything you need within the hour. I'll be very displeased if we get to our destination and you don't have adequate clothing."

She nodded, though her knees still shook and her legs were weak enough that she worried about being able to walk the distance to the closet.

He turned and walked crisply away, leaving her alone in the vast emptiness of his huge bedroom.

CHAPTER 27

*R*en arched her face into the bright sunshine as they disembarked the small jet. Salt air danced through her nostrils and in the distance she could see the emerald splash of the Caribbean.

Cole motioned to one of the stewards who immediately piled their luggage on a cart. Cole then slid an arm around Ren's waist and ushered her toward a waiting car.

He hadn't said a word about his plans. Ren had obediently given him a list of things she'd need for swimming and a warmer climate and he'd arranged for everything she could possibly need to be delivered within a few hours.

Then he'd spirited her to the airport where Damon's jet awaited and they'd flown here to an island. What island she had no idea. A tingle of excitement jittered over her body as the car pulled away and the ocean view got bigger through the windshield.

"Where are we staying?" she asked, unable to keep the excitement from her voice.

Cole's smile was indulgent. He absently rubbed his fingers up and down her upper arm as she leaned into the curve of his arm.

"You'll see."

She wanted to huff but that would only earn her one of his looks. And the promise of retribution later. It was obvious he wanted to surprise her and she was determined not to ruin it by being a brat.

She settled back into the seat and snuggled deeper into his side. His arm tightened around her and his lips brushed across her hair.

"If we had more time, I'd pull you onto my lap and fuck you right here in the backseat," he murmured.

Her mouth went dry and then she leaned back and stared accusingly at him.

"You did that on purpose."

He grinned. "Maybe."

She sighed. "You're an evil, evil man. Would serve you right if I fucked your brains out right here and now."

He snorted. "Is that a threat? Am I supposed to be contrite and promise to be a good boy now? Because it's so not happening if that's my punishment."

She stared darkly at him. She opened her mouth to retort when the car slowed and she faltered. Cole pulled her against him to steady her and she turned to look out the window.

They were at a marina. The smell of fish was strong as was the salty air. Boats dotted the water, some small and some really huge.

Cole got out and then reached back for her hand. She clambered out and stared at the array of vessels and the expanse of jewel-toned water that spread out as far as the eye could see.

The driver began unpacking the luggage from the trunk and Cole motioned her toward the pier that jutted over the water. At the very end, a large yacht was stationed with the steps lowered to the wooden walkway. Cole stepped aside and gestured for Ren to board.

"I'll be right behind you. Watch your step," he cautioned.

At the top, a man about Cole's age dressed in white shorts, a polo shirt and wearing what looked like a captain's hat appeared and offered Ren his hand as she got closer.

"Welcome aboard," he said in slightly accented English.

She stepped over the side and Cole followed. He shook the captain's hand.

"You must be Cole Madison. I'm Captain Mike. I'll be at your service for the next several days."

Ren stared agape at the deck. Toward the back there was a large hot tub, several lounge chairs and a couch, mini bar, grill and a Ping-Pong table.

"I plan to kick your ass later," Cole said, following her gaze to the table.

"Ping-Pong?" she asked with a laugh.

"Yeah, and if you hit the balls overboard, you have to go in after them."

She laughed harder and followed him to the doorway leading to the interior. They were shown into a luxurious bedroom and a moment later, their luggage was brought in.

"If you'd like to change into something more appropriate . . . say a bikini, the captain has said we'll leave dock in just a few minutes."

"A bikini, huh."

He grinned. "Absolutely. The fewer clothes you wear for the next several days, the happier I'll be."

"How did you arrange this?" she asked, looking around, still stunned by the sheer opulence of the yacht. Cole was a wealthy man, yes, but this wealthy?

"Connections," he said smugly. "It always pays to have friends in high places."

She went into his arms and hugged him tightly. "Thank you. I'm so excited I can't see straight."

He returned her hug and held on to her for a long moment.

"We're going to anchor off a small private island. You can swim right off the boat or we can boat into shore and laze on the beach or we can sunbathe right here on deck. Whatever your whim is, I'm here to fulfill it."

She pulled away and shook her head. "Sometimes I tell myself you can't possibly be real."

"Bet you won't say that with my dick inside you later," he said in a silky voice.

She shivered and goose bumps prickled across her arms.

He smiled and then leaned in to kiss her. "Get changed. Meet me topside."

When Ren stepped back onto the deck, she didn't see Cole anywhere. Assuming he was with the captain, she walked gingerly across the deck but quickly realized she wasn't going to take a tumble.

Gaining more confidence she went to the rail, gripping it tightly as she stared over the ocean. It was like looking over a lake on a calm day. The only ripples were caused by the yacht as it plowed through the water. And it was so brilliantly blue that it hurt her eyes to look at it.

After a moment, she relaxed and rested her forearms on the side so she could lean forward. The breeze whipped at her hair and she vaguely thought she should have put it up.

A few days on the water with nothing more pressing to do than soak up the sun? Heaven.

A firm hand slid over her bare ass and remained there, caressing boldly. "Oh I like," Cole murmured as he fingered the string of her thong. "So easily accessible. The question I ponder is whether I should take your pussy or your ass. This position is ideal for either."

Shock thrilled through her veins and she started to rise but Cole's hand pressed down on the small of her back.

"Oh no, stay right where you are, darling."

She heard him unzip his jeans. He hadn't changed into swim or loungewear.

Was he really going to fuck her right here on deck where anyone could see them? Not that there were many people. So far she'd only seen the captain but wasn't there usually a steward? And could the captain see them from wherever he was piloting the boat?

She had no further time to contemplate the what-ifs. Cole spread her ass cheeks and his cock nudged impatiently at her pussy. As soon as he fitted the head to her opening he shoved forward, seating himself deeply within her body.

She gripped the rail to brace herself as the force of his possession sent her forward. Already she was teetering on the verge of orgasm. The excitement of him taking her right here in the open had her on edge. And he was big inside her. She was tight around him. She hadn't been fully prepared for his entry and she gripped him like a fist.

He was relentless, not giving her time to adjust. He too seemed to like the tightness. His fingers dug into her ass and he made low noises of satisfaction as he drove into her.

"I wonder if you have any idea how fucking sexy you are," he growled. He pressed in close, his body flush against hers, his mouth hovering just over her ear. He buried himself in her flesh, gripped her hips, held her in place and fucked her some more.

"When I came on deck and saw you standing here against the rail, wearing just that thong and a bikini top that barely covers your nipples, I damn near swallowed my tongue."

She closed her eyes, leaning back into his chest, entranced by his words of praise.

"Your legs are spectacular. You're lean but curvy in all the right places, and your skin, my God, your skin. It reminds me of twilight, dusky and creamy, soft and so goddamn beautiful. And your hair. I have the most perverted fantasies about wrapping my cock up in your hair and coming all over it."

Her breath hitched and caught. Her fingers tightened around the rail until they were white and bloodless at the tips. It fascinated her that both he and Lucas loved her Korean features. Not just accepted but found her exceptionally beautiful and celebrated the traits that marked her Asian heritage.

Like Cole, Lucas loved her skin and her hair. Loved the lilt of her eyes and the unusual mix of brown and green.

Lucas was a match to her dark hair and skin. Cole was her opposite. Light to her dark, his hair a muddy blond, his eyes blue and piercing where Lucas's were dark and sometimes menacing. Not that Cole was all sweetness. He could be as formidable as Lucas but perhaps it was more incongruous on him.

In her most secret fantasies, she wondered at what a child of hers and Cole's would look like.

"Am I boring you, Ren?" Cole asked menacingly. He bit into the column of her neck, inciting a yelp from her. He slapped her ass with a stinging blow that had her immediate attention.

"What the fuck is your problem? You're zoning out. Does my dick not interest you? Should I ram it up your ass? Will that get your attention?"

He pulled out of her, wrapped his arm around her waist and jerked her back from the railing. He pushed her roughly to her knees, his hand wrapped in her hair.

"If you aren't enjoying my attentions, you'll at least see to my pleasure."

The blunt head of his dick bumped against her lips. She opened her mouth, not even trying to defend herself. He was right. She'd given him the ultimate disrespect when he was giving her nothing but the best.

He slid to the back of her throat and stayed there several long seconds, until her eyes watered and her throat convulsed. Only then did he let off and allow her to catch her breath.

His hand wrapped tighter in her hair and he pulled her head up, angling her jaw so that his entry was better. Then he pushed in again and began fucking her mouth with long, ruthless strokes.

"Kneel there and take it," he gritted out. "Make it easier on yourself, Ren. Don't fight me."

No, she wouldn't. Later, she'd fight because she remembered the turn-on for them both when she resisted and he subdued her, forcing her to his will. It was a practice she'd never dared with another man. Not even Lucas. She'd always been afraid of what would happen if her partner went too far, got too caught up in the act.

But Cole wouldn't hurt her. Had never hurt her. No matter what he thought or felt guilt for.

Would he remember pinning her down, her being helpless and him slaking his lust? Would it still be a source of arousal for him?

It hadn't come to her until now. A sharp memory brought on by his command for her not to fight. Was he even now telling her the opposite?

No, he looked too pissed. Too firm. Far too disapproving. He wouldn't be playing a game now. He wanted to punish her and she'd take it because it was what she deserved.

His other hand slid over her cheek, over her ear and into her hair on the other side. He gripped her head with both palms and held her in place as he fucked her noisily. The wet sucking sounds, mixed with her gag, filled her ears.

Her body was electrified. Her nipples hardened painfully. Her pussy spasmed as sharp pleasure coiled in her pelvis and spread through her stomach.

His control and dominance over her aroused her in a way she could never hope to explain. She simply couldn't describe the euphoria that accompanied the bite of discipline. She panted around his cock, so far gone that she was barely cognizant of her surroundings.

But then his voice. Like a whip. Cutting through the haze.

"Tell me, Captain, is she not the most beautiful sight you've seen? There's something about a woman swallowing a man's dick that fires the senses."

Her eyes flew open and her gaze locked on the captain standing a short distance away, the bulge between his legs evident even at such a distance. To his side stood another young man, his gaze raking over Ren as Cole shoved his cock farther down her throat.

Her entire body trembled and fire swept through her veins. Oh God, she was going to come and there wasn't a damn thing she could do about it.

She closed her eyes, trying to ward it off but it pooled in her groin and tightened unbearably. She let out a cry around Cole's erection and then went utterly senseless as her orgasm lashed her like the slap of a leather crop.

Just as suddenly her mouth filled with semen. She choked at first but his fingers wrapped cruelly around her jaw and she heard his warning from a distance, breaking the fog that surrounded her.

"Don't you fucking spill a drop. Hold it in your mouth. Don't swallow. And don't lose a drop."

She was smart enough to obey even though she was completely undone by the sheer power of the moment.

He jerked at his cock, coaxing every bit of his release onto her tongue. Then he thrust again, sliding deep, coating his cock with the cum in her mouth.

"Tighten your lips and clean every bit off my dick as I pull out."

She did as he ordered and he slowly dragged his cock over her lips, coming away from her mouth as clean as she could manage.

"Now let them see," he said. "Let it slide over your lips and down your chin. Make them imagine that they just came all over your pretty mouth."

She relinquished her hold on the warm liquid and allowed it to seep over her lips and down her chin until it dripped to the deck below.

"Goddamn," the second man, the one she guessed was the steward, said in a hoarse voice. "Fucking amazing."

"Yeah, she is," Cole said, his voice tight with pride. "And she's mine."

The captain turned as if to go, but Cole stopped him.

"Gentlemen, if you don't mind. I have a punishment to mete out. I'd like you to stay and observe."

CHAPTER 28

Captain Mike nodded his head. "As you wish, sir."

Cole looked in C.J.'s direction. The young steward looked like he'd swallowed his tongue and a little like he was in love. Ren had that effect on men. Who could possibly resist a beautiful, willing, submissive woman who made the art of submission look elegant and spiritual.

Ren's calm acceptance of Cole's demands awed the other two men. By the time he was through with her punishment, she'd make slaves of both the other men, which amused Cole since she was the submissive. But then, wasn't he himself an absolute slave to her every want and need?

She had all the power in this relationship. She had the ability to break him or make him the happiest man in the world. He had control because she gave it and for no other reason. She reveled in it and she was so damn beautiful that his teeth ached.

"Your belt, please," he said calmly to Captain Mike. Then he looked to C.J. "I assume you have an oar of some type? It must be a smooth piece of wood. Coated and treated with no possibility of splinters."

"I have a decorative oar, or rather the c-captain does," C.J. stammered. He looked apologetically in Captain Mike's direction. "That is, if you don't mind, sir. The one on your wall is a perfect size."

Cole stifled his smile. The young man looked so eager to witness what came next that he seemed afraid that if he didn't proffer the perfect piece of equipment that there would be no punishment.

Mike nodded. "Fetch it."

Cole decided to tease them a bit and up the stakes. He waited patiently, Ren on her knees in front of him the entire time, his cum still smeared on her face, until C.J. hurried back with the small oar.

He handed it to Cole and Cole inspected it, turning it over and over, feeling for any sharp edges, splinters in the wood or any grooves that would hurt Ren more than necessary.

Then he lowered the oar to his side as Mike handed him the belt he'd been wearing. He turned his attention to Ren, staring down at her upturned face.

"You'll take your punishment and if you make a single sound, you'll suck the cocks of both men while I fuck you from behind. And I won't be easy, Ren. I'll fuck your ass and I won't be nice and prepare you."

C.J.'s mouth fell open and he shifted in agitation but nothing he did could hide the bulging erection he sported.

"On your feet."

She rose, faltered and then regained her footing. He put a gentle hand to her elbow so she didn't fall and then guided her toward the railing where he'd fucked her just minutes ago.

"Hands on the rail. Chin up. Legs apart. If you make a single sound, I'll make good on my threat."

Mike and C.J. closed in and stood to the side. C.J.'s eyes were wide but Mike's glittered with lust. Cole knew he was hoping like hell that Ren broke. Cole knew better.

"No lashes to count, Ren. I haven't decided how many. I'll quit when I'm satisfied with how your sweet little ass looks. And then I'll probably fuck you, provided you don't lose your discipline first. If that happens, I'm afraid your pretty mouth is going to get quite the work out."

She trembled underneath his touch and he couldn't discern whether it was in anticipation of the punishment or perhaps because she was turned on by the idea of sucking the two men's cocks. Regardless, it was all in her hands.

He chose to use the belt first. He handed back the oar to C.J., who took it eagerly, his face flushed with excitement. Cole carefully doubled over the wide leather belt and gave it an experimental pop.

Ren flinched and he smiled.

The first lash was one of the hardest for her not to react to. He knew it and made it purposely sharp. The two men watching leaned forward in anticipation of hearing a sound escape Ren's lips.

The second, she showed more restraint and took it stoically as she did the third and the fourth. And the next several. But then it became a test of her endurance as he continued to stripe her buttocks, working over the entire area so he didn't strike the same place two times in succession.

He worked below her buttocks to the undersides of her legs but he didn't venture above her ass to the small of her back. Ren was especially sensitive in that area and he made it a point never to strike her there.

C.J. looked near desperation by the time Cole discarded the belt and reached for the oar. Mike just looked pissed. Cole gave her a moment to gather herself. The purpose wasn't to break her down or cause her so much pain that she lost sight of her purpose. And because he knew her so well, by the time the last blow from the oar fell, she would be so near to orgasm that it would take little effort on his part to send her spiraling into the abyss.

He smacked the oar over one cheek, making the globe shake delectably. She jumped but still, not a sound escaped those disciplined lips. Pride swelled deep inside Cole. She'd rather die than show him the disrespect of disobeying a direct order. If indeed she broke and uttered a sound, he would have pushed her too far.

Her ass was delightfully red. Glowing with the marks of the belt and now the wood. He hadn't struck her hard enough to leave bruises or break the skin, but her ass would be red for hours and the welts would be visible equally as long. Which is why she wasn't going to cover that delectable little behind for the rest of the day. He wanted to see his mark on her. He'd probably fuck her senseless as many times as he could get it up until he wore them both out. That's what she did to him. Made him ache from the inside out.

C.J. was nearly beside himself, clearly agitated that Ren hadn't broken. There was grudging respect in Mike's eyes. His gaze grew more tender with each blow that fell on Ren's ass. His lust had turned to something else. He looked as though he wanted nothing more than to gather Ren in his arms and offer comfort—and perhaps praise.

Cole let the oar slide from his fingers. It hit the deck with a clatter and Ren's shoulders slumped forward. His hands glided over the swell of her ass, red and marked. So very beautiful.

His own cock was about to burst out of his jeans again, so he well understood Mike and C.J.'s frustration. With clumsy fingers, he unzipped his fly, pulled out his cock and pushed into Ren, feeling the warm snugness of her pussy swallow him whole.

She fluttered wildly around him, already in the throes of her orgasm. She threw her head back and he leaned into her, wrapping his arms around her, holding her against his chest as he murmured words of praise in her ear.

"It's okay now, Ren," he murmured. "Darling, Ren. Let me hear your pleasure. It's okay now."

She moaned softly and then louder. His words seemed to catapult her even further over the edge. She went liquid around him. Hot satin, flowing over his cock, stroking him so intimately that he could feel it in his soul.

"Cole," she whispered. His name was like the sweetest of endearments falling from her lips. It sent a thrill coursing through his veins. Like a drug. One he couldn't get enough of.

His name. No one else's. Her acceptance of his ownership.

He cupped her breasts, rubbing his thumbs over her tight nipples. Then remembering her account of the night at the club with Lucas, he turned her away from the railing until she faced Mike and C.J. He was still buried deep inside her but he'd stilled, wanting to ward off his orgasm so he could bring her to release again.

"Touch her," he said hoarsely. "Touch her but be gentle."

C.J. fell to his knees, his eyes so dark with lust that Cole wondered if he'd already come in his pants. His hands trembled as he reached tentatively to touch her breasts. Then he glanced up at Cole as if seeking permission for more.

Cole nodded. "Touch her any way you like. With your hands, your mouth. But don't hurt her. You'll show her the respect she's earned. I want her to enjoy every minute."

As soon as C.J.'s mouth closed around her nipple, she moaned and stiffened. Her pussy tightened around Cole's cock and he moaned along with her.

Mike forewent her body and angled in from the side, his hand cupping Ren's face just before he kissed her. It was a savage kiss, like he meant to devour her. It was an odd sensation to have another man kissing his woman so passionately while Cole was fucking her from behind, but he was unbelievably aroused and so was Ren, judging by her frantic movements and the sudden wetness around his cock.

Wanting her to have as much pleasure as he himself was finding, he slid out of her body. At first C.J. pulled back and even Mike took a step away, as if assuming that Cole was calling an end.

But Cole merely repositioned himself at her ass, spread her a little further so the angle was adjusted and then he carefully began to work himself inside her.

He hadn't used any lubricant and he knew her wetness wasn't enough to make it bearable. He wanted that fine line between pain and pleasure. He didn't want to hurt her too badly, so he patiently worked at getting inside her.

Some pain was good. He wanted that edge. He wanted to feel her reject his cock and press forward anyway. She would want it too.

"I have oil," Mike said gruffly. "Suntan oil. It's here in one of the compartments."

Cole smiled. Already Ren had made another conquest. As much as Mike had wanted to witness her punishment, he now couldn't bear the thought of her being hurt.

He gathered Ren's hair in his hand and pulled slightly back. "Tell him, Ren. Tell him how you want it. Do you want it easy? All slicked up so I glide right into your sweet little ass? Or do you want that bite? Do you want to fight my invasion and have me force your surrender? Tell him so he knows."

He could just see the glitter in Ren's eyes from the angle he looked down on her face. Her face was suffused in color and heat and so much anticipation. She had a drugged look and her lips were swollen from another man's kiss. It made him want to savage her mouth, to replace Mike's mark with his own. But he'd sworn this would be about Ren's pleasure now that she'd withstood her punishment.

"I want the pain," she said hoarsely. "I want it hard."

Cole's hands moved down to her hips until he gripped her hard, giving her nowhere to move to, no way to fend off what was coming. Then he thrust hard. "Like this?"

She shuddered and convulsed around him, pinned to his body, helpless. "Oh God, yes. Just like that."

"Then stand there and take it. Tell your men to touch you while the one who owns you fucks your ass."

"Touch me," she pleaded, her gaze finding Mike and C.J. once more.

C.J. needed no urging. As before, he dropped to his knees and cupped both breasts in his hands. He looked like a kid in a candy store. His mouth closed around one nipple and the wet sucking sounds he made spurred Cole on.

Mike took her mouth again, but this time he slipped his hand between Ren's thighs.

"That's it," Cole said in approval. "Give her what she needs. Use your hands to show her what two cocks feel like."

Then to Ren, "Tell me what it feels like, baby. Are his hands inside you? Are his fingers long and thick like my cock? How does C.J.'s mouth feel on your nipples? Are you wishing that I'd let them fuck you? What if I let them take you right here on the deck while I watched? What if they fucked you so long and hard that you couldn't walk tomorrow?"

She let out a cry and he knew she was gone.

"Son of a bitch," Mike murmured as he reclaimed her mouth. "She's coming all over my hand."

C.J.'s hands slipped around to the backs of her knees as Cole continued his ruthless ass fucking. C.J.'s mouth never left her breasts. He sucked and licked like a man starved. He acted like he'd never been that up close and personal with a woman's breasts in his life and he seemed determined to make the most of the experience.

Mike's mouth gentled on Ren's. He kissed her with reverence and then stroked her cheek with his other hand, pushing aside a strand of her hair as he stared into her eyes. Then slowly, he pulled his hand away from her pussy and Ren sagged, still impaled on Cole's cock.

"Hands behind your back," Cole ordered.

Ren gave him her hands and he captured them at the small of her back, holding her captive as he bent her forward so he could finish. He slapped against her ass, hard, with the purpose of orgasm. His release gathered in his balls, put a stranglehold on his cock and raced up the head until it felt like he was going to explode.

And then he started spurting deep inside her ass. It vaguely occurred to him that he hadn't used a condom this time. He couldn't conjure any real regret. She belonged to him. She was his. His to use. Her body was his.

Mike slid a hand into her hair and supported her head as Cole bent her further forward as he rammed into her ass, shaking with the last of his release. Then finally he shuddered to a stop and remained locked inside her for a long moment.

When he finally pulled away, semen slid from her ass and left a wet trail down the inside of her leg. He viewed the result with deep satisfaction.

Yeah, she was his. Marked. Possessed. Owned.

He gently separated her hands but kept hold as he guided them back around to her sides. He waited until he was sure she had her footing and then he took a step back.

"Turn around, Ren. Show them whose cum slides from your body and over your skin. Show them who's marked you, who owns you."

Slowly she did his bidding, turning so that her back was presented to Mike and C.J.

"Good girl."

Then to Mike. "Take her below. Make sure she gets into the bathroom safely and wait outside in case she needs something. When she's finished cleaning up, have her come back topside. This time, no swimsuit. I want her naked so I can see the marks on her ass."

CHAPTER 29

Cole stripped down topside and pulled on a pair of swim trunks. C.J. had gone to prepare refreshment for Cole and Ren and now Cole just waited for Ren to return.

He hadn't planned the scene as it had gone down. But he'd known in advance that Captain Mike was well used to observing such things. The man who owned the yacht was a hedonist at heart and more often than not, he had his latest submissive, aboard, fucking her six ways to Sunday.

While he doubted C.J. had ever participated or even observed for that matter, he wouldn't doubt that Mike had joined in his fair share of sexual escapades. Or at the very least, he'd seen it all. C.J. had to be new or at least still green because he'd damn near come undone at the opportunity to touch Ren.

It was good to have friends with expensive toys and who employed staff who either looked the other way or were discreet above all else.

With the salary that both Mike and C.J. received, it was doubtful they'd report a murder if it happened right in front of their noses.

Cole would have to remember to thank Jon again for the last-minute use of his yacht. It served its purpose well. It got Ren away from any potential run-in with Lucas and it isolated him and Ren from the rest of the world. A few days to live and love and do nothing more than enjoy each other would hopefully go a long way in cementing the fragile relationship that had begun repairing itself from the moment he and Ren had reunited.

His body leapt to life as soon as he saw the top of Ren's dark head clear the top of the steps leading belowdeck. She climbed slowly up, her naked body gleaming in the sunlight. Her hair streamed over her shoulders, the ends lifting and blowing this way and that. She honest to God took his breath away.

Mike followed a discreet distance behind, carrying a tube of sunblock and two towels. Ren stopped in front of where Cole lounged in the deck chair, awaiting his next directive.

Damn, he was a lucky bastard. Ren fit him and his needs so perfectly. Never would he be able to find a woman who was so quietly content to give herself into his keeping.

"Turn around," he said softly.

She did as he asked and turned until she faced away, her plump little ass still red and bearing the marks of his punishment. Damn if he didn't want to pull her down and fuck her again until one of them couldn't walk. Probably himself.

"Beautiful. Don't you think so, Mike?"

"Yes, indeed," Mike murmured.

Just then C.J. came bearing a wheeled cart with several trays, a bottle of wine and several bottles of water.

"Good timing," Cole said in approval. "I'm sure Ren is hungry and thirsty as well. However, before I feed her, her needs must be met.

She'll need sunblock. I won't have her burned. I'd like for the two of you to take care of the matter for me."

C.J. visibly swallowed and Mike twisted the tube in his hand, his hungry gaze going to Ren. It was probably damn cruel to have the two men apply the sunblock since Cole had no intention of allowing them to fuck her, but Ren would enjoy it and this was all about Ren and no one else.

"Come lie down, darling. Face down first so they can get your back. Then you can roll over so they get your front."

Ren took the lounger beside him and gracefully stretched out to lay on her stomach. He reached over to flip her hair up over her shoulder and then let his fingers wander down her back, just to let her know he was near and watching. Always watching, always protecting.

Then he motioned for Mike and C.J. to do the job.

Mike pointed C.J. to Ren's other side and then took position opposite C.J.

"Don't get in a hurry," Mike instructed C.J. "And be mindful of her welts."

Cole smiled. Yep. Total conquest.

"Very good," he said approvingly. "I want Ren to enjoy this. Make sure she does."

Ren sucked in her breath the moment the unfamiliar hands began to glide over her flesh. Even knowing where each man was positioned, it was easy to know whose hands were whose. Mike was more . . . knowledgeable. That was the word she searched for. He was patient. Didn't get in a hurry. He seemed to know exactly how to touch a woman.

C.J. gave it very good effort, but he was excited and he kept having to slow down as if remembering what he was supposed to be doing.

Gradually they settled into a rhythm. Stroking, caressing. Warm, soothing. The heat of the sun coupled with their sensual exploration of her back had her nearly asleep and so drugged on pleasure that she couldn't have moved if she wanted to.

They worked down to her ass and Mike took over there, as if he didn't trust C.J. not to hurt her. She heard him tell C.J. to work on her legs and then both his palms covered her still-aching behind.

She sighed in bliss as he very tenderly worked the lotion into her skin. Her ass still tingled and was hypersensitive to every touch. But Mike was exceedingly gentle and he covered every inch of her flesh.

After several long, glorious minutes of him cupping and massaging her behind, he slid his hands down her legs to her feet and began to rub the soles. He pressed into her arches and rubbed the tops of her feet, even running a finger over each of her toes.

She made a sound. Maybe she'd tried to talk. It came out as a garbled, incomprehensible mess. Cole laughed softly beside her. She opened one eye to see him stretched on the lounger, hands behind his head, looking like a sun god. So confident and supreme she wanted to jump on him and lick him up one side and down the other. But that would require effort and she didn't have any to spare at the moment.

"Enjoying yourself, darling? Are they doing a good job?"

"Oh God, yes." She whimpered again when Mike hit just the right spot on her foot.

"Turn over," Mike said gruffly. "We need to do your front."

Her hands and arms shook so badly that she couldn't push herself up from the lounger to rotate over. Mike took her arm and carefully maneuvered her until she was on her back.

The lust was back in C.J.'s eyes as he stared down at her breasts. She wanted to laugh. The guy was obviously a boob guy. He didn't see anything else once he locked on to those.

"Don't maul her," Mike muttered as he squeezed more lotion onto his hand.

Cole chuckled. "Indeed."

They started at her neck and worked down to her chest. Mike was more cautious. He touched her breasts experimentally at first and then as if reassuring himself he wasn't hurting her, he began to massage lightly, working a pattern around her nipples that had them so stiff and taut that the slightest breeze over them made her ache all over.

C.J. was more enthusiastic. He caressed, rubbed and pinched her nipple between his thumb and forefinger. The dual sensations, so very different, had her so worked up she was about to fidget out of her lounger.

"This is supposed to be relaxing," Cole said in amusement.

She cracked an eye open again to glare at him. "Oh really? So you're telling me if two gorgeous women were running their hands all over your cock, that you'd be all relaxed and ho hum?"

He grinned. "Only if that gorgeous woman was you."

"Oh you're good," she muttered.

"Relax, darling. This is all for you. Enjoy it."

She closed her eyes again and surrendered to the male hands that explored her body, rubbing sunblock in areas that would probably never see the sun.

Mike slid his fingers between her thighs and she parted her legs automatically. He found her bare lips and ran his thumb up and down the soft folds until she was all but purring.

"Do you want him to make you come, Ren?" Cole asked quietly.

She opened her eyes to focus on him once more. She stared into his eyes, looking for the right answer, but as it had been with Lucas, it wasn't a trick question.

"Yes," she whispered. "Please."

"Ask him then. Ask him prettily and maybe he'll give you what you want."

Her gaze drifted down to Mike's tight features. He was dark brown from hours in the sun. There probably wasn't a part of him that hadn't been kissed by the sun. It was hard to know his ethnicity because of the tan. She couldn't place his accent, though he looked to be at least part Latino. Either way the man was damn sexy and he was looking at her with those soft black eyes that said he'd do anything at all to please her. What woman could resist that?

"Please make me come."

"Address him properly," Cole admonished.

"Please make me come, Captain Mike," she amended.

"It will be my pleasure," Mike said as he slid his fingers through her folds to the already damp flesh beyond.

He rolled his thumb over her clit while he stroked a circle around her entrance with his middle finger. All the while he stared directly into her eyes and she found herself unable to look away. She had no idea what C.J. was doing or if he was even still touching her. There was only the magic of Mike's eyes and fingers as he lazily stroked her most intimate flesh.

"Would you like me to use my mouth?" Mike asked.

Her gaze flew to Cole. He looked pleased by her reaction but nodded his permission, effectively leaving it up to her.

"Oh God, yes," she breathed. "Please."

"Spread your legs and place your feet on either side of the lounger," Mike directed.

She did as he bade and planted the soles of her feet on the sun-warmed deck. Her pussy was spread and bared and she was completely vulnerable, a sensation that sent a heady thrill through her body.

Mike straddled the lounger and scooted up until his hands covered the tops of her thighs and slid warmly up to her pelvis. He lowered his mouth at the same time he spread the folds of her pussy with his thumbs. Holding her open, he dipped his tongue down and licked her from her entrance to her clit.

She nearly came off the lounger and would have but she suddenly realized where C.J. had gone. He was holding her shoulders down so she couldn't move. Her gaze went helplessly to Cole who surveyed her with lazy arrogance.

Mike nuzzled her flesh, the scruff on his jaw abrading her sensitive areas, driving her crazy. He licked and sucked, gently, so very gently. The man was a God when it came to oral sex. There wasn't a woman alive who wouldn't throw herself at a man who had a mouth like this.

And man was he patient. He didn't tire. Didn't grow impatient when she didn't come right away. He was content to work her up slow and easy. He licked her deep, sliding his tongue as far inside her as he could reach. Then he'd work his way up to her clit where he'd tongue her and suck lightly at the quivering bundle of nerves. She was ready to scream because she was so on edge but she just couldn't get there yet.

"She needs more," Cole said softly. "She needs that edge. A little rough. Push her a little more and she'll come."

Oh how he understood her. Even watching another man go down on her, he could read her like a book. Knew she was close and what she needed to achieve release.

Mike nipped lightly at her clit and then rubbed the bristle of his beard growth through her folds. He slid two fingers inside her while he nibbled at the taut bud above her entrance and then began finger fucking her.

"That's it," Cole said. "Don't be afraid of hurting her. She likes it rough. Don't you, Ren darling?"

"Yesss."

The word came out as a long hiss because just as Cole had given Mike further directions, Mike added a third finger and thrust hard.

"Come in my mouth," Mike said hoarsely. "I want you to come all over my tongue. I want to taste you. I've never tasted anything sweeter."

Those words, so sweetly said, did more than the bite of pain and the hard edge of his fingers. She catapulted over the edge, her entire body drawing up and then exploding with the force of a bomb.

She quivered from head to toe and she was only aware of Mike licking her. Of him sucking every bit of her release into his mouth. She moaned and melted into the lounger, so boneless that she couldn't move. Her legs sagged limply to the side. As Mike raised his head from her pussy, she couldn't even muster the strength to close her legs so they remained gaped open like a complete wanton.

"Bring her to me."

Cole's quiet command drifted over her ears and soon she found herself lifted from the lounger and delivered into Cole's waiting arms. He cuddled her to him and held a glass of cold water to her lips. She drank thirstily and then sagged against his chest as he stroked his hand up and down her back.

"Lay here with me, Ren. I'm going to feed you delicious food and we're going to watch the sun go down."

She sighed a blissful, happy sigh and burrowed a little tighter into his embrace. Oh, but he did love to spoil her so.

CHAPTER 30

"*W*here did you wander off to today?"

Ren lay in the lounger, wrapped in Cole's arms as the sunset put on a fiery display worthy of the gods. The sky was painted in vibrant golden hues with brushes of pink and lavender. And just over the horizon, the sun was a giant orange orb, sinking lower and lower, hanging on with a weakening grip.

She didn't pretend to misunderstand. She knew exactly what he was asking. It was the source of her punishment and the catalyst for everything that had happened since. Put in that light, she couldn't very well regret what had happened but she could at least make him understand.

"I was thinking."

"About?"

She flushed, embarrassed at the first thing that had drifted her off course while Cole was fucking her.

"Ren?" he prompted.

"I was imagining what a child of ours would look like," she mumbled.

He went utterly silent. So still against her. Disconcerted, she chanced a peek at him to gauge his reaction and was stunned by the raw hunger in his eyes. He looked . . . wistful.

"I think she would be beautiful like her mama," Cole said quietly. "Dark skin, dark hair. Who knows what kind of eyes with your mixture of brown and green and my blue eyes. But I'd lay odds she'll be stunning."

"And a boy?" she asked with a smile.

"I picture him like you too. A miniature Ren with your mischievous smile."

"Would our children inherit nothing from you?"

"Just my love of you."

She was flattened by the statement. Had no response. She felt like she was swaying while the world went still around her.

She lay her head back on his shoulder afraid to dream further.

"When you began the punishment, I remembered when we were young how we used to act out those scenes where I said no and you forced me."

Cole stopped his lazy exploration of her skin. "Did I frighten you?"

She shook her head. "That's not why I brought it up. It made me remember. It . . . excited me. It excited me then."

"And now?"

"You're still the only person I would ever trust in a situation like that. I've never taken things that far with anyone else."

He touched her hair, ran his fingers absently through the strands. "Not even Lucas?"

She shook her head. "Lucas is intense. One, I don't see him really appreciating such a situation. He's much too serious. And impatient with games. Two, it's entirely possible that he'd push too far. I don't think he'd get carried away. I mean, I trust him. I guess I've just never wanted to see that side of him. He can be intimidating."

"That wasn't what I was doing. Earlier, I mean. You . . ." He looked pained for a moment as if he didn't really want to say what was on his mind. "You get to me, Ren. Like no one else has ever been able to. I look at you and my instinct is to dominate and not just because it's a sexual aspect that turns me on. It goes much deeper than that with you. I want to protect and cherish you. I want to get so deep inside your mind and skin that you can never shake me. That probably scares the hell out of you but I can't be any more honest than that."

Fright was the very last thing on her mind. Warmth curled around her insides, fluttered through her chest and seeped into her soul, comforting her from the inside out.

"What if I told you that was precisely what I needed? What I want? More than anything."

"But would you be happy with those things no matter who provided them?" he asked grimly.

She sucked in her breath, stung by the almost accusation even as she understood why he asked it. It was a valid question. In his shoes, she'd be wondering the same thing. But instead of answering or perhaps by way of answering, she turned it back on him.

"Would any woman do for you? Would you be happy protecting and cherishing any woman or is it just me?"

He looked pissed and she instantly regretted the little demon that prompted her to ask it.

"I'm not even going to acknowledge, much less respond, to that question. I believe I've more than answered it. You, on the other hand, have yet to answer mine. That's not like you, Ren. You've been honest and straightforward on every other occasion. Even to your detriment."

She sighed. "I'm sorry. It made me angry and frustrated me a little."

"Care to share why?"

He'd relaxed a little the moment she'd admitted the emotion behind her question, and he began stroking his hand over her arm again, offering comfort. The man really was too good to be true, and here she was about to be the biggest most ungrateful bitch alive.

"Because I couldn't respond and say what I wanted to say. Not while being truthful. I'd love to be able to tell you that like you, I could only be this way with you. That I'd only want these things from you. But I'd be lying and I won't lie to you, Cole. I can't."

"Lucas."

That one word said it all. The grim resignation in Cole's voice told her without any other explanation that he knew well that Lucas was the one exception. The one thing standing in the way of her total and complete acceptance of what she and Cole had together. Because she'd shared much of the same with him. Because she trusted Lucas and she cared for him. No, that wasn't even being honest with herself. She loved him just like she loved Cole. Even knowing that he might be finished with her. Even knowing that he'd hurt her horribly just days earlier.

A part of her couldn't accept what she feared was true until she was presented irrefutable evidence, and in this case it would mean facing Lucas and having him tell her.

It made her stupid. It made her . . . It made her someone she didn't want to be. She hated it. But God, how do you just stop loving someone? How? It wasn't like flipping a switch. She'd been with Lucas an entire year. She'd only been back with Cole a few days.

She couldn't cheapen her love for Cole by being as fickle as to say she no longer loved Lucas. What would that say about what she felt for Cole?

The words burned in her throat and she knew she had to tell him. She had to explain. And oh God, if he didn't understand, if he grew angry, she didn't know what she'd do because there was nothing left for her but the truth.

She opened her mouth but the words stuck. How she hated this horrible paralysis that gripped her.

Then Cole's gentle hand slid over her cheek and turned her more fully to face him.

"Talk to me, Ren. There's such torment in your eyes. I can't stand to see you this way."

Her throat swelled and then tightened into a vicious knot that she could barely breathe around.

"I love him," she whispered.

Something died in Cole's eyes. His hand drifted slowly down until it lay on his leg. It was then that she realized that she'd never been honest with her feelings about *him*. Everything had happened so fast and she'd battled so many conflicting emotions. There was never a doubt in her mind that she loved Cole deeply. Always had. But she hadn't told him and now she'd just blurted out that she loved Lucas and in Cole's mind that meant she was choosing him over Cole.

She put both hands to his face, forcing him to look at her as she pleaded with him with her gaze. But instead of saying anything she pressed her lips to his in a hungry kiss and poured every ounce of her feelings for him into that kiss.

"Please forgive me," she whispered. "I'm so terrible at something that is so important. Please just listen while I explain."

"What else is there to say?" he asked hoarsely.

"I love you, Cole. I love you so damned much."

His brows furrowed and he looked utterly perplexed. "But you just said . . ."

She nodded. "I did. I just thought all this out in my head but instead of thinking it, I should have been saying it to you. I love you. I've always loved you. Even when I was so hurt and devastated by you leaving me. My loving Lucas doesn't change that. It may sound ridiculous. Maybe you don't even believe me. But it's true.

"I've been with Lucas for a year. It took me a long time to sort out my feelings for him. I already told you that in the beginning I was using him. Not maliciously. But I clung to him because he was an anchor in a tumultuous time in my life. I needed him. He provided so much of what I needed to get back on track. I respected him. I liked him. He was a friend and a lover. I'm not even sure when all of that changed and became something deeper and more meaningful. Maybe I didn't even realize it myself until he took me to you. Because it hurt. It hurt more than I could have imagined that he walked away from me so easily. It was like swallowing a torch and being burned from the inside out.

"But then there was you. So damn perfect. So caring and loving. Seeing you again was like having the past hit me like a tidal wave. I immediately knew that if I'd ever told myself that I'd stopped loving you, I was a damn liar.

"But oh God, Cole. I love Lucas too, and I don't know what I'm supposed to do. I can't just turn that off. Even if he has left me and moved on. I don't know how I'm supposed to deal with that. I don't want to hurt you. I don't want to disrespect you. But I can't pretend like this isn't tearing me up inside. I can't pretend I don't love him when I do. But I can't—I wont—have you think that I don't love you with every thing I have."

Her breath came out as a sob, stuttering over shaking lips. She hadn't realized how badly she was shaking all over until Cole gripped her arms with his hands and simply held her.

"I love you, Cole," she whispered. "I'm sorry if I ever made you feel like you were second best or that I didn't love you or that, God forbid, you were a substitute for Lucas and that any man could give me what I want and need."

He pulled her into his arms and held her tightly, his chest heaving against her. "Ren. My darling, Ren. I love you too. So damn much. So honest and so tormented. I wish you'd talked to me before. I hate that you've been feeling torn and afraid."

"I didn't even know myself what to say or what to do," she said, muffled by her mouth against his throat.

She inhaled his scent, closed her eyes as his pulse beat against her lips. Steady and reassuring. Just like he always was. Her Cole.

"I love you," she said again, because it seemed the right and best thing to say. Perhaps the only thing out of all the other stuff that mattered.

He kissed her hair, stroked her skin and simply held her as she clung to him.

"It will be all right, Ren. I swear to you," Cole finally said. It was a vow. So firm that hope and comfort took hold. "We'll find a way, darling. We'll find it."

PART 3

ren

CHAPTER 31

$\mathcal{F}$or several long, glorious days, Ren lived a pampered, idealistic existence. Cole saw to her every need, emotionally and physically. Captain Mike and C.J., were equally attentive whether it was to smooth sunblock over her skin or to bring up food or drink whenever she or Cole requested it.

She and Cole swam in the sea. They snorkeled along a reef not far from the boat and she delighted in all of the sea creatures she got to interact with.

One afternoon, they took the small outboard to the island they'd anchored off and picnicked on the sand. They played in the surf, took a nap in the shade of a palm tree and then motored back to the yacht at sunset.

Their two weeks were almost up, but neither broached the subject even though it weighed heavy on Ren's mind. But she knew Cole thought about it too because she could see the way his eyes changed when he thought she wasn't looking.

On the morning of their seventh day, she woke to Cole parting her legs and plunging deep inside her. He hadn't worn a condom since that first day on the boat and she'd been fiercely relieved. It wasn't as if they'd been completely irresponsible.

Both were healthy and had discussed their histories at the onset of their time together. It had been Lucas who'd insisted Cole wear a condom and he'd done so because he hadn't wanted another man to have what was his. He'd wanted Ren to hold something back. Not let Cole enjoy the same privileges as Lucas had.

But neither Ren nor Cole had been willing to continue that line of respect in light of Lucas's actions. And it had more to do with their own deep, personal connection than any regard or disregard for Lucas.

She wrapped her arms around Cole's neck and let her palms slide over his shoulders to his back and down to his lean waist and over his firm buttocks.

He was such a gorgeous man. Toned. Muscled. But not hulking and huge. Just perfect.

"We have to go back today," he murmured as he nibbled at her ear.

She wrapped her legs around his waist and pulled him deeper. "I know."

"Mike's already weighed anchor and we're heading back to the island where the jet is waiting."

She sighed her regret. Their return to reality was inevitable, but still, the few days they'd been able to escape were a fairy tale she'd never forget. Perhaps an extremely kinky adult fairy tale, but a fantasy nonetheless.

He continued to rock into her until her release slid warm and pleasurable over her. Like the sun caressing the earth at dawn. She kissed him. Held on to him as he lowered his body to hers.

For the longest time they remained there, legs intertwined, their breaths mingling until finally Cole rolled over so that Ren was sprawled atop him.

"Let's take a shower together and get dressed," he said in a regretful tone.

She lowered her mouth to his and allowed the sweetness of his kiss to reassure her. He'd said they'd work it out and she believed him.

"Last one in the shower's a rotten egg," she threw out just as she lunged from the bed and ran for the bathroom.

"You little cheat!"

She laughed madly as she turned the water on and waited for it to warm. A moment later, his arms closed around her and his mouth found her neck. Then to her utter shock he hauled her into the shower and shoved her underneath the still-cold spray.

She shrieked and then began laughing as goose bumps broke out over her skin. The water began to warm and suddenly she found herself forced against the wall of the shower. Cole spread her legs and lifted her just enough that her feet left the floor and she was angled so he could penetrate her easily.

Her palms slapped against the wet shower wall and she turned her head so that her cheek was flush against the now-warm tile. She closed her eyes as he ruthlessly fucked her from behind while water rained down over them both.

There was no leisurely love making as there had been just moments earlier. He thrust hard and fast, with the sole purpose of release.

Her hair wasn't completely soaked yet and he wrapped his hand through the tresses before yanking her down so she knelt in the shower. He angled the showerhead away and began stroking his cock with his free hand, directing the spurts of semen into her hair.

The thin ropes of cum landed in intervals and dripped onto the floor where it disappeared in the swirling water down the drain. When he was finished, she expected him to sink into her mouth and have her lick the remaining stickiness from his cock, but instead he wiped himself with her hair, smearing the liquid through her tresses.

For several long moments he simply stared down at her with glittering eyes as she knelt in front of him. Then he smiled a slow, arrogant smile that told her he was well satisfied with himself.

He ran his fingers over the stickiness in her hair before finally pulling her to her feet and once more directing the shower nozzle directly over her.

He shampooed her hair and rinsed it thoroughly before washing the rest of her body with gentle hands. He sent her out ahead of him while he finished his own shower, and she toweled off and went back into the bedroom to dress.

Breakfast was served topside and Ren watched as the island they'd anchored off of became smaller and smaller on the horizon. Then she smiled because no matter what happened in the future, she'd always treasure the memory of these last days with Cole.

"What has you smiling?" Cole asked.

Her gaze moved to him and her smile widened. "I was thinking of beating you again at Ping-Pong on the trip back."

Cole's eyes narrowed. "What do you mean, *again*? I clearly won our last bout."

She shook her head. "You cheated. I won."

He sputtered and set down his glass of juice. "You accuse me of cheating?"

She nodded solemnly. "I do. But another match should clear things up. Winner takes all. Claims championship rights for the entire trip."

"You're on."

What before had been a friendly game turned quickly into a competitive bloodbath as both were determined to emerge the victor. The ball flew fast and furious.

Ren sank her teeth into her bottom lip and let her competitive nature take hold. Over her dead body was he going to beat her.

"Game point," she taunted.

She blew a strand of hair out of her eyes and stared grimly across the table at him as she prepared to serve. If she lost this one, they'd tie and then she'd have to win by two. Cole seemed every bit as determined to win as she was. It was now or never.

Instead of slapping the ball toward the corner, she put a wicked backspin and barely put it across the net. Cole, who'd stood back, anticipating the hard hit, lunged forward, paddle outstretched. He just caught the ball as it fell over the side and he popped it up high. She backhanded it viciously to the opposite side and he had no prayer of getting to it in time.

She grinned triumphantly as he shot her a disgruntled look.

She sauntered around to his side and slid her paddle back onto the table. "My game."

"So it is. I don't like to lose, you know."

She raised an eyebrow.

"Turn around. Hands down on the table."

Delicious chills danced up her spine when she saw he was still holding the paddle. Her pussy tingled and her breasts tightened and swelled, suddenly super sensitive to the slightest touch.

He reached around to unfasten the fly of her jeans. Then he pulled her pants down just below her ass. With no preamble, he brought the paddle across her cheek with a smack.

It felt like fire. The very best kind. Edgy pain that quickly turned to hot pleasure.

He struck her other cheek and then stopped to caress the marks on her ass. "Very pretty. But do you know what would be even prettier, Ren?"

"No," she whispered.

"You sucking my cock while your pretty ass gets marked."

A jolt of excitement seared through her belly. This she hadn't counted on. It both terrified and titillated her beyond measure.

"Who should I ask to do the job, Ren? You choose. Shall I get Captain Mike? He obviously has experience and he's given you great pleasure these past few days. Then there's C.J., who you've made a conquest out of. But he's young and exuberant. I bet he'd get carried away and his blows would hurt a hell of a lot. But then you might want that."

"Captain Mike," she managed to get out. Because then, oh God, she could fantasize about him fucking her red, sore ass while Cole fucked her mouth. Just the thought of it had her so hot that with one touch she could go off like a rocket.

"Awfully quick with your decision," he taunted. "Lucky for you he's standing just behind me. He's been watching while I paddle your bare ass. I think he's itching to get in on the action."

She trembled and closed her eyes. Her fingers curled into balls against the Ping-Pong table. Then suddenly she was jerked away. Cole's arm curled around her waist and he lifted her in the air, tossing her over his shoulder as if she weighed nothing.

Captain Mike tossed one of the thick cushions from one of the loungers down onto the deck and Cole tumbled her onto it. "Get on your hands and knees."

She was quick to obey his order and placed her palms down as her knees dug into the padding. Cole sank to his knees in front of her face and he shoved his hand into her hair, yanking her head toward his erect cock.

"Suck it."

The crude directive incited her arousal further. She opened her mouth and slid her lips over his thick erection. He didn't give her any time before he grasped her head and began fucking her in long, powerful strokes.

She's forgotten all about Mike until fire seared over her ass. She gasped and got a throat full of cock in response.

"Yeah, baby, open that mouth up like that again. I'll stuff it full. You decide. Every time you gasp like that, I'm going to stick my dick as far down your throat as I can."

She trembled and shook, and then Mike paddled her again. She tried. She really tried not to make a sound, but then he struck her again, harder, and she cried out.

Cole made a sound of triumph and he pushed deeper until her throat convulsed around him.

"Oh hell, just like that. Love when you gag around me like that. It feels fucking insane."

Mike's blows were methodical, well placed and he acted like a man who was well disciplined when it came to punishment. Or pleasure. Because this sure as hell wasn't punishment. Ren liked to think it was her reward for winning because she couldn't think of a better one.

Her ass was on fire. There wasn't an inch of her skin that was untouched. It was so hypersensitive that if he so much as breathed on her burning flesh, she whimpered. And that only caused Cole to fuck her face even harder.

"Fuck her, Mike. Fuck her. She wants it. Look at her. She's got a mouthful of my cock and she wants more. She's all but shaking that pretty red ass at you. If you want her, take her, but take her hard."

Cole thrust into her mouth and ground his pelvis against her chin until his balls were resting just below her lips. And he stayed that way. She sucked desperately for air through her nose and tried to settle so she didn't fight. If she fought him right now, he'd probably turn her over and face fuck her just like he'd fuck her pussy. It wouldn't be easy. It wouldn't be for her pleasure.

Rough hands gripped her ass. Tears burned her eyelids as she fought the urge to push at Cole. Then suddenly he withdrew and as she gasped for air, Mike rammed into her, opening her in one swift thrust.

Cole gripped her head and pushed back inside her mouth and both men began fucking her so ruthlessly that she felt utterly powerless between them. She gloried in that feeling. Embraced it and held tight to it.

She lost all awareness of where she was, only that she was being fucked by two powerful men in an animalistic fashion that should have appalled her. Maybe it did. But it thrilled her in equal parts. She only wished she could see it. But she could damn sure feel it.

After a while her pussy burned, as did her throat from the rough thrusts.

"She's getting dry," Mike said as he pulled out.

She winced at the sheer size ravaging its way out of her pussy. Cole abruptly pulled away from her mouth and walked around to the back of her. Mike withdrew completely and suddenly Cole was inside her, thrusting hard.

"Take off your condom and fuck her face for a while," Cole said. "I'll come inside her and you'll have plenty of lubricant to fuck her some more."

Oh hell, it was all she could take. She was bombarded by the words, the images and the reality of these two men having their way with her on every possible level.

Cole's possession hurt. He was big, bigger than Mike, and she fought his invasion with every thrust. And he loved it. It made him even more forceful and she moaned just as Mike gripped her hair and forced his way into her mouth.

"Just a moment longer and you can have her back," Cole panted.

Mike didn't seem to be worried. He sank into her mouth and moaned softly as she swallowed him deep. Her entire body shook with the force of Cole's thrusts and then suddenly her pussy was bathed in sticky, liquid warmth.

He coated her passageway with cum and continued thrusting until she felt warmth travel down the inside of her leg.

Then he pulled out and slapped her on the ass. "Oh hell yeah. I'm going to stay back here a moment while I watch Mike fuck a pussy that's full of my cum. Mine, Ren. That pussy is mine. I'm letting him borrow it, but it's all mine."

Mike dutifully pulled out. She heard him tear another condom wrapper and then his big hands were gripping her waist again and he slid in to the hilt.

He pumped rapidly and then to her surprise, he pulled out and positioned himself at her anus. What was Cole telling him to do? Or was he taking the initiative himself?

Oh God.

The moment he breached her ass and pushed the blunt head in past her resisting opening, she started coming. She tried to cry out but Cole was stuffing his semen-covered cock back into her mouth with harsh orders to suck it all.

Mike fucked her ass while cum leaked out of her pussy. It was on his cock and inside her ass as well. Cole's release.

And Cole was still leaking into her mouth, still spurting light streams against the back of her throat. She could no longer keep herself up and sagged onto the cushion.

Cole slid from her mouth, but Mike followed her down, relentlessly pushing his cock into her ass, even when she was forced by his weight to lie flat on the cushion.

He rode her hard and long until she was delirious. Then and only then did he shudder against her and force himself deep while he came. He rocked over her, pulling at her hair as if tugging on reins.

Then he stopped, still buried deep in her ass, astride her like he owned her.

Cole chuckled above her.

"I wish you could see this, Ren. Your ass all wide open and his cock stuffed inside. If I hadn't already come, I'd make him pull out and I'd come inside your sweet little hole as it gaped open."

Then Mike lifted himself off her and pulled his cock out, making her moan as she lay there, belly down, exhausted.

Cole knelt behind her, slid his fingers into her pussy to scoop out some of the semen. Then he slid his fingers into her ass, depositing the cum there.

Slapping her on the ass once more, he got back up and made a sound of satisfaction.

"Now that is a damn gorgeous sight, Ren. My woman, my possession all sprawled on the ground with my cum leaking out of both holes. You look well used. Get up and thank me and Mike for fucking you."

She pushed herself up and stood on unsteady feet. Mike was still standing there, his cock erect and bare of the condom he'd worn just a moment ago. Cole stood beside him, stroking himself back to erection.

Knowing what was expected, she dropped to her knees in front of them both and circled both their cocks with her fingers.

"Thank you," she whispered as she closed her mouth around Cole's erection.

She sucked a moment and then pulled away to slide her lips over Mike's dick. "Thank you," she said to him as she sucked greedily at his thickness.

"Oh hell yeah," Mike muttered. "I love the way you thank a man, sweetheart."

Cole smiled. "Isn't she pretty? Now make us come, Ren. I don't care how long it takes. I want you to have a mouthful of our cum and I want you to swallow every drop."

CHAPTER 32

It was raining when they landed in Houston. A cold drizzle had set in and showed no signs of letting up any time soon. Cole hurried Ren into a car where the heat was already running and he began the drive back to his house.

She curled up in the front seat and turned to face him, watching him as he drove. It was a bit of a shock to be back in the real world as she called it. The last days had been surreal. Like they'd taken place in an alternate reality. Paradise. Fantasy land.

Her body was deliciously sore from being used so hard and she'd never felt better. She wanted to stretch like a cat and purr.

Cole turned to her as he maneuvered through traffic. "Enjoy yourself?"

She smiled and nodded. Then she cocked her head to the side. "Why did you do it?"

He lifted one eyebrow in question.

"I mean, why did you let Mike do what he did? I would have thought you would never let another man take what you consider yours. You've said many times you don't like to share."

"I knew it was what you wanted," he said simply.

Her eyes widened. "You let him fuck me because it was what I wanted?"

"Can you think of a better reason? I knew it turned you on. I can read your body language. As soon as he touched you, your pulse went up, your breathing sped up and you were instantly aroused. You wanted it and so I gave it to you."

She touched his cheek, stroking the strong line and exploring the light rasp of stubble. "Thank you. For everything. Not just Mike and C.J. and all the pampering. But thank you for those memories. It was a wonderful few days."

He captured her hand and kissed the inside of her palm before letting it go once more. "You're quite welcome."

They arrived home a few minutes later and Cole ordered her to bed. He did it laughingly because he could see she was falling over with fatigue. She gratefully crawled between the covers and melted into the pillows. She didn't even remember him coming to bed. She slept long and hard but when she awoke the next morning, he was wrapped around her, a reminder that she belonged to him.

She smiled and then kissed his neck. Then she began extricating herself from his hold.

"Where you going?" he mumbled sleepily.

"Work," she answered softly. "I want to work for a while. I haven't written in days. I want to finish."

He kissed her forehead. "Okay. I'll check on you later."

And he did. But she was so immersed in her writing and her drawings that she waved him away, her lips pursed in absolute concentration. She was compelled to finish the story and the drawings. They were so clear in her head that she feared if she took even a break that everything would disappear before she could get it down.

She worked through the day and into the night. Cole brought her a tray of food and left it on the desk beside her but crept quietly away, not disturbing her or insisting she stop.

After over twenty-four hours of work, she sat back in her chair and rotated her stiff neck. Her back was killing her. Her muscles were stiff and sore and her eyes felt like sandpaper every time she blinked.

But she was finished.

She closed the journal where she always completed the preliminary draft and caressed the aged, soft leather. Then she secured the ties around the floppy manuscript and held it to her chest.

Already she knew what she would do with it. She had a hard copy on her computer. She'd scanned in her drawings and compiled everything into one file to send to her publisher. But this copy would go to Cole. She could hardly wait to show it to him. Would he recognize the story? Would he see himself and Ren in the pages?

Wiping the sleep from her eyes, she clutched the journal to her chest and hurried off to find Cole. He wasn't in the living room or the kitchen so the next logical place to find him would be his office.

She stopped outside his door when she heard his voice through the cracked door. He was on the phone.

She pushed open the door to peer inside and her gaze connected with Cole's. He motioned her inside and held up one finger to signal he'd only be a minute.

She wandered in and took the seat in front of him. She settled back and let her gaze drift over him and his surroundings. She'd seen his office but she'd never really spent any time in it. Certainly not when he was conducting business.

He was even dressed for the office. Sort of. Or at least he had been.

At one time he'd been wearing a tie, a long-sleeved white shirt and slacks. At the moment his sleeves were rolled halfway up his arm and his tie was loosened so it hung halfway down his chest.

Or maybe he'd even gone to a meeting while she'd been closeted in her office.

He rang off then put his phone down, turning his gaze on her. "Hey. You okay? You look tired."

She pulled the journal away from her chest and placed it on the desk. "I finished."

She pushed it toward him, suddenly nervous. What if he hated it? What if he didn't see the parallels between the story played out in the pages of a children's book and their own?

"You want me to read it?" he asked hesitantly.

She nodded. "It's for you. I mean, this is. I always do my rough draft in a journal such as this and I keep them but I want you to have this one."

"Is it okay if I read it now? I'll call down for breakfast. You can go down and eat or I can have it brought up here. Entirely up to you."

She nodded. "I'll eat up here with you if that's okay."

He smiled. "I'd like that. Make yourself comfortable."

Taking him at his word, she found the couch, but more than the comfort it offered, she wanted away from him where she couldn't see his facial expressions as he read her story.

He leaned back in his chair and carefully opened the journal. She watched from the corner of her eye as he turned each page, his forehead creased in concentration.

A moment later, a knock sounded and the woman Cole employed to run his kitchen came in bearing a tray of breakfast for Ren. She set it on the coffee table in front of the couch where Ren sat and then backed away, disappearing as quickly as she'd come.

Ren smiled. All her favorites. A cup of hot chocolate. A toasted bagel with cream cheese with scrambled eggs and bacon piled on top.

She settled down to eat but she still kept subtle watch on Cole. When she finished, Cole was still deep in concentration, and she knew she couldn't be here when he finished.

She rose and wiped her hands down her pants. "I'm, uhm . . . I'm going to go grab a shower. I've been up forever. Need to brush my teeth. Do all my girlie stuff."

Cole looked up from the journal, blinking as if he'd forgotten she was there. "All right. I'll find you later."

She fled the room, grateful to have an excuse to leave. She did shower but did none of the girlie stuff she'd hinted at. She didn't even dry her hair but rather combed it straight, dressed and then went outside into the garden.

There was a nip in the air and she breathed deeply, enjoying the scent of smoke either from burning leaves or perhaps a nearby chimney.

She wandered down one of the spiraling pathways to a fountain in the center of the garden. She sat on the bench and listened to the soothing bubble of water splashing over the rim.

She was finished. Another book done. With each project she completed, though there hadn't been many yet, she always feared being able to duplicate the creativity that went into creating the story. What if she couldn't do it again?

Lucas had laughed over her fear and told her that she was brilliant and that only brilliant people worried about not being brilliant any longer.

It hadn't made sense to her but she liked the idea that someone found her intelligent. She didn't always feel smart for some of the choices she'd made.

For how long she sat, soaking up the peace and tranquility around her, she wasn't sure but she heard footsteps and looked up to see Cole walk toward her, the journal in his hand.

Her mouth went dry. Why did his opinion matter so much? She should be able to shrug it off. Subjectivity and all that jazz.

He sat beside her and for a long moment didn't say anything at all. Then he turned to her, his eyes full of wonder.

"You're amazing, Ren. I'm so damn proud of you."

Her cheeks warmed and she went limp with relief. Joy shot through her veins like a dose of adrenaline.

"You liked it?"

"Liked it? I think like is way too tame of a word to describe my reaction. You're so talented. The pictures, the way you turn a phrase. Your writing is very evocative. It's very . . . nostalgic. God, it made me think of so many things in my childhood that are bittersweet."

He reached up to touch her cheek, smoothing his thumb over her skin. "And it reminded me of us."

Her chest ached and her throat knotted. "It was us. In a way. Perhaps a younger and more innocent us. A fledgling friendship but a relationship that meant the world to them as ours meant the world to us."

"Yes, I could see that. Reading it made me ache, Ren. I'm so damn proud of you. It was an amazing story. I'll treasure the draft you gave me always. And even when it's worth millions of dollars because you've become rich and famous beyond words, I'll still treasure my copy and keep it safe and private."

She leaned into his side and wrapped her arms around his waist. "Thank you. That means the world to me. For so many years I felt so . . . adrift. Only in the last year have I begun to think I know what I'm meant to do and be. It probably sounds silly and melodramatic but it's taken me a long time to get to this point where I feel like I have direction."

He kissed the top of her head. "I don't think it's silly at all. Sometimes it takes some longer than others to find their way. It doesn't make their contribution any less valuable."

She smiled and hugged him tighter. "I love you."

"And I love you, darling Ren."

She snuggled a little deeper into his arms and closed her eyes.

He let her remain there a moment longer before carefully prying her away. "What do you say I take you to bed now? You've been up well over twenty-four hours. You have to be exhausted."

She nodded ruefully. "I am. I feel like I could sleep forever."

He rose and then pulled her to her feet beside him. He wrapped an arm around her shoulders and walked her back toward the house.

CHAPTER 33

"Lucas is here."

Ren's head shot up at the grim statement. She was sitting at her desk checking e-mails and taking care of things she'd let languish during the time she was with Cole and when she'd been working.

She wanted to be calm but her hands shook, betraying the turmoil that churned inside her. She stared at Cole who stood just inside the door, trying to get a read on him.

His features were impassive. There was no expression on his face. His eyes were shuttered.

She pushed herself upward and she walked haltingly toward the door to stand before Cole.

"Where?" she croaked.

"Outside."

She pushed by Cole and walked down the stairs, her pace quickening with each step. By the time she arrived at the door she was nearly running. Her hand closed around the knob and she drew in steadying breaths as she tried to calm her raging emotions.

Then she flung the door open and stepped outside.

Lucas's car was parked just a few yards away and he stood, leaning against the passenger door, looking as arrogant as ever. He seemed relaxed while she herself was a flaming mess.

He was here but now what? Was he saying good-bye? Had he come to bring her things?

And then he simply opened his arms and she flew across the gravel to launch herself into his embrace.

He wrapped his strong arms around her and held her tightly. To her shock he shook against her. Every bit as much as she shook.

"You came," she whispered. "You came."

He hoisted her up in his arms until she straddled his waist and he was holding her up on eye level. "I'll always come for you, Ren. Never doubt it."

His dark eyes flashed with tenderness, clear affection, but this time there was something much stronger there. Something beyond sweet regard.

He pressed his lips to hers in a gesture so gentle it nearly undid her. There was no control or dominance in the kiss. It felt as unsure and as relieved as she'd been.

"I thought you were leaving," she said in a cracked voice. "That this was your way of moving on. Of making sure I was taken care of. I thought you were tired of me."

He cursed colorfully under his breath and gently lowered her to her feet. Then he tipped her chin up to meet his burning gaze.

"I did this for you, Ren. Only for you. I have no intention of leaving you. Ever. Do you understand that? Do you know what it is I'm really saying? Because I don't think you do. These two weeks have been hell for me and I've counted every goddamn minute until I can come re-claim what is mine."

She couldn't seem to breathe right. The words registered but she didn't know quite what to make of them. Relief stormed through her senses. Lucas was here. He hadn't deserted her. He wanted her back.

Then her stomach dropped. Cole.

Oh God, Cole. Cole whom she loved. Cole who loved her. Cole who she wanted to be with every bit as much as she wanted to be with Lucas.

She turned, her every intention to go back in. To somehow find a way around this mess. But what? How? How could she possibly find a solution? What the hell was she supposed to do?

And then she saw him. Standing on the steps looking at her and Lucas.

Again with that impassive face. Those cool eyes. Barely flickering as his gaze passed over her. She made a sound like the cry of a wounded animal.

"I'll arrange for your things to be delivered," he said. "Good-bye, Ren."

"Good-bye?" she whispered. "But Cole, you said . . ." She bit her lip painfully not wanting to make a fool of herself. But then what else was there for her? There was no pride in love. She'd already laid herself bare before him. Before both men. "Cole? You promised. You told me we'd find a way."

But Cole wasn't listening. He nodded in Lucas's direction and then simply turned and walked back into the house. Ren's mouth dropped open and hurt splintered through her, throwing jagged shards into her soul.

She started after him. She had to know why he'd lied. She wanted to know how he could do this again. *Why?*

Lucas caught her hand and tugged her back. "Come away, Ren. It's over now."

"But he said . . . He promised . . . ," she choked out in anguish. "I can't go yet, Lucas. Please."

She tugged against him, fighting him for the first time ever. Never before had she challenged his dominance. She turned back to the house, trying to get back to Cole even as she stared at the door he'd closed behind him.

Lucas gathered her gently into his arms and steered her toward the passenger seat of the car. He opened the door, got her into the seat and carefully buckled her seat belt. Then he brushed his lips over her forehead.

"I hate myself right now for what I've done to you. I never wanted to hurt you. It's the very last thing I wanted to do. I'm sorry, Ren. Come home with me. Let me make this right."

She sat numbly in the seat, her gaze fixed on the front door to Cole's house. He'd come back, right? He'd realize what a terrible error he'd made. He'd remember his promise, wouldn't he?

Lucas slid into the driver's seat and started the engine. It roared to life and he began to pull away. Ren turned so she could still see the door, tears streaming down both cheeks.

Please, please come back. Just open the door. I love you.

But it remained solidly shut as Lucas drove away and the door disappeared from view. She turned and bowed her head, allowing her hair to cover her face as she wept silent, aching tears.

Beside her, Lucas reached his hand over and tentatively curled his fingers around hers.

"It will be all right, Ren," he said softly. "I swear to you, it will be all right."

She shook her head because it would never be all right.

*   *   *

Cole stood in the upstairs window in brooding silence as he watched Lucas's car pull away. Then he stared down at the journal in his hand. He had the sudden urge to hurl it across the room but he hugged it close to his chest instead. It was a precious gift and one he'd treasure always.

Ren was gone and she'd left behind a gaping hole in his soul. His heart. His mind. She'd taken the most essential part of himself with her. His love. Always his love.

He'd watched her with Lucas. Seen the relief and the ache in her eyes. Had seen how torn she was the moment she realized that Lucas hadn't abandoned her. He knew then that he'd lost.

Ren would never choose between the two men and neither were going to let her go. But one of them had to. It was the only way. Ren would tear herself apart and above all, Cole wanted her to be happy.

So he'd made the decision for her. He'd sent her away because it was the only thing for him to do. If he stood and fought for her, even if he won, she'd never be happy with him because Lucas would always be between them.

If he let her go, eventually she'd get over her sense of betrayal, just as she'd done before and Lucas would be there every step of the way. She'd be happy again.

Together they'd both be miserable. Apart, only *he* would be miserable. It was a hell of a note and two days ago he'd have said that nothing on earth would keep him and Ren apart. But it was a selfish vow and an unrealistic one at that.

He'd been a fool to barge into her life again and manipulate her as he'd done. He knew exactly why Lucas had agreed to the bargain. Lucas had taken a calculated gamble and the bastard had won.

And once again, Cole had lost the only thing that had ever mattered to him.

CHAPTER 34

"*W*hy did you do it?" Ren choked out.

She sat huddled on the couch in Lucas's home, a home that hadn't been hers for two weeks. An eternity. She clutched the blanket around her, more for comfort than for true warmth. It was perfectly comfortable in Lucas's house. As it always was.

She glanced around, half expecting things to be changed. Her presence somehow washed away. But it was still littered with many of the things she and Lucas had chosen together. And there were her things as well. Her books. A purse. A pair of her shoes. A scarf. Things that ordinarily should have been put away, but it was as if he'd left them out as reminders.

Lucas stood staring out the window a short distance away, his body tense and brooding. Silence fell between them and she pushed where before she'd never have dared. She wanted—deserved—an answer.

"Why did you send me to him? If you weren't tired of me. If you weren't moving on and seizing the opportunity to make sure I was taken care of. If none of those are the reasons, then why, Lucas?"

He turned then, something fierce flashing in his eyes. "Because I bloody well love you. All right? Happy now that you've managed to strip me to the barest of layers? I'm bleeding before you, Ren. I'm as vulnerable as a man can be when the woman he loves sits crying over another man."

She blinked in astonishment and then she gave him a bewildered look. "I don't understand. If you loved me then why did you look right through me when I saw you at the restaurant? If you loved me, why on earth would you send me back into the arms of a man who once hurt me so badly? Are you *insane?*"

He laughed, a dry, humorless laugh that made her wince.

"*Insane?* That's one word for it. At the restaurant . . . Do you even know why I was there?"

She shook her head.

"I was there because I knew it was where you'd be and I wanted just a glance. I wanted to see how you were. If that bastard was taking care of you. And what did I see? I saw you smiling and laughing and looking so damn happy that it damn near killed me. And I knew if I looked at you, I'd damn well be on my knees begging you for forgiveness and asking you to come back with me that minute. But I gave my word and you looked happy," he said in a bitter voice.

She covered her face with her hands. And then he was there in front of her, kneeling on the floor as he gently pulled her hands away from her face.

He held her wrists captive in front of her as he stared into her eyes. "You asked me why, Ren. I'll tell you why. Because when you met him again, I saw something in you. I saw a spark of something that made me uneasy. Seeing that also made me realize several things. Mainly that I loved you and the thought of losing you made me crazy."

Her mouth popped open but he released one of her wrists and put his finger across her lips. "Let me finish."

She nodded and he let his hand fall away.

"I had to come to terms very quickly with the fact that you weren't like other women I'd been with. What I felt for you wasn't just sexual or me fulfilling a kink. And it befuddled me. I've made a practice of not getting emotionally entangled with women. But you snuck up on me. I can't even tell you the point in which my feelings for you changed. Just that they did. With any other woman but you I would have sent you to Cole and been happy to do so. I wouldn't have felt like my guts had been ripped out and I wouldn't have counted the days until I could return for you. I would have moved on as you accused me of doing."

"I still don't understand," she said tearfully.

"I wanted you to be happy, Ren," he said quietly. "If Cole was the person who was going to make you happy, then I wanted you to have your chance with him. Did I want you to go? Hell no. But I thought you *should* go so that maybe when you returned to me—*if* you returned to me—you could let go of the past and embrace your future . . . with me."

She swallowed and stared at him in wonder, trying to digest everything he'd just admitted. Her heart was bursting but she wasn't sure if she was happy or devastated. How could she be sure when she hurt so much?

He moved onto the couch beside her and pulled her into his lap. For a long moment he held her tightly against his chest and caressed her arm.

"I was wrong, Ren. I'm sorry. I never wanted you to be hurt. I should have known this would put you in an untenable position. I wasn't thinking that way. Maybe I thought it would be an easy choice. Your past or your present. I'm a black-and-white kind of person, but you aren't and I should have seen this coming. I swear I only wanted to try to be unselfish and to give you the happiness you deserve."

Lucas didn't often admit he was wrong. It wasn't that he was too arrogant to ever think or admit he was wrong. He simply wasn't often wrong.

"I don't know what to do, Lucas," she whispered.

He went still against her and then in a low voice he said, "If you want to go back to him, I'll drive you over."

Tears stung her eyes. Eyes that were already red and swollen and that she hadn't imagined had any more tears to shed.

"It's not that easy. It'll never be that easy."

"Why? Talk to me, Ren. Tell me what you're thinking."

She pushed herself up so she could look into his eyes. She owed him that much at least.

"I love him."

The dullness in his eyes hurt her more than she could have ever imagined. Lucas wasn't one who often showed emotion. Ren could never remember him appearing vulnerable. He was strong, disciplined and he was always in control.

She palmed his face, unable to bear the pain in his expression or the bleakness that had entered his gaze.

"I love you too, Lucas. I was so miserable with Cole."

Lucas frowned. "But—"

"It's so twisted. I was miserable because I realized after you left that I loved you. Everything else was already there. Trust. Respect. Friendship. Desire. I was distraught because I'd convinced myself you had dumped me on Cole and I'd never see you again. But at the same time, being with Cole made me incredibly happy. Satisfied. I realized that I loved him too. That I've never stopped loving him."

Lucas's expression softened. There was relief mixed with sadness. He stroked her cheek even as she held his face in her hands.

"Have you ever been torn between two impossibilities and knew in your heart that no matter which way you went or which path you chose that you were doomed to unhappiness?"

"Oh God, Ren. I never meant for you to feel this way."

He leaned his forehead to press against hers. He cupped her face and kissed her, wiped away her tears with his thumbs.

"I'm so sorry, baby. We'll find a way. I promise."

She stared at him, grief overtaking her until the words nearly choked her. "He said that too. He told me that we'd find a way. That he wouldn't let me go. And yet at the first opportunity, he walked away. Again."

Lucas enfolded her in his arms and rocked back and forth as she buried her face in his neck.

"I'll make it right," he whispered. "Somehow I'll make this all right for you."

She clung to him but blocked out the promise. She didn't want any more promises. She only wanted truth. The hard, ugly truth.

"I love you, Lucas. I do. I want you to believe that. I don't want to be without you no matter how it may sound. I'm hurting right now, but I'll survive. I survived before. Just please be patient with me. Don't be angry because I can't give you one hundred percent of me just yet. I'll get there. I swear it."

She made the vow because she was determined that it would be so. Cole had walked away from her once before and she'd been devastated then. Now? She was destroyed. It hurt worse the second time. But she refused to allow it to dictate the course of the rest of her life.

Lucas was the best of men. She loved him and he loved her. In time she'd be able to embrace her future with him. But first she had to lay her past to rest.

CHAPTER 35

"*O*n your knees."

Ren slid to her knees and focused her attention on Lucas, waiting for his next command.

He stared down at her, his gaze probing and assessing. He was more patient of late. Almost as if he weighed every single command or perhaps he was afraid he was being too hard on her. Ren wasn't sure, but she knew she needed this. In her very unstable world, she needed the constant that was Lucas. She needed him hard and firm. Unyielding. Because if he wasn't, then her world really would crumble.

She wanted to tell him that she wouldn't fall apart. That she needed his dominance and routine now more than ever. But she refused to sound that weak and needy. Besides, he knew. He could see right into the heart of her, which was why he was treating her with kids' gloves.

She sighed unhappily and forced herself to await what came next.

"Choose tonight's instrument," he said, and took her back so many nights ago to one similar as this. The same evening they'd eaten out in a restaurant and the course of her future had forever been altered, though she hadn't known it at the time. It was the night Cole had seen her.

She licked her lips, suddenly indecisive. She would have loved to have said a belt, but the bite of leather reminded her too much of Cole. He'd liked the belt and had used it often. He'd never, ever touched her with a whip. She wondered if he'd even ever laid hands on one after all those years ago.

Even asking for wood brought back the memory of being on board the yacht when Cole had used the wooden oar. A shiver stole over her as what had followed came back to her with startling clarity.

"Your hand," she finally said.

"Was it such a hard decision?" he asked mildly.

If he only knew. But she shook her head and said instead, "I was weighing my options. I prefer your hand."

"Perhaps later you'll tell me why," he murmured. "Very well. Rise to your knees and come with me to the chair."

She took the hand he offered and allowed him to help her to her feet. He took his time moving to the chair that faced his bed and then he sank onto the cushion and motioned for her to lay across his lap.

She closed her eyes as he ran his palm over her bare ass, cupping and caressing the cheeks. When the first blow fell, she embraced it. She focused on herself and isolated herself from everything but Lucas and the comfort he offered.

She was so tightly immersed in the zone that she didn't even realize when he stopped. To her horror, when she came to awareness, he was holding her shoulders as she knelt between his thighs and he was staring hard into her eyes.

"Oh God, I'm sorry," she whispered.

To her further horror, a tear slid down her cheek. And then another and yet another until there was a steady stream of moisture wetting her face.

Lucas didn't say a word. He simply rose from his chair and then leaned down and swept her into his arms. He carried her to bed and gently laid her down on the mattress.

He climbed in beside her and pulled the covers up over her shoulders. Then he pulled her into his arms and curled his leg over hers until she was surrounded by him.

"Sleep now, my love," he murmured next to her ear. "And know I love you."

She closed her eyes and snuggled deeper into his embrace until she had no awareness of where he ended and she began. And she slipped to a place where there was no pain. No sadness. No Cole. Only her and Lucas before Cole came back into her life.

"You're an idiot," Damon said mildly.

Cole's lips twisted into a snarl but he bit back the explosive response.

"Yeah, I'd say you fucked up royally this time, man," Micah added.

Cole lost the battle not to respond. "What the fuck was I supposed to do? She loves him. She was hurt by the idea that he'd given her to me and that he'd moved on. But then he shows back up for her and it's obvious he has no intention of calmly letting her walk away from him to me."

"Who gives a fuck about him?" Micah asked. "Ren was happy with you, was she not? You said she loves you. If all that's true then that tells me she'd be happy with you again. But you wouldn't know that because you let her go."

Damon held up a hand. "He knows what a mistake he made. The real question here is how he's going to rectify it."

"I'm not," Cole said grimly.

"You're an idiot." Micah echoed Damon's assertion in disgust.

"Oh like you were Prince Charming with Angelina?" Cole snapped.

Micah's nostrils flared. Angelina was a sore subject with him and Cole knew what buttons to push. He was being a first-class asshole, but he couldn't help himself. He was in a foul mood.

"I may have treated her like shit and I may have done my damndest to drive her away, but I eventually pulled my head out of my ass and got on my knees and groveled my ass off. Think you'll ever get to that point?"

Cole blew out his breath. "Look, she loves Lucas. Yeah, she said she loves me too. I don't think she lied. But she loves him too. That tells me she'll be fine with him. Hell, she's probably better off. I can't seem to ever make the right choices around her."

"It doesn't sound like either of you deserve her," Damon said darkly. "She isn't a piece of property to be pawned, bartered and shoved back and forth. She's a beautiful, intelligent woman with feelings and she shouldn't be toyed with."

Micah smiled. "Ever the polished gentleman, eh Damon? I wonder if you've ever fucked up with a woman in your life."

Damon sent him a shut-the-fuck-up glare.

"Apparently you and I are the only ones who don't have sense when it comes to women," Cole muttered toward Micah.

Damon rolled his eyes and shook his head in Cole's direction. "Look, if I had pulled this kind of lame ass stunt with Serena, I would have never heard the end of it from you. You'd sit there and remind me of how you once walked away from a woman and that it was the worst mistake of your life and that I shouldn't do the same. Come to think of it, we had this very conversation about three weeks ago where you admitted that leaving Ren was the absolute worst thing you'd ever done. So what would possess you to do it all over again? Are you a masochist or are you just that stupid?"

Micah chortled and choked on his beer before setting the bottle down on the table. "He's got you there."

"Swear to God, if we weren't in a public place . . . " Cole bit out.

"Not sure Cattleman's serves as a civilized place," Damon said. "I've never quite seen the appeal myself, so by all means, act as though we aren't in a public setting."

"Ya know, Cole is a rich son of a bitch too but he never acts like Cattleman's is beneath his pampered palette," Micah drawled. "You just don't like it because the girls have their nights out with Drew the bartender here."

Damon sent him a quelling glance. "There is no price tag on taste."

"How is Serena?" Cole asked.

He desperately wanted to change the subject. Talking about Ren made the pit in his stomach grow larger. He hadn't slept in nights. Every time he closed his eyes, it felt like he was hurling over the edge of an abyss with no way to catch himself. That was what every day without Ren was like. Hell, it was dramatic, but he was fucked and he damn well knew it.

"She's fine. Growing more restless by the day. Her doctor thinks that perhaps her due date was miscalculated and that she'll deliver sooner. She's scheduled to have a sonogram this week so more accurate measurements can be taken."

"And how are you taking this news, Daddy?" Micah asked.

"It scares me shitless," Damon admitted. "I'm not prepared for this. I'm supposed to be the strong and in control one and it's Serena who is constantly having to calm and reassure me. It's damn embarrassing. The idea of something happening to Serena terrifies me."

Cole could understand that because the idea of Ren being hurt paralyzed him and made his blood run cold. An uneasy feeling settled into his stomach. Was she okay now? Was she happy? He hadn't ensured anything before he'd let her leave with Lucas. Ren had feared that Lucas was moving on and no longer interested in her. Cole had never ever gotten that from the other man but Ren knew him better. Had he only arrived to take Ren because his ego dictated such? What if he'd discarded Ren? What if she was out there alone?

He closed his eyes and pinched the bridge of his nose between his fingers. He could call Lucas, but would Lucas be truthful with him if he had tossed Ren out? Would Ren even know how to contact Cole if she was out there on her own? Would she want to?

"I'm an idiot," he said in disgust.

Micah sighed in exasperation. "Have Damon and I not been saying this for the last half hour? What made you see the light now?"

Cole stood and tossed down a bill for his drinks. "I've got to go. Damon, please keep me informed of Serena's progress. I'll want to know when she goes into labor."

Damon turned a little green at the mention of labor but nodded.

"Good luck, man," Micah said, his eye serious. "I hope this means you aren't going to sit back and let her walk out of your life."

Cole grimaced as he pushed his chair back in. "I may not have a choice."

"There's always a choice," Damon said. "It's what you do with that choice that matters."

"I really can't stomach you when you get all philosophical," Cole growled. "I'll see you two later. Much later."

Micah chuckled as Cole strode toward the door.

The cold air hit him in the face as did the heavy mist in the air. It was a rotten night to be out but an even worse night to be home alone with only his regrets for company.

If Ren were with him, they'd spend the evening in front of the fire and then she'd go down on her knees, her hair shimmering in the glow of the flames while he slid into her mouth.

Hell, who was he kidding? If he had any chance of being with Ren tonight, he'd be on his damn knees in front of her begging for another chance.

He drove home, unsure of what he was going to do or if he'd do anything at all. All he knew was that his demons were beating inside his head. Relentless and vicious. And they were all screaming at him that he'd been wrong. Again.

He was tired. He hadn't slept in nights. But when he pulled into his driveway and rounded the bend to see Lucas's silver Mercedes parked in front, his pulse bolted up and a shot of adrenaline rocketed through his veins.

Instead of continuing on to his garage, he pulled up behind Lucas's car and it was then he saw Lucas standing outside the driver's side door, hands shoved into his pockets.

Cole's eyes narrowed as he shut down the engine and opened his door. He stepped into the raw night and realized that whatever Lucas wanted, he'd come alone. Ren wasn't with him.

"What the hell do you want, Holt?"

Lucas leaned against the side of his car. "Invite me in, Madison. I think you'll be interested in what I have to say."

Cole shut his door and stared at Lucas for a long time. The other man didn't so much as blink. Or give any hint of what he wanted to talk about.

"This better be good," Cole muttered as he headed for the front door.

He stepped inside, flipped the lights on and led Lucas into the living room. The same living room where he and Ren had been just three weeks ago. Cole swore he could still smell her in his house. As such, he hadn't had it cleaned since she left.

"Drink?" Cole asked as he walked to the liquor cabinet.

"Nothing for me," Lucas said.

"I think I'll need it," Cole said in a low voice. He poured himself a glass of Irish whiskey and took a fortifying sip before turning his attention to his visitor.

"Now, what is it you wish to discuss that I'll find so interesting?"

"Ren."

Cole sucked in his breath. "Well you have me there. I'm definitely interested in anything you have to say about Ren. Is she okay?"

"Do you care?" Lucas asked sharply.

"I don't have time for your bullshit," Cole said coldly. "I didn't run you down and arrange to spend two weeks with a woman I care nothing for."

"Let me just tell you how Ren sees it. She spent two weeks with a man she once loved beyond reason. The same man who walked away from her and devastated her when she was young. She realizes during those two weeks that she still very much loves this man and he makes her a promise that he'll find a way. A promise she clings to when she's uncertain of how things can possibly work out. Then at the end of the two weeks, this same man walks away from her yet again. So you tell me, Madison. Does that sound like a man who gives a damn?"

Cole stared at him in stupefaction. Then he shook his head. "There are so many what-the-fuck issues with that bullshit you just spouted that I don't even know where to begin. But let's start with why the hell do you care? Why are you here? And for that matter why point the finger at me when you hurt her so badly by A. giving her to me in the first place, which immediately made her assume the worst and that you were dumping her and B. looking straight through her like she didn't exist when she saw you outside Cattleman's."

Lucas's face was locked in stone. "Just tell me why you left, Madison. Why did you give her up when you once swore to me you'd fight for her with every breath you had. You pretty much told me that you'd do whatever it took to ensure she never came back to me. And yet it seems to me that you couldn't get rid of her fast enough."

Cole slammed his drink down on the sideboard with enough force to make the liquid slosh over the rim. "I didn't goddamn walk away from her. I let her go because it was the right thing to do. She loves you, and she was never going to choose between us. Never. She loves us both but one of us had to lose. I just want her to be happy even if I'm fucking miserable in the process."

Lucas sighed. "I thought it might be something like that, you fucking martyring bastard."

"Don't piss me off. I've spent the night deciding just what a dumbass I was. This is the only warning you're going to get. I'm coming for her."

Lucas stared at him for a moment as if studying or perhaps deciding whether or not he wanted to say what it was he wanted. And finally he spoke. "I had in mind something different."

Cole was at the end of his patience. He was tired. He was pissed. And what he really wanted was to knock Lucas on his ass and then go find Ren, throw her over his shoulder and haul her back to his cave. In that order.

"Just get to your point."

"I think we should share Ren," he said in a low, grim voice.

CHAPTER 36

*C*ole stared wordlessly at Lucas. The man was out of his goddamn mind. "Share her? Like a piece of meat or something?" He couldn't help but remember Damon's angry assertion earlier that evening. Hell, but Lucas's suggestion made it sound like it was exactly what they were treating her like.

Lucas made an angry, frustrated sound. "Look, what I'm suggesting isn't easy for me. No, I don't think we should pass her back and forth like some tasty treat. I think we should give serious consideration to entering a relationship wherein she belongs to both of us. Full time. All the time. Which means that you and I would have to come to an understanding. And we'd have to make a hell of a lot of decisions about living arrangements."

Cole's eyes widened as realization dawned. What Lucas was suggesting was a permanent, full-time arrangement. Hell, they'd live together and be in constant contact. They would truly share Ren. There were so many potential pitfalls that Cole couldn't even wrap his head around it.

But the one thing that stuck out in his mind the most was that he'd have Ren. She'd be happy. She wouldn't have to choose. Was he insane for even considering it for the barest of seconds? And for not tossing Lucas out on his ass? What kind of a freak did it make him?

And then he remembered that Micah had lived just such an arrangement. Before Angelina. He and his best friend had shared the same woman. A woman who Micah had married but had shared with his best friend. She'd belonged equally to both of them.

But they'd been best friends. There had been a level of trust already established. There was nothing between Lucas and Cole except animosity.

"Jesus," Cole muttered. "Is this what Ren wants?"

Lucas's lips tightened. "I don't know if it is or not. I haven't talked to her about it. I wouldn't do anything to get her hopes up or potentially upset her. I wanted to talk to you first so that if it isn't an option, it's never mentioned to her as one."

Yeah, he understood that and grudgingly gave the other man respect for protecting Ren.

"You'd really consider this?" Cole asked incredulously. "I don't share well. It's not something I've ever considered."

Lucas made another rude sound. "I've shared her with men at the club. You shared her with Captain Mike and some guy named C.J. Yeah, she told me all about it. It's the same principle only now we'd be sharing her with each other. And preferably no one else."

"That was different," Cole bit out. "She didn't love Captain Mike or C.J. They gave her pleasure but she didn't feel anything for them."

Lucas's lips thinned. "Ah, so now we get to it. She loves me and you'd feel threatened by that."

"Are you telling me you wouldn't feel threatened by the fact she loves *me*?" Cole demanded. "Because I don't buy it. I don't buy it for a minute. You're way too intense of a guy. You're way too possessive. You're way too bloody like me for it not to bother you."

"Sit down, Madison. You and I have a lot to discuss and I'm not going to stand here like two circling wolves all damn night. I don't like leaving Ren alone for this length of time and in particular when I know she's not herself."

Cole froze and some of the irritation fled. He lowered himself onto the couch as Lucas did the same in a chair across from him.

"How is she?" Cole asked hoarsely.

"Not good," Lucas returned. "But that's to be expected. She's in love with two assholes who've done everything wrong. Which is why I'm here so that maybe, *maybe* we can do something right for a change."

Cole couldn't even take offense. Holt was dead right. They were two of the biggest assholes on earth. They'd manipulated, played with and hurt Ren. And yeah, maybe it was time to step up, work together and fix the situation.

"How is this supposed to work?" Cole asked wearily. "You're domi-nant. I'm dominant. Ren's only one person."

"I'm not asking you to submit to *me*," Lucas said in amusement.

Cole's lip curled up at the corner and he glared at the other man. "Ha-ha, very funny."

"Look, I don't have all the answers. It's something we'd have to work at, and more than that, be *committed* to working at. Every damn day. I don't expect it to be easy. What is? What I do know is this. I love Ren. I'm not letting her go. You love Ren. You let her go because you thought it was the right thing to do. Ren loves us both and is hurt by the idea that you walked away from her and that I gave her to a man who'd already hurt her once. That makes us both dumb as shit assholes who have a hell of a lot to make up to her."

Cole sighed. Damn but the man was making way too much sense.

He wanted to hate him. He didn't want to respect him. But the fact that Ren was at the forefront of his every thought had already earned him Cole's regard.

"Ren would be submitting to two men. Not just one. And I don't expect it would always be easy with us pulling her in two different directions, which is why we'd have to set aside our differences and work together to make sure she's taken care of and not overwhelmed. In the end, it has to be her decision because her life changes the most."

"It should be her decision anyway," Cole said quietly. "You and I have already made too many decisions for her. I've walked away from her twice because I thought it was best for her. But I never asked her what *she* thought was best."

Lucas nodded. "And I brought her to you because I thought it was best for her to face her past. I think it's time we stop thinking for Ren and let her make her own decisions."

"Yeah, agreed."

Lucas rose from the couch. "I've been away from Ren for too long. She's not been herself. She goes through the motions. She needs the routine and the discipline of submission but her heart's not in it." He stared hard at Cole. "Think about what I said, Madison. Think hard about it. Then whatever objection you have or however you think it's going to affect your life or whatever sacrifices you think you'll be making, consider Ren, and ask yourself if your objections are worth more than a life with her. When you make up your mind, give me a call. We'll approach her together. Until then I won't say a word to her."

Cole watched Lucas go, unsure of whether he was supposed to thank him, curse him or dismiss him all together.

What a goddamn mess.

Or was it?

Was it a mess or was it the solution to an impossible situation?

In a perfect world, Cole would have Ren to himself and he'd never have to share her with anyone. In the shitty world where he currently existed he didn't have Ren at all. Lucas did.

That there was enough to make compromise not look so damn bad after all.

He pulled his cell phone out of his pocket and punched the contact button for Micah. Micah would at least understand the situation and he could likely offer Cole some been there done that if nothing else.

He had a feeling this was going to involve a lot of alcohol.

CHAPTER 37

"*M*arry me."

Ren stiffened in Lucas's arms and pushed away from his chest to stare at him. "What?" She couldn't have heard him right. Ren didn't even equate marriage with Lucas. It was traditional. Lucas was anything but. He was a free spirit. Liked things his own way. He wasn't one to uphold tradition. He was much too likely to forge his own, separate from the ideals of the majority.

She didn't doubt that he loved her. His confession had been painful and almost angry. But it had been raw and honest and she knew without a doubt he spoke the truth.

But marriage? She couldn't even wrap her head around it. For that matter, she wasn't sure *she* was a traditionalist in that sense.

"Marry me," he said again softly.

Her brain synapses were firing but she couldn't seem to get her tongue to work.

Lucas chuckled. "I see I've managed to make you speechless."

"Marriage?" she finally managed to croak out.

"Yeah, you know, that thing that people do when they're in love and want to commit to a future together? It's customary to participate in a ceremony of sorts, exchange rings or other meaningful symbols of their love and they make promises to remain faithful, et cetera, et cetera."

"Smart ass," she muttered. "I know damn well what it is. I just didn't imagine that you were the marrying type. I'm pretty sure you've told me in the past that marriage wasn't an institution in which you were swayed to participate in."

He grimaced. "Sometimes I can be a dumbass. And other times I'm wrong. I want us to get married, Ren. I want that commitment from you but more than that, I want to offer my commitment to you so that you'll know without a doubt that I'll love and cherish you for the rest of my life."

She made a sound of impatience. "Lucas, if you're doing this so that I'll feel secure, I assure you I don't need a gesture so grand."

"It's what I want, Ren. Okay?"

She blinked. "Well okay then. In that case . . ." She bit her lip, suddenly overcome with the magnitude of the moment. This wasn't something to be taken lightly even if she'd never quite imagined herself in such a position.

But isn't it what she wanted? Deep down? Hadn't she dreamed of love and children and happily ever after? She certainly had once with Cole.

"In that case?"

She took a deep breath. "Perhaps we should wait. Just a bit. Maybe when things aren't such a . . . mess."

He cupped her cheek and stared into her eyes until she was disconcerted by the intensity in his gaze. "Tell me something, Ren. What is your first impulse? What was that very first gut reaction telling you right before you started to overthink the situation and come up with reasons why you shouldn't?"

She licked her lips nervously. "I would have said yes."

Triumph gleamed in those dark, delicious eyes. A predatory smile carved the hard lines of his mouth.

"Then that is what you should do."

"You would marry me even knowing that I was in love with another man?" she asked quietly. She hated to bring Cole up again but it wouldn't be fair if they didn't at least take her feelings into consideration before making such a huge decision.

Lucas kissed her gently, his lips moving warm and tender across hers. "Do you love me, Ren?"

"You know I do," she said huskily.

"Then that's all that matters to me."

She drew in a deep breath. "All right then. If you're sure. Then yes, I'll marry you."

Even as she said the words, it felt like she was closing a concrete seal over a tomb. Her heart ached with grief. For Cole. For a man she had loved and did love. Would always love.

But perhaps in time it would dim and fade and she wouldn't think of him so much. She'd done it once. Had gotten on with her life when she hadn't been able to imagine doing so. And she hadn't had Lucas then. Not for nine long years. But she had him now and no matter what she felt for Cole, she did love Lucas with all her heart and soul.

A kernel of peace settled over her soul. In time she wouldn't feel so raw. She just had to get through the present.

She smiled up at Lucas, her heart full of love.

He smiled back and gathered her hand in his. He traced a line around her ring finger with the tip of his.

"It's customary for a man to give his intended bride a glittering, expensive token of his love and devotion."

She laughed. "Indeed it is."

"I think perhaps we should choose one together. I would want you to have a ring you're happy with."

She leaned forward to kiss him. "You make me happy, Lucas. Not a ring or a promise. Just you."

His expression became serious. "You'll be happy again, Ren. Trust me to ensure it."

"I do," she said softly. "Just be patient with me."

He kissed her, his mouth sweet and possessive. "Always."

Cole stood outside of Lucas's home and stared up at the cozy mixture of stone and wood. Somehow he'd expected something a little more imposing. More in keeping with Lucas's aloofness. But the house was warm and inviting. It had the look of an English country cottage. Only bigger. The grounds were immaculately rendered. Even in winter, the shrubbery was bright and alive with the promise of spring blooms.

It was a place that looked like it would be alive with love, laughter and children running about shrieking with delight and playing hide-and-seek.

There was a hole in his stomach that seemed to yawn wider with every minute he stood here trying to make up his mind whether to go in or not. Lucas had been explicit. Show up or don't show up. But this was it. Do or die. If he didn't take the opening now, it would never be extended again. The door would effectively be shut on Cole forever.

Even after an all-night conversation with Micah, he didn't feel wholly reassured. Micah had been sympathetic to Cole's position but thought he was crazy if he didn't leap at the opportunity to have a life with Ren even if it meant sharing her with another man.

But then to Micah, the arrangement seemed almost normal. He

wouldn't even blink an eye over the nontraditional arrangement. If only Cole could embrace it as easily.

He curled his fingers into tight fists at his sides. Inside the large wooden doorway just a few feet away, Lucas was positioning Ren. He was taking her through the paces of a scene that Lucas had carefully constructed. All that was missing was Cole.

All he had to do was walk in that door and he'd see Ren again. But fear held him back. What if she had no desire to see him again? What if he'd used his allotment of second chances?

What if Ren really was better off with Lucas?

Ren walked to the center of the living room and stood in front of the stone fireplace facing Lucas, who sat sprawled in an armchair. He was in a mood tonight, one she couldn't quite figure out.

He'd bathed her, pampered her endlessly, brought her wine in the tub and fed her bits of cheese and fruit. And when she was done, he'd dried her and brushed her hair until it sparkled and shone.

Once he was finished, he'd instructed her to come to the living room in just a dressing robe. Then he'd left her in the bedroom and gone down ahead of her.

Her skin tingled in excitement as she stared into his enigmatic eyes.

"Disrobe."

The simple command made her shiver. She tugged at the tie holding the lapels of her silk robe together and then shrugged out of the sleeves, letting it fall to the floor.

The warmth from the flames warmed her back but it was Lucas's gaze that warmed her from the front. There was approval, lust and . . . love in his eyes.

She stood proudly before him, her head a little higher than it had been in the last week. It was still hard for her to sleep at night but Lucas had brought her a measure of peace with his attentiveness.

Standing here looking at him and seeing what she now recognized as love on his face, she was tempted to break discipline and throw herself into his arms. Hold on and never let go.

But pleasing him was more important to her and now more than ever she needed his quiet dominance.

"You're lovely, Ren. I could sit here watching you all night. There is such an elegance about you. Your features are so striking. But I think what I love most is your smile. You've not had much to smile about in recent weeks, but tonight I hope to remedy that."

There was an odd note to his voice. Almost caressing. She basked in the warmth in his tone, unconsciously leaning forward as he spoke.

"Tonight you'll decide how we start. Tell me what your fondest wish is and I'll grant it."

"Me bound. Utterly submissive. To you. My dearest wish is that tonight you have me in any manner you desire," she whispered.

His smile was tender as he rose. "Do you know how I see you, Ren?"

She shook her head.

"I imagine you on a pedestal, displayed to your best advantage. Beautiful inside and out."

He went to the window and pushed out the square leather ottoman. It was huge, an accompaniment to the leather sectional in the library, but Lucas had always kept the ottoman in here because he liked to position her on it.

It elevated her to a perfect height for her to kneel and be on level with his cock to either suck or for him to fuck her from behind. And it was plush and comfortable on her knees. She could remain on it for hours and never complain.

Tonight he pushed it to the center of the living room, a distance from the fire so she wouldn't become too warm but would still enjoy the warmth in the otherwise cool room.

Then he left the living room for a moment and returned with two metal posts attached to heavy bases. He positioned them on either side of the ottoman and then left to get two more. When he was done, there were posts about two feet out on all four corners of the ottoman.

Without a word, he picked up Ren, curling her into his arms and carried her to the leather cushion. He turned her on her knees and stroked a hand over the curve of her back and then to her buttocks.

"Stay here. On your hands and knees. I'll be back in a moment."

She put her palms down, enjoying the sumptuous feel of the buttery-soft leather. Then she spread her knees at a comfortable distance and positioned herself according to Lucas's instructions.

A moment later he was back and he came in behind her. First there was the warm clasp of his hand around her ankle and then next she felt the slight abrasion of rope. She closed her eyes and sucked in her breath as he wrapped the length around one ankle.

It was then she realized the purpose of the posts. He secured the rope binding her ankle to the post, pulling it tight in the process. Then he repeated the process with her other ankle until her legs were spread wide and her feet were splayed outward, opening her completely from behind.

"Lower your head," he ordered quietly.

She dipped her head down.

"Lower. Rest your cheek against the ottoman."

She complied, tilting her body down so that her ass was higher than her head and she pressed her cheek to the soft leather.

He pulled one arm out beside her so that it dangled over the edge of the ottoman and then he wrapped rope around her wrist. Then he pulled outward until her arm was stretched and he tied the rope to the corresponding post.

When he finished with the other hand, she was effectively trussed hand and foot, secured to the ottoman and vulnerable to whatever he chose to do to her.

"I've left you just enough slack that you can raise your head when necessary," Lucas said. "For now you can rest your cheek as you are. When I tell you to move, you'll lift your head so that your mouth is as accessible as your ass and pussy."

She nodded her understanding.

He hesitated a brief moment, his hand resting on her head. "Before we begin, there is something we need to have an understanding about."

She frowned, though her expression was hidden by the veil of hair obscuring her face.

"We haven't discussed a safe word since the beginning of our relationship. You've never used it. I need to be sure you remember it so that if anything occurs tonight that is not to your liking, anything at all, you will simply say the word and it will all stop."

She was confused and a little worried at his tone but she nodded. She trusted him to stop. Absolutely.

"Say the word. This once so I know you remember it."

"Butterfly," she whispered.

"Good girl. Now choose your instrument. I have a desire to mark your pretty ass tonight."

She closed her eyes for a moment. "A belt."

His hand went still on her shoulder. "A belt? Interesting choice. Not one we've used before."

She should have said a crop. She should have just gone with the familiar and not put Cole anywhere into this scenario, but she couldn't take the words back now.

"You can use mine."

Her head whipped up, putting a painful strain on her arms as she twisted her head in the direction of that voice. She blew at her hair to move it from her eyes and ground her teeth in frustration when it wouldn't budge.

Then Lucas gently pushed the hair from her face, collected it in his hands and pulled it around to her back so her vision was no longer obscured.

Standing across the room just inside the doorway was Cole.

CHAPTER 38

$\mathcal{R}$en couldn't breathe. She was so in shock that she couldn't even process the simplest thought. What was he doing here? And why was Lucas standing there, holding her hair, so calm and measured that it could be anyone at all in his living room.

Her chest hurt. Her eyes stung. Her pulse was thudding hard in her ears and all she could hear was a dull roar.

"Remember your safe word, Ren," Lucas murmured.

And finally it all made sense. Somehow, someway, they were here together and the reminder of her safe word was Lucas's way of ensuring she was okay, not just with sex, pain and having her boundaries pushed, but with everything. Him, Cole and whatever the two of them had planned.

Cole stared at her with his piercing blue eyes and then he slowly walked forward, closing the distance between them. He came to stand directly in front of her and Lucas tightened his grip around her hair, forcing her chin up even farther.

Then he leaned down and kissed her. Hard. So savage that her oxygen-starved lungs screamed for mercy. Then he pulled away and took one step back.

Lucas's hand relaxed and he settled in against her back, rubbing lightly. Then to Cole. "Your belt?"

Cole unfastened the leather belt, pulled it from his pants and handed it over to Lucas. Her neck ached from holding herself in such an awkward position but she couldn't look away, no matter the strain on her bound wrists.

She had so many things to ask. So many questions burning her lips. But neither man had given her permission to do so. Which brought up yet another issue. Who was she to submit to? She closed her eyes and lowered her head, confused and aching.

"Look at me, Ren. You'll look at me while he uses the belt on your ass."

She jerked her head back up, her eyes flying open.

"Better yet," Cole murmured as his hands went to the fly of his pants. He unzipped himself and let the pants gape open as he pulled out his cock. He stroked once and then twice and moved forward until the tip of his erection was a mere centimeter from her bottom lip.

"Open," he directed.

She opened her mouth but he made no move to enter. Not until . . .

The first lash of the belt cracked across her skin, shocking her. She'd momentarily forgotten. Her concentration and focus had been on Cole.

As soon as she cried out, Cole slid deep into her mouth, pushing to the back of her throat.

"Beautiful," Lucas said in approval. "That's my girl. Suck his cock while I play with your ass. Please him or you'll be punished."

But she was already being punished. Having Cole here, commanding her like he had the right had her heart in tatters. What could she have possibly done to have deserved such a cruel, heartless thing?

Cole gathered her hair in his hands, wrapped the strands around his fingers and pulled her forward to meet his thrust. Lucas popped the belt across her buttocks again and it was like laying down a strip of fire.

She gasped and was rewarded with another mouthful of thick cock.

"Relax, Ren," Cole said. It wasn't an order as much as an encouragement. His voice was tender, and just the fact that he was here, in front of her, speaking so sweetly, to her brought tears to her eyes.

"Let us bring you ultimate pleasure tonight," he continued. "Let us show you how it can be."

How could he be so cruel?

Anger. Grief. Love. The three conflicting emotions swelled in her chest until breathing was impossible. What game was he playing? Was this some sick taunt? A final farewell and, oh by the way, this is how it could have been between us?

Tears crowded, stinging her eyes. Her nose drew up. She couldn't force air into her lungs.

Lucas brought the belt down over her ass, but it was no longer pleasurable. Each blow was painful. Sharp. The euphoric haze that normally surrounded her when Lucas laid leather to her flesh had evaporated, leaving her cold.

She strained against the bonds, panicking for a moment because she was utterly restrained. No give. She was helpless with no way to stop what was happening to her.

Cole shoved into her mouth. There was no longer any beauty to the act. For the first time, she felt used. Degraded. *Mocked.*

How could he do this to her? How could he be here when he'd walked away from her a second time? Worse, how could Lucas *allow* it? Did he want her to have closure? Because she was sick to death of decisions being made for her.

She struggled against the bonds but Lucas and Cole both followed her movements. The pain of the belt stopped and she went weak with relief for a moment. Lucas had recognized that she didn't want this.

But then he slid into her, hard. Deep. His hips slapped against her sore ass as Cole continued to use her mouth. They had no mercy. Had no idea that she was dying on the inside.

Butterfly.

The word floated through her mind and she seized upon it, realizing it was the only way to make this stop and to make them go away.

She struggled fiercely again. This time Lucas paused, his hand sliding over her hip as if he was concerned. The moment Cole withdrew she yanked her mouth away and tried to say the word but it caught in her throat that was swollen with grief and unshed tears.

When Cole cupped her jaw to guide her back to him, she shook her head in silent rejection and then finally, her voice came to her.

"Butterfly," she croaked out.

Lucas went completely still. He pulled out of her instantly and when Cole would have taken her mouth again, Lucas bit out, "Stop! It's her safe word."

Cole released her immediately and backed away. She didn't look up. Couldn't bear to look up. Behind her Lucas fumbled with the rope around her legs.

"Get her untied," Lucas ground out. "Quickly."

With both men working to untie her, she was free in just a few moments. She sagged onto the ottoman, refusing to meet either of their stares.

"Ren." Lucas's voice came to her, low and urgent. "Ren, what's wrong. Did I hurt you? Are you all right? Tell me what's wrong."

He tried to touch her. He would have picked her up, but she warded him off, slapping at his hands, pushing him away.

She pulled herself into a sitting position and dragged her knees to her chest in a protective measure. She hugged them to her body, buried her face between her knees and rocked back and forth, silent tears streaking down her cheeks.

"Please just leave me alone," she said in a hoarse, ugly voice.

A hand dropped tentatively to her shoulder. Cole.

And then on her other side, Lucas. He threaded his fingers through her hair and pressed in close until the heat from his body bled into her.

"Ren, look at me," Lucas pleaded in a soft voice. "I can't leave you alone. Not until I know what's happened. Have I hurt you?"

She raised her tear-ravaged face then and the two men swam in her vision. She could see the stark worry reflected in their eyes. They looked . . . tormented. Unsure.

"I just need this to be over. I can't do this anymore. How could you do this? Either of you? Haven't you done enough? Did you really think this would help me? Or make me feel not so abandoned?"

Lucas, who was never at loss for words, stared at her as if he had no idea what to say or that he even understood what she'd burst out with. Maybe it didn't even make sense to her. She just knew she was bleeding to death and there wasn't a bandage in the world that would stop the flow.

Cole looked bleak. He rubbed his hand through his hair and then over his head to clasp the back of his neck. "I shouldn't have come. I shouldn't have done this."

It made her furious and she wasn't even sure why his statement made her snap, but she was suddenly so very angry that it was like being infused with a shot of liquid fire.

She flinched away from Lucas's touch and he backed away as if sensing that she desperately needed space.

"No, you shouldn't have come!" she shouted. "Why did you come, Cole? Why? Is this some sick twist? It wasn't enough you walked away again after promising me we'd find a way. Is this some kind of final farewell where you show me how it could be but can never be because you have no intention of ever keeping your promises to me?"

Both men looked shocked by her outburst.

She dropped her face into her hands as some of the tearing sobs finally clawed their way from her chest. The sound was ugly in the silence but she could no longer control the horrible grief swelling inside her.

"Ren, oh God no, Ren," Cole said hoarsely. "No, no darling. That isn't it at all. Oh God, you have to listen to me."

He tried to tug her hands away from her face but Ren resisted and turned away, hunching into a miserable ball.

She was naked and vulnerable and not in the physical sense. She had no care for her actual nudity. It was just flesh. But her soul was flayed open. Her heart lay in shreds. She'd never been so intensely vulnerable in front of someone else in her life. Not even in complete submission. The most intense scene. No matter what paces she'd been put through. No matter how wholly she gave her obedience. Never had she felt so stripped of her self before. And it wasn't a good feeling.

She felt ugly, dirty, used . . . betrayed. Betrayed by the very men she trusted and loved with everything she possessed.

She turned then to Lucas because her anger was a terrible thing, wrapping her in its heartless embrace.

"How could you let this happen? How could you do it? You knew how badly he hurt me. I told you everything, Lucas. *Everything.* You were supposed to protect me. You asked me to marry you and then you let him come here and *use* me and throw back in my face everything I'm trying to forget. How will him walking away a third time make me anything but more miserable?"

Those damnable tears slid endlessly down her cheeks. She wiped furiously, wanting to remove the signs of weakness. She wanted to be strong, now of all times. She couldn't afford to be weak when the very men who swore to always keep her strong had utterly failed her.

"I'm not leaving you, damn it!" Cole roared. "Goddamn it, Ren, I made a mistake. One I'm never going to repeat if I can goddamn well help it."

She pulled her gaze from Lucas to see Cole towering over her, bristling with anger and frustration. But when she met his stare, all she could see was endless pain and despair, a perfect match to her own.

Lucas slid his fingers over her chin, gripped her jaw and gently turned her back to face him. "I would never do anything to hurt you, Ren. Not intentionally. I love you. You're my fucking *life*. Neither of us deserves your trust right now but I'm asking you to listen to us. Listen to what we have to say. Please."

The *please* threatened to shatter her control. Lucas never asked for anything. He certainly never begged but this was as close to him being down on his knees before her as it was possible for him to get without actually being there.

There was a rawness to his eyes that grabbed at her gut and twisted hard. What she saw in his gaze made her ache all the more because it wasn't confidence, arrogance or even anger she saw. What reflected in those dark eyes was vulnerability and fear. Two things she'd never imagined seeing in this man's face.

And then to her utter shock, both men moved in unison. Both knelt awkwardly in front of her, down on their knees so they were on eye level with her.

Lucas reached for her hand and brought her palm to his lips as he bowed his head. "We're at your feet, Ren. Give us a chance to explain. It's all we ask."

Cole took her other hand, threaded his shaking fingers through hers and pulled it to lay over his heart.

"I'm not too proud to beg," Cole said hoarsely. "For you I'll get on my knees. I'll do or say whatever it takes to make you give me one last chance. Just one, Ren. It's all I'll ever ask of you again."

CHAPTER 39

*R*en stared back at the two men on their knees before her and a fresh round of tears squeezed from her already burning eyes.

"Please don't cry," Lucas said in a tortured voice. "You're killing me, Ren. I'd do anything in the world not to make you cry."

"What is it you both want to say?" she asked in a husky, strained voice.

Relief was stark in Cole's eyes. His grip tightened around her hand but she could still feel the tremble in his fingers. He seemed terrified. Nervous. More unsure than she'd ever imagined him looking about anything.

"There's a decision we want you to make," Cole began.

She sucked in her breath and jerked her gaze between the two men as panic welled in her chest. Choose? She'd never be able to choose between them. How could she?

Lucas touched her cheek and wiped away the dampness from underneath her eye. "We aren't asking you to choose between us, love.

Never that. What we're asking is if you can submit to two very dominant men."

She looked first at Lucas and then to Cole before moving her bewildered gaze back to Lucas. "I don't understand."

Cole moved in closer, his hand sliding across her leg to rest on the top of her thigh. "What we're asking isn't easy. But then what ever is when it comes to love? If you chose to submit to us both, it would be difficult at times. We're both demanding. You'd be pulled in opposing directions though we'd vow to work together as often as possible to alleviate any stress on you and our relationship."

"Relationship?" she croaked. "Cole, I'm confused. What are you asking me here? Are you wanting to trade me back and forth? A week at your place then a week at Lucas's?"

Lucas made a strangled sound and his lips came together in a thin line. "Hell no. We want you with us all the time. The both of us. What Cole is so delicately trying to say is that the three of us would enter into a relationship. Together. With you as the common glue, to put it crudely. You would be what binds us all together. We'd live together. Work out our differences. We'd swear to love you always and do everything in our power to make you happy."

"Oh."

It came out as a shocked whisper. It was the very last thing she'd imagined they'd say. A rush of hope so powerful that it made her dizzy blew in but close on the heels of that bittersweet emotion came doubt and a hundred questions.

"You asked me to marry you," she whispered.

Lucas nodded. "I did. I want and need that commitment from you."

"Then how?" she took a breath because her head had begun to pound. She rubbed at her eyes and then dug her fingers into her temples.

"We would still marry, Ren. As a couple we'd be inviting Cole into our lives. As a permanent member. Instead of one man in your bed, you'd have two. Instead of one husband, you'd essentially have two."

Ren found Cole's gaze, needed desperately to know his thoughts. What was he thinking? How could such an arrangement work when he was basically an outsider looking into a legal, established relationship?

"I made a mistake," Cole said in a tortured voice before she could voice her own question. "I thought I was doing the right thing. I wanted you to be happy. I swore I'd never walk away again but then Lucas came for you and I saw how that affected you. I saw how happy you were. How relieved. And then I realized that making you choose would make me the biggest asshole in the world and I couldn't force you to do something that would, in the end, make us all miserable. I hoped by me walking away that you could find happiness with Lucas. But I can't let you go, Ren. I can't be the better man here because I'm only better if I'm with you."

Her breath left her in a silent exhale, her chest caving in at the agony in his voice. "Is this what you want? Would you be happy in such a situation? You're okay with *sharing* me with another man?"

Her heart was about to beat out of her chest. So many questions. So much uncertainty. The only thing she knew for sure was that she loved both of these men, heart and soul. And if there was a way . . . any way . . . of her having a life with both, she'd be a fool to walk away, wouldn't she?

His expression became fierce. His eyes sparked with determination and when he spoke, the conviction in his words was crystal clear.

"I love you, Ren. I love you so goddamn much I can't sleep, I can't eat and I've got a hole in my gut that's never going away. So yeah, if I've got even a small chance at having a life with you? Then yeah. Hell yeah. I'd share with you Satan himself."

"I hardly think I'm the equivalent of Satan," Lucas said dryly.

She smiled and oh God, did it feel good. She wanted to weep again but now of all times she didn't want to dissolve into another weepy mess. This was too important—the most important moment of her entire life.

Hesitantly she turned to Lucas. "I don't think we should get married."

Lucas blinked. Then his brow furrowed. He opened his mouth, no doubt prepared to argue but she put a gentle finger over his lips to silence him.

"Think how you would feel if Cole and I sat in front of you talking of marriage and inviting you into our relationship," she said gently. "If this is going to work—if it has a prayer of working—the relationship has to begin on equal footing. I don't ever want Cole to think that he's less important in my eyes. I don't want *you* to ever think you're less important."

Cole's hand tightened around her leg and when she glanced from Lucas to him, she was shocked to see a glitter of tears in his eyes.

"Do you have any idea how much I love you right now?" he whispered.

"I want you to marry me," Lucas said stubbornly. "I'll find a way for you to marry us both if that's what has to happen. But I want you tied to us, legally, emotionally, physically and mentally."

"Now the man is speaking my language," Cole muttered. "And finally we find common ground. See Ren? The one thing that unites us is you. You're the one thing we both love beyond reason. You're the one reason we'll put aside our stubbornness and be willing to compromise. Because neither of us wants to face the prospect of losing you. I've lost you twice. Two of the most goddamn miserable moments of my life. The one thing I can promise you above all other things is that I will never willingly walk away from you again. You may not trust that yet, but in time, I'll prove it to you. I swear it."

It was hard to believe they were on their knees in front of her having a perfectly civil discussion about entering into a relationship where both men would have to share the woman they loved with each other. The amount of sacrifice involved boggled her mind.

She turned to Lucas and stared a moment at this hard, unapologetic man. Her throat knotted again at what she suspected and she was moved to find out. She needed to know if her suspicions were accurate.

"Was this your idea? Did you go to him?"

Lucas sighed. "Does it matter?"

She nodded. "Yeah, it does."

"I may have gone to see him to inquire as to whether he'd be open to such an arrangement."

She launched herself into Lucas's arms, knocking him flat on his back. She kissed him and then hugged him tight. "I love you so much," she whispered. "You've always understood me better than anyone."

He stroked her hair and kissed her long and leisurely, seemingly content to lay there on the floor with her perched atop him. "I love you too, Ren. I want you to be happy. We want you to be happy."

She pushed herself back up and glanced shyly at Cole. He stared back at her, his heart in his eyes for her and the world to see. So much love. And honesty. Vulnerability. In that moment she realized how much power she truly had over both men.

It wasn't a moment of triumph where she relished victory or was smug to have such power. It was more a quiet awe and a vow to always respect the hold she had on them.

"I love you," she said simply. Because what other words held as much power?

Cole's eyes lightened and joy flushed away the wariness. "I love you too, my Ren. We'll work it out. It may not be solved tomorrow. Or next month. But we'll get there. As long as I have you, I can bear anything."

She went into his arms and circled his neck, hugging him tightly as she burrowed her face into his shoulder. He squeezed her to him until she could feel each ragged breath burst from his chest.

"Can this really work?" she whispered. "I'm so scared. And excited. And terrified. And happy. I don't know how to feel or what to think."

Cole pulled her away and then eased her back onto the ottoman so she sat in front of the two men once more.

"We'll make it work," he said simply. "What else is there for us to do? We love you. You love us."

She smiled then, relief sliding through her heart.

"Come here, Ren," Lucas said gruffly.

It wasn't the command of a dominant to his submissive. It was the low growl of a lover desperate for his mate. Slowly she stood, naked but not nearly as vulnerable as before. Lucas rose to stand in front of her and then he swept her off her feet, cradling her in his embrace.

He strode toward the bedroom and deposited her on the mattress. He and Cole made quick work of their clothing. In seconds they were both naked and both bearing down on her. Lucas came down on her left, his eyes tender and loving. Cole settled on her right, warm desire shining in his blue eyes.

Wordlessly they began a sensual assault on her senses. Lucas claimed her lips while Cole tugged on her nipple with his mouth. They kissed and caressed every inch of her body. Their hands worshipped her. Their lips cherished her. And soft, sweet words whispered from their lips.

They told her they loved her. Told her how beautiful she was. How lucky they were to have her. Tears pricked her eyelids but this time they were happy tears. They were lucky? She had to be the luckiest woman in the universe. Who wouldn't die to have two sexy as sin alpha males absolutely love and adore her?

Lucas moved over her first, sliding between her legs and rocking his big body over hers. He entered her in a gentle thrust that threatened to undo her. He claimed her mouth just as he claimed the rest of her. And he didn't stop at her body. He claimed her heart, her mind, her very soul. Sliding deep where she was unraveled and carefully putting her back together piece by piece.

After a few moments he carefully withdrew and before she could protest the loss of his warmth and possession, Cole was there to take his place, his body blanketing hers as he pushed inside her.

So loving and heartrendingly beautiful. His body undulated over hers as he nibbled at her neck and then he whispered in her ear that he loved her, would love her forever.

Each promise he made her, she took to heart, letting his words heal so much of the hurt and anguish she'd endured. She wrapped her arms around him, holding him close as joy enveloped her. So much happiness. She was afraid it was all a dream. A crazy, marvelous dream that she would wake up from cold and alone.

Cole thrust deep, pressed his body to hers and then he slid his arms underneath her and holding her tightly, turned so that she was atop him.

She let her legs slide over his so that her knees found purchase in the mattress. His hands roamed down her back to her ass. He cupped the cheeks and squeezed gently before lifting his hips to thrust again.

And then the bed dipped. Lucas's hand slid up her spine, pressing her downward until her body was flush with Cole's. A shiver of delight overtook her as she stared down into the eyes of a man she'd feared was gone from her life forever.

Cole cupped her ass more firmly and then spread her just as Lucas positioned the head of his cock at her opening. Lucas leaned down and kissed the center of her back and then whispered softly as he delicately probed her tight entrance.

"Relax, my love. Let us both take you. Let us show you how much we love you."

She melted all over Cole. Lucas pushed more firmly and her body gave way to his persistence. He slid inside and she moaned at the instant fullness of having both men buried inside her body.

It was . . . magic. The two men she loved beyond measure. Both deep inside her body. Both commanding her, dominating her, cherishing her with words and actions.

She wanted to be consumed. Completely overtaken. Used. Controlled. Owned. This was her reality. Her existence. Between two strong men. Pampered, spoiled . . . *loved*.

It was more than she could have ever imagined. Tonight there were no belts, no crops. No harsh words meant to incite desire. No orders, no commands. Just love. So much love she was drowning in it.

Their gentleness was her undoing. They moved with a sensual grace that made her ache with desire. Every movement. Every thrust. Each push inside her body was done with complete caring. Infinitely sweet. Strong and yet so adoring.

They covered her, surrounded her, touched her, kissed her . . . loved her.

"This is how it will be, Ren darling," Cole whispered so close to her ear. "Every day for the rest of your life. Us loving you. Taking care of you. Always protecting you. We may command you, but it's you who own us heart and soul."

She smiled and reveled in the beauty of his words. Lucas's lips brushed across her nape and he nipped lightly as he covered her from above.

"Love you," he said huskily.

"I love you too," she whispered back. "I love you both so much. I want this. I want a life with you. The both of you."

Cole shuddered beneath her. Lucas stilled and his body trembled as he sought to maintain his control. But it was as if her words drove them both over the edge. Their control was a thin thread that unraveled the moment she embraced the life before them.

With a harsh groan, Lucas began thrusting, his cock pulsing already with his release. Below her, Cole grasped her hips and surged upward, matching Lucas's rhythm as they both poured themselves into her body.

She laid her cheek against Cole's heaving chest as Lucas settled over her like a heavy blanket. Both men were breathing hard as they remained buried inside her. She smiled, suddenly having a very good picture of the future.

Between two strong, dominant men who loved her beyond reason and would cherish her on a daily basis.

The future had never looked so utterly wonderful.

EPILOGUE

Ren's mouth turned up into a smile as she watched Cole and Lucas stride into their Vegas hotel suite. She lounged on the sofa, her feet curled beneath her and watched hungrily as Cole loosened his tie and Lucas kicked off his shoes.

Their gazes immediately found her, swept over her, warming her to her toes with the love and desire that was so clearly reflected in their eyes.

Lucas's nostrils flared and Ren rose, heeding the unspoken command. As she walked toward them, they closed around her, their heat circling her and pulling her into the haven they provided.

Cole slid his arms around her from behind, pulled her against his back as his mouth slid sensuously up her neck to her ear. She sighed and shivered as goose bumps danced across her skin.

"I missed you," he growled.

"You didn't have to go with Lucas," she said innocently.

Lucas frowned at her and she held back her laughter.

Over the last year, Lucas and Cole had gone beyond an uneasy truce. Their relationship had been one of tolerance in the beginning and it had been far from hearts and roses. Ren had danced delicately in the early days, always afraid of upending the tenuous peace.

But as things had progressed, so too did the friendship that had sprung between the two men. Lucas had drawn Cole in, had asked for his advice and business expertise in running the nightclubs.

More often than not, the two men arranged their times between their respective businesses so that they worked together and so their time with Ren could be planned. The only exceptions were when it was required for one of them to be out of town. They never both left her. One remained so she was never alone.

"What are you thinking?"

Lucas's question drew her attention back to the present. She glanced up to see him watching her thoughtfully.

She settled more comfortably into Cole's embrace and smiled, allowing all of the happiness inside her to shine through.

"I was thinking about us." Her throat tightened and she had to work to get the words out around the sudden catch. "I was thinking how lucky I am. And how happy."

Lucas reached for her hand and tugged her away from Cole, into his arms until he was wrapped around her, their noses just inches apart.

"That's funny, because Cole and I were just remarking on what lucky sons of bitches we were that you hadn't tossed us out months ago."

Her smile grew broader and she leaned up on tiptoe to offer him her mouth. His hand tangled possessively in her hair and he pulled her to him, devouring her lips in a breathless kiss. Then he pulled her away, his hand still solidly fisted in her hair. His eyes glittered with desire and she shivered at the raw power that emanated from him.

With his free hand, he traced a line along her cheekbone and then softly over her lips. "So very beautiful. So very perfect. And you belong to us."

"Always," Cole growled softly from behind her. "Never doubt it, Ren."

Tears pricked her eyelids and her vision became swimmy. One escaped, trickling down her cheek, landing into Lucas's hand. He looked instantly alarmed. His gaze softened and he released her hair to cup her face with both hands.

"Ren, love, what's wrong?"

Cole was at her side, shoving in instantly. His eyes narrowed and he glanced accusingly in Lucas's direction. She looked at both of them, took in these strong, dominant men. Men who loved her, adored her, cherished her every single minute of every single day.

"Ren?" Cole prompted. "What's wrong, darling?"

She smiled again, so wide that her lips felt as though they would split at the corners. "Nothing. Nothing at all. In fact everything is so . . . right. So very right."

She pushed in close and wrapped an arm around both their waists. She rested her cheek against Lucas's chest but held on tightly to Cole. Cole slid his arm around her until she was held by both men. Loved. So very loved.

"I love you both so much," she whispered.

Cole kissed her temple and Lucas brushed his mouth over the top of her head. "We love you too, Ren," Cole said.

The men pulled away from her and then Lucas took her hand. "Come with us. There's something we have for you."

Cocking her head to the side, she followed obediently, but inside she was like a kid at Christmas. They were forever showering her with little surprises and she enjoyed being spoiled as much as they enjoyed spoiling her.

Lucas stopped to pick up several bags that she hadn't seen them bring inside the door. Cole led her toward the bedroom and Lucas followed closely behind.

Lucas set the bags onto the bed. "Put on everything we've bought. Dress, stockings, shoes. There is jewelry. And combs for your hair. I'd like you to put it up tonight."

She opened her mouth to ask what they were doing, but Cole slid his lips over hers, smiling against her mouth. "Just get dressed, darling. Lucas and I will be waiting."

It took an hour for Ren to dress, do makeup and arrange her hair. The dress was stunning. White, floor-length. It hugged her figure perfectly. The bodice was tight and just at the hips, silk flowed to her ankles, swirling delicately about her legs. There was a long slit up one side that bared a sexy glimpse of her stockings and the shoes were killer. Cinderella shoes. Clear but crusted in diamonds.

Leave it to her men to buy shoes that cost more than a house.

Ah well, she'd reward them later by giving them a show in just those shoes and those decadent stockings that she'd loved pulling up her legs.

She gasped softly when she opened the velvet box containing the jewelry. Gorgeous dangly diamond earrings and an equally stunning necklace. There was also a diamond-crusted bracelet that was dazzling when it caught the light.

She looked and felt like a million dollars. She looked and felt . . . cherished. Pampered. Spoiled beyond measure by the two men she adored.

At the door leading out of the bedroom, she paused, suddenly nervous to face them. She knew she looked stunning but it wasn't herself she wanted to see in the mirror. She wanted to see herself in their eyes. Wanted to see the instant flash of approval and desire. The pride and the fierce possessive glint they always wore when they looked her way.

Taking a deep breath, she opened the door and stepped into the living room of the suite. Both men turned and looked her way. They had changed and both wore expensive slacks and formal white shirts. They'd showered and Lucas's hair was still damp. They both looked so damn sexy, she wanted to strip them both naked and ride them, wearing nothing but those to-die-for shoes they'd bought her.

"Come further into the light," Lucas said in a low voice.

She stepped forward, her heels clicking on the Italian marble floor. Then she stopped and slowly turned for their inspection.

When she finished her rotation, Cole's gaze was fixed on her. "Ren, darling, you look absolutely magnificent."

Lucas said nothing and held out his hand. Only when he'd pulled her close did he speak. "Words fail me. There aren't words to adequately describe how beautiful you are tonight."

Not that Cole and Lucas weren't always complimentary, but tonight there was something decidedly different about their regard. She looked inquisitively at them, but they were giving nothing away.

Lucas leaned forward to kiss her forehead, likely so he wouldn't muss her lipstick, not that he normally cared about such things.

"Let's go," he murmured.

She cocked her head. "Where?"

Cole arched an eyebrow. "You'll find out in good time."

At one time Lucas had maintained a residence in Las Vegas, but after he, Cole and Ren had forged ahead in a committed relationship, he'd sold his apartment because he didn't feel it reflected his commitment to Ren.

They spent much of their time in Houston. Both men had been willing to sell their homes and for them to choose a new one together, but Ren hadn't wanted that. In the end, they'd decided to keep Lucas's home and Cole sold his.

Now when they came to Vegas, they stayed in one of the sprawling, posh suites at one of the hotels on the strip. Ren loved the nightclubs and the excitement of Vegas. She liked being in the middle of all the hustle and bustle and the nightlife.

Cole wasn't as sold on it as she and Lucas were and it had been an adjustment on his part, but he went where Ren went. Every time. No complaint and Ren had even gotten him on the dance floor with no small amount of coaxing.

Blackjack and poker were her two games of choice when it came to gambling and Cole and Lucas bankrolled her willingly. She had to admit to a decadent thrill to have two gorgeous men hover at her sides, watching over her while she played. She drew looks of envy from women and undisguised interest from males.

They spoiled her shamelessly, getting her drinks, making sure she was comfortable, her every whim satisfied. But the nights when they were back in their suite, alone, sheltered from the world, were her favorites. Those were the times they demanded her obedience, showered her with love and gave her all she needed and more.

In the elevator, rushing down to the casino level floor, she nestled closer to Cole's side, enjoying his scent and the natural warmth that radiated from his body. He curled his arm around her waist just as the door opened and she exited, flanked by both men.

They walked through the busy crowds, past blackjack, roulette, baccarat, pai gow and craps tables. One arm was linked through Lucas's while she held Cole's hand on her other side. Cole scowled when one man who'd obviously had too much to drink teetered too close into Ren's path.

Once they reached the exit, they ushered her to a waiting limousine where the driver stood holding the back door open for them to duck in.

Ren settled back, content to await whatever the night held for her.

A few minutes later, they pulled into the parking lot of Lucas's nightclub that was just a block off the strip. The car pulled to the very front and Ren frowned to see the parking lot completely empty save for a few other limousines.

The door opened and Cole got out and reached back to help Ren. Lucas climbed out behind them and then tucked Ren's hand into his.

She glanced sharply up at Lucas because she could swear the man was nervous. His grip was too tight and his whole body language was tense like he was uneasy.

She glanced over at Cole, trying to get some clue as to what was up, but he looked similarly unsettled.

And then the doors to his club swung open. Two men, dressed formally in dark suits, held the doors open as Cole and Lucas started forward again, bearing her with them.

When she stepped inside, she gasped. It was Lucas's club, but then it wasn't. It had been completely and utterly transformed into something she couldn't quite describe. Magical. Fairy tale. Something straight out of a book. And then she realized it *was* out of a book. *Her* book.

"Oh my God," she whispered. "Oh my God!"

She took another step. And another. Shaking off their hands, moving further into the wonder before her.

It was her garden. The magical place she'd created within the pages of her story. The place her characters—and she—had retreated to. A place of comfort and refuge.

It was her drawing come to life.

There was an honest to goodness koi pond to the right with a fountain spilling water over its sides. Flowers. Flowering vines. Stone benches. A beautiful flowering archway.

"How?" she whispered. She turned round and round, staring up at the ceiling where it gave the appearance of a beautiful sky just after sunrise. "How on earth did you do this?"

Cole and Lucas stood smiling, their eyes bright with excitement as they watched her. It was only then she realized they weren't alone. She turned again, suddenly taking in that there were many people here. People she knew.

Damon and Serena, their baby daughter nestled on Serena's hip. Micah and Angelina, their daughter held securely in Micah's arms. Other friends she'd gone on to make in the year she'd been with Cole. Connor and his wife, Lyric Jones, the famous pop star. Nathan Tucker and his wife, Julie. Gray Montgomery and his wife, Faith. And Pop. Surrogate dad to them all.

The management team from Lucas's Houston club. His employees here at the Vegas club. Two people from his Dallas club.

And they were all looking at her, smiling, excited.

She sensed this moment was huge, but she couldn't make her mind work beyond the shock of the setting and the crowd of people assembled. She turned again in bewilderment, seeking out Cole and Lucas who were now mere feet away, their expressions serious.

They both reached for her hands, simply holding out theirs. She didn't hesitate, sliding her fingers over their palms.

Lucas cleared his throat, and again he looked nervous. It was odd to see him appear anything but self-assured and in complete control. Cole looked little better.

"Ren, we—Cole and I—brought you here tonight because it was important to us to have a symbolic ceremony that binds us together. We brought our friends here, not only to witness our binding but to celebrate our union and our love for you."

Cole squeezed her hand and took over as Lucas went silent. "We love you. We want you to marry us and of course the only way to legally do so would be for you to marry *one* of us. We don't want that. We want you to marry us both. We don't give a damn about society, legalities or what anyone thinks. We want a wedding. We want one hell of a reception to celebrate our marriage and we don't give a damn if we don't have a piece of paper that declares it all legal and binding. All we care about is that you pledge yourself to us and that we pledge our lives to you. That we'll promise to love, cherish and take care of you for the rest of our lives. It doesn't matter what anyone else thinks or knows or accepts. It only matters to us that we know and that *you* know how much we love you and are committed to you."

Her heart pounded furiously. She battled tears, biting her lip to keep from ruining the moment by bawling like a baby. Her nose burned. Her eyes burned.

Then before she could respond, they both slowly went to one knee, each holding one of her hands. Cole reached into his pocket and pulled out a glittering diamond ring. Lucas took out a platinum band with three intertwined ropes.

"Marry us, Ren darling," Cole whispered.

Lucas found her gaze and stared intently into her eyes. "Marry us tonight. Right here in front of the people we care most about. Let's throw one hell of a party to celebrate your marriage to two men who love you more than it's humanly possibly to love anyone else."

No longer able to control herself she rushed forward, nearly tripping as she threw her arms around them both. They caught her against them, ensuring she didn't fall.

"Yes," she whispered fiercely. "Yes!"

They held on to her as tightly as she held on to them. She buried her face in Lucas's neck, trying to compose herself but she shook uncontrollably.

When she was finally able to pull away, she still shook. Shook so badly she couldn't get to her feet without their help. They slowly rose, holding tightly to her and they held her between them. Safe. Protective. Always a shield. Constant.

She wiped her face, not caring if it messed up her mascara or smudged her eye shadow. To Lucas and Cole she was perfect. The rest of the world? Didn't matter.

An older man pushed forward to stand just underneath the floral arch. He smiled at Lucas and motioned them forward.

"This is Father Hillman," Lucas said in a low voice. "He's a good and loyal friend of many years. When I explained our situation, he was more than happy to perform the ceremony so that we are joined in God's eyes as well as ours. All we lack is paper, Ren. Just paper."

She turned, love shining in her eyes. "We lack nothing, Lucas. We never will."

She stepped to the priest, her hands tightly in the grips of Lucas and Cole. She glanced between them, love overwhelming her, welling from so deep that she couldn't contain it. She didn't want to. Now more than ever she wanted them to be able to see, never to doubt, how very much she loved them. How much she trusted them and that she embraced their lives together with no reservations.

She pulled their hands until she held them both in front of her, clasped tightly to her heart. Then she smiled and nodded at the priest.

"Dearly beloved . . ."